The Blind Dog Gospels

By Tim Arthur

Published by Whirling Chair Publishing
4 Coolinge Road, Folkestone, Kent
CT20 1EW

—

Copyright © Tim Arthur 2011

ISBN 978-0-9568147-0-8

Tim Arthur is Comedy Editor of Time Out Magazine and Director of Time Out Live. Apart from 20 years experience as a journalist he has written over 20 plays including 'Dark Tales' which ran for four months in the West End. He has also been Managing Director of Cardboard Citizens Theatre Company, Artistic Director of Trinity Theatre in Tunbridge Wells and of Derby Playhouse Community Theatre. He has presented various television and radio shows none of which were very good and one was downright embarrassing. His first book 'Shadow in Tiger Country' was co-written with his late wife and published around the world by Harper Collins - it's still in print in Germany for some reason. His parents were famous children's television presenters and folk singers in the 70s as well as being white witches (which was always kept a little quiet). He has a daughter, Caitlin and a dog, Dusty. In 2009 he came second in the prestigious Male Tournament of Tease burlesque competition. He is a reluctant atheist and a terrible flirt.

The Blind Dog Gospels

Chapter 1

These are the Four Gospels of Sex and Drugs and Death – the Holy Trinity of life. They speak of pain and loss. They tell tales of love and agony. They offer the hope of redemption, though promise only that dying alone will put an end to all suffering.

I am the blind dog that is kept alive by a misplaced act of kindness – suffering and stumbling through its last days. I'll scribble down as much as I can before the lights go out permanently. My final role, that of apostle. The message I bring is one of lives lived in darkness.

I lie here trying to work out how this became my final resting place and all I know is that I must be close to the end but that I don't know when it will finally come to release me. As my eyesight fails, I have been given a wonderful gift, one final twist. Through the blindness I have a second sight and stories to show and tell. But like the whole of my life, I can't tell you what the point of my gift is or of the stories I can see. Perhaps if I tell you, you can make sense of them. Perhaps you can interpret the jumble of pictures and fragments of lives that live with me in this sticky tropical heat and the encroaching darkness. Perhaps I am not meant to understand the whys or wherefores. I may just be the carrier passing on a virus that lives within me but never touches me, perhaps my job, my reason is just to spread it.

Perhaps you are the one who'll be affected by the illness. Perhaps?

'It was most unlike him.' Was all she could say when the reporter asked her for a comment about her husband's suicide.

I got married in a small snake-and-fire chapel in Buttfuck, Texas, to a screaming hellcat bitch from Mexico. She had spent the last two days fucking me to within an inch of my life in a sweaty motel room. Flies buzzed in the crackling heat and swarmed, desperate to get in at the window. The air conditioning unit hummed and whined, fighting a losing battle. I only noticed it in the brief moments when she slept. Those moments of peace between her biting and scratching and moaning and barking were filled with the noise of the room and the insects. There was a scrabbling in the plasterboard press-stud wall at the head of the bed. When I shut my eyes, I could see the recess filled with a million cockroaches climbing endlessly over each other. Mandibles chewing their way through the powder-dry cardboard, eager to get to our naked cum-covered bodies.

I had met her on a Reservation in an Indian Casino. I couldn't make out her name when she said it. It sounded something like 'Juanita Breggaga' or 'Chickita Fetardo'. I asked her twice – both times I couldn't catch it, so I gave up asking. I called her 'Baby' and she called me anything she liked.

He had just flushed the toilet, zipped up his flies and put his hand out towards the door when it was blown off its hinges into him. In the split second it took to happen, he saw – or thought he saw – a flash of fire, but that might have been his head reinterpreting the facts after the event, creating a set of memory images to fit his injuries. What was real though was the force of being thrown across the cubicle, his legs smashing against the toilet bowl, his head cracking off the wall, the crunching pain and then the blackout.

He didn't know how long he was out for but when he came round, he was lying in a small gap under the door. It was resting at a forty-five degree angle on the chipped porcelain water tank. He pushed at it and heard debris slide off its smooth easy-to-clean beige Formica surface.

His eyes scanned the scorched walls, shattered mirrors, leaking twisted metal pipes and a ceiling hung with the mess of live wires which had been attached to the now fractured strip lighting. There was acrid choking smoke throughout the place and his spinning head was finding it hard to take in all the information around him. He was in a state of sensory overload. He wanted to faint; he was sweating, cold and shaky.

There was a man lying on the floor next to a urinal with most of his leg blown off. The bleeding bloody stump was not as distracting though as the huge chunk of the man's face that had been sliced away by some flying debris – where there had once been a cheek and jaw, there was now blood and dripping strands of flesh through which a severed tongue and shattered teeth could be seen. Various other victims of the bomb lay amid the devastation, some moaning and alive, some silent and dead.

The bomber himself had almost entirely evaporated as the incendiary vest he was wearing had gone off twenty minutes early. There hadn't even been time for slight surprise or a final comical 'what the fuck!' A jolt and a wire had touched something it shouldn't have and he was no more. His final act, the decimation of a motorway washroom.

He regained some of his wits and started to make his way shakily out towards the exit. As he passed what remained of the hand basins, he looked at himself in the splintered shards of a mirror. He took a comb from his jacket pocket and ran it under a running cold tap. He smoothed his hair down. He ran it under the tap again. Blood flowed from its teeth. He turned his head and saw that he was cut and bleeding somewhere under his thick black hair. He had had this experience before. It also appeared there was blood running from both his ears. That would explain his muffled hearing. He presumed the high-pitched tinnitus that was consuming his entire brain and driving him slowly mad was due to the boom of the blast. He brushed dust off his shoulders and found they were also soaked in blood. He washed this off his hands, straightened his tie, and coughing slightly as the smoke plumed around him obscuring his reflection, stepped over the crumbled masonry out into the open air of the car park.

Police cars and fire engines were arriving at the scene. He knew their sirens must be sounding but all he could hear was a sound like the sea pulsing through his head and a squealing, whistling constant white noise. Everyone seemed to be running into the burning building behind him. He was a one-man tide flowing in the opposite direction. No one approached him, no ambulance man tried to examine his wounds, it was as if he was invisible to everyone. He reached his car and felt in his pocket for his keys. They were there. He pushed the button on the keyring to disable the car's alarm. He pressed it again. The central locking clunked open, not that he could hear it. He had a moment of panic that, in the fall, he might have lost something. He did his ritual check – keys, wallet, mobile phone. All were there. Anything else, he could live without. His mobile phone was telling him he had received a text message. A little graphic of an envelope sat at the top of the screen. He opened it.

'Bartholomew has been sent home with earache.'

She loved keeping him in the cage. Ever since he'd been in there, she felt a weight lifted from her, everything was rosy in the garden. For the first time in years she might get to see what her arms looked like without bruises. On the first night he'd been in it, down there in the cellar, she'd played Supertramp at full volume to cover his screaming. It was the first time since she'd got married that she'd been allowed to play it in the house.

She had been planning it all for a long time. Ever since the first time he broke her nose. The slap crushing the cartilage and slicing membrane, so that her thick blood ran all over her chin and down on to her new sneakers. She had promised herself that she would get him back one day, somehow.

A year ago she had taken to fucking or blowing anyone in her small town she thought might me able to help. She half-hoped she'd catch something she could pass on, something he might think he'd caught off one of his many inbred extramarital fucks.

After sucking on more cock than many of the local hookers, she met Max. Max made things, things that might be useful to her. Whenever she could escape from the house for ten minutes to get the shopping or pick up the dog's anal tablets from the vets, she would always take a detour down Echo Lane, to Max's house. She would rarely speak; there wasn't really time. Leaving the pick-up's door open, she would wander into his workshop, sink to her knees, unzip his work trousers and reach inside to grab a handful of his huge cock. Then she'd suck him hard and fast, one hand kneading his balls. If she were really short of time, her saliva-wet fingers would slide on into his arse. He came almost instantly then. On those days she refused to wash her hands and made sure she touched every bit of her husband's food as she prepared it. She would smile as she gave him his burger and fries. Eat up, you evil bastard, eat up.

'I want you to make me something?' She was wiping his warm cum off her chin as she said it.

'What?' Max asked doing up his flies and picking up his saw to start working again.

'A cage to keep a bear in!'

'Sure!'

As far as he could work out, he had been tripping for somewhere in the region of eighteen years. He had taken acid for the first time after a gig he'd done in Camden Town in 1976 and had just kept on going. He'd chased the dragon, regularly met with Charlie, sped his way through weeks in seconds and loved a whole generation of strangers on 'E' for months and years on end. There was never a good reason to stop and there was always a thousand perfect reasons to keep going, to keep hiding inside himself.

When he got the phone call from his aunt telling him about his mother, he was lying on the floor of his flat watching an infinite mass of spiralling butterflies circle his lampshade, dancing to an old KLF album he had found under a pile of forgotten clothes. There were bits of his brain that were lost forever, however, this news somehow reached deep inside his psyche and dragged him out like a newborn baby, kicking and screaming. It was time to reassess. It was time to go home.

After nearly two decades of losing everything – his band, his wife, his child, his ability to play guitar, his sanity and the keys to his car which he had left to rust and rot in the garden – he found himself walking up the garden path to the house he'd been born in. The same house his mother had died in just two days before.

His aunt met him at the door with a cup of tea in hand and a smile. He could only just remember her. In his mind he tried to smooth out the wrinkles on this old woman's face in an attempt to discover the person she must have been before he went mind travelling. She looked at him.

'My God, Steve! What happened to you? Are you under there somewhere? Where's the little boy that used to ride a trike down this path to meet me?'

He wasn't accustomed to non-drug related conversations. Nobody he knew now knew anything about his past. Most didn't even know his name. Just hearing it said out loud was a novelty. These kinds of questions were dangerous and unsettling. He closed his eyes and began an ancient cine film of a childhood he had lost and thought never to reclaim. In it he saw himself and his mother and father and his dead sister. The tears fell from his eyes before his brain had time to realise he was upset and crying – his body and his mind had got out of sync and it took a while for one to catch up with the other.

His aunt held him in the doorway. It was warm and comforting, like newly-baked bread.

'Come on in. Here, you drink this tea, love. Now come on, hun, stop crying, there's a good boy. Oh dear, look at you, you're getting your beard all wet.'

Without realising it, he had, over the years, become obsessed by this lawn. It was the only thing he was allowed to call his own. It was half an acre of perfect green. Sometimes if he had inhaled enough of the poppers he kept in the biscuit tin in the shed, it would appear to glow. The vibrant colour would rise up from the grass – a dancing undulating iridescent hue six inches above the short clipped uniformity. Today though, there were no poppers, just the ritualised cutting. This was an art to him, a thing of beauty, his own suburban equivalent of the Japanese tea ceremony. He would mow a series of perfectly straight horizontal lines for fourteen minutes approaching and then away from the house, followed by perfectly straight vertical lines for twelve minutes. The resulting chequer board pattern gave him a deep sense of calm.

As he mowed the garden that day, he found his mind drifting in and out of consciousness. His thoughts had been cluttered these last few days, a nasty ugly feeling of panic had been making him gag. Bile from some deep pain inside him had been rising into his throat, its burning acid making him chew almost continuously on indigestion tablets.

Over the top of the noise of the mower, he could hear occasional snatches of Puccini wafting down to him on the wind from the stereo in the living room. It floated out through the French windows and down to his aching heart. The fact that the music was playing meant that Jill, his wife of some twenty-odd years, was out. She was either at her sister's, at another suffocating coffee morning or out on the golf course doing what Oscar Wilde had described perfectly as 'ruining a perfectly good walk'.

He hated golf and the people who played golf and the clothes people wore while playing golf, and the drinking in the clubhouse and the smugness of it and the manicured sculpting of otherwise wild and beautiful countryside. He hated a lot of things, but he kept a special place in his dark heart for golf.

Jill spent at least some part of every day up there with 'the ladies'. This was one of the game's only redeeming features. She would leave the house for a few blissful hours and he would play opera. When she was in the house, there was to be no classical music played, it was 'noise' interrupting Radio 4. She didn't really 'get' that kind of music he had heard her say time and time again at countless mortuary-like dinner parties they had attended over the years. This, he had come to realise, was one of the many outward signs that she had no 'soul'. She was nothing but a walking carcass – flesh and bones and muscle walking and slowly decaying. At forty she was fighting to keep herself beautiful and desirable, and many thought her pushed-up breasts and short skirts with her gym-toned legs made her just as sexy as she always had been, but all he saw was an ugly machine once beautiful and natural now showing the first signs of the sagging and wrinkling which would destroy her self-image. The hundreds of small lines caused by years of sucking on cigarettes made her mouth look like an arsehole. He liked this image as it explained the sheer amount of shit that poured forth every time she opened it.

As the lawnmower pulled itself forward dragging him with it, he thought of his brother who'd died of cancer eight years earlier. The accident had happened when they were children. Nathaniel had been balancing tin soldiers on the blades of his father's push mower. He had been marching around the machine doing an impression of their nanny when he lost his footing. He fell against the handle causing the mower to jump forward a foot or so with just enough force to get the slicing metal blades revolving, just enough force to cut off a finger. His brother had bled profusely. That blood that would in later life turn bad and suffocate him.

He missed his brother. His nine-fingered cynicism and dry, mocking humour would give voice to the thoughts he could never speak. He had been an involuntary mute for much of his life.

Ironically, the last words he heard his more talkative sibling say were.

'More morphine, less talking.'

Chapter 2

I took Baby to Las Vegas. She said her mother was there and she wanted to show her that she had found herself a nice man. It was a mistake. I met her mum after she'd finished a long shift at the mall where she worked on the checkout counter. She told me she liked my English accent. I told her I loved her daughter. We were both lying. We went out to eat and Baby let me pay for everything, she was good like that. We ate ribs, a lot of ribs. The place we went to had all these paper bibs you could wear to stop getting the sticky sauce all over yourself. It kept the juice off Baby's clothes but her face was covered. It reminded me of the way she sprayed my cum all over her face when she jerked me off. It was an image I had captured with my camera. I clicked away at the table thinking I could match the images at a later date.

'Why are you here?' Her mother asked me, whilst picking a large chunk of muscular flesh from her teeth.

'To meet you.' I said plainly.

'No, why are you here in America? It's a long way from home, no?'

I didn't really have an answer. I was lost.

'I guess to see things. New things.'

'Why?'

'So I can take pictures of them.'

She slugged down half her beer in one go and then patted her sternum gently until she burped.

'This is what you do for money? You take pictures?'

'No.' I said. 'I have some money. I am lucky that way.'

'You are lucky. You can lose it all here, however much you have. This town can eat it all up. You would be wise not to stay here. It's like a disease. I see it all the time.' Her strong Mexican accent made him smile. 'It is much better to be poor here. When you have nothing to lose, it is just like living anywhere else. This is no place for her.' She pointed a rib at Baby.

'Well, I don't know how long we'll be here.' I said looking at Baby. She stared out of the window, obviously bored with the conversation. She hardly spoke during the meal and halfway through put her headphones on and started singing along with something on her iPod. She took some money from my wallet and went down the road to buy some cigarettes. While she was gone, her mother just ate, belched, drank, and sometimes smiled at me. She only asked me one question.

'What is wrong with your head?'

I put my right hand up to the top of my head and ran fingers across my shaven spiky hair. I felt the ridges she referred to. Then Baby came through the door. She was smoking in a lazy way, with the cigarette hanging from the side of her mouth, glued to her glossy lipstick.

'Will you take my mother home? I have to do something.'

I told her that that would be no problem. She reached into my wallet and took out a couple of hundred crumpled dollars – it was all the cash I had left except for the odd note in my jean pocket. She kissed me on the cheek without removing her cigarette and wiggled her gorgeous little arse out of the door. I took a picture of her through the smoke-stained glass window. She walked out of my life as quickly as she'd walked into it. She appeared a silhouette against the bruising evening sky behind her, which I guess she was really. She was a shadow wife not a real one.

Max made the cage to her exact specifications; it was to be an eight-by-eight-by-eight cube. The bars were to be no more than four inches wide and there would be a box built into the front of the cage that could be used to push food through. It also had to come in small enough parts to be easily taken down into her basement and assembled there. She drew a picture of it, complete with a bear inside, on the back of a beer label she'd peeled off a bottle.

To get him to finish the project and assemble it while her husband was away, she agreed to let him fuck her and her friend, Loretta, at the same time. Loretta worked in the local bar and it was rumoured she could do things on the pool table with a cue that would win her a place in the Guinness book of records. Loretta would sleep with anything, it was even rumoured that she had had knowledge of a particularly handsome German shepherd – for money, naturally.

The deal was Max could video if he wanted, and of course he wanted. He got a friend of his, Hank, to come and film it and his payment for filming was to fuck both of the girls in the arse. Hank had a big sweaty body. While he pushed her head down into the carpet she could feel his distended stomach using her arse as a shelf to rest on. The only consolation was that his cock was tiny and after having been fucked wide open by Max, Hank barely touched the sides. Hank liked to take his teeth out before fucking, he didn't like the way the denture plate bounced up and down as he pumped in and out, he said the sound of it clacking against his real teeth was like a 'fucking castanet'. So while he humped away, his two front teeth and one from either side watched her from the arm of the sofa. He had lost them in a bar fight a few years back and as he mounted her, she thought of the fist that had done it punching into his face over and over again. The only other good thing about being fucked by Hank, apart from his small dick, was his speed. No sooner was he in you than he'd shoot his load.

After giving her a minute to drink some beer, Max was back at the job, and while she didn't particularly enjoy it, she didn't actually dislike it either. Not disliking it meant it came pretty high on her list of sexual encounters. It was equivalent to most people's idea of great sex. Her husband had more or less habitually raped her from the moment they'd gotten married. Well, it wasn't rape in any legal sense, it was his conjugal right after all, at least that's what her pastor had told her when she'd asked him about it. After all, she didn't actually say no, she was too scared he'd hit her if she did, but she never actively went out of her way to engage in intercourse and she always felt he had done it to her rather than with her. Sometimes she'd be so disgusted by it that she'd throw up after.

Anyway, Max got his videotape of her and Loretta. The entire thing didn't last much longer than a half hour and after that, Max and Hank went out back to the truck to get the cage. They huffed and humped the stuff down to the basement.

'Hey, Shirley, what you want a bear cage for down in your basement anyway?' Hank asked, as he mopped the sweat from his brow with a red-and-white bandana.

'Did I ask you why you wanted to fuck my arse?' Was all she replied, as she brought them down a glass of homemade lemonade.

'I knew a fella once who kept a gator on a chain in his kitchen, just to keep his mother-in-law out the house. Damn she hated them gators. Only thing was, one night while he was asleep, the thing bit off its own paw and took itself and its bloody stump through the house looking for the one who'd chained it up. The guy just about survived the attack but lost a leg and now he has to shit in a bag 'cos the thing took a great chunk out of his stomach. His wife wasn't so lucky. Still with the wife dead an' all, at least that bitch of a mother-in-law ain't comin' round no more. If you ask me, he ain't got it so bad, he just sits there watching Sally-Jesse and drinking beer and eating chips and he don't even need to get up to go to the can. Pretty sweet, eh?'

'You're a fucking moron, Hank.' Loretta said as she headed out of the door for her car. She was bored and had already got her twenty dollars.

Shirley watched them as they bolted the thing together and then screwed it to the basement wall. It took up more of the basement than she had planned. It was roomier than she had expected and she felt a little annoyed. Finally, they hung the front onto two great hinges and swung it to.

'Here,' said Max handing her two giant padlocks. 'You lock it here and here and there ain't no bear nor nothing getting out.' She took the locks and practised closing them.

'You coming over later?' Max asked her as he and Hank started up the stairs.

'Why?' She stood staring at the cage.

'Thought we might fuck some more.'

'Not tonight. I'm gonna be kinda busy.'

He sat in his mother's living room for three days, waiting for the funeral. Everything in the house, he thought to himself, was the same but different. After her stroke five years earlier, she had had the place altered for her new wheelchair-bound existence. He'd never seen her in this semi-paralyzed state. She had been a healthy middle-aged woman when he'd last had any contact with her. She had kindly told him that he was a disgrace. Think of your children. He did and it hurt. When she slammed the door and left, he reached for his pipe and smoked some crack to numb it all away.

Everything had been automated to help her live as normal a life as possible. Her armchair had a large remote control on it which made it go up and down. It could slide almost entirely flat or prop her upright to balance a tray on the arms so she could eat her dinner. There was a track running across the ceiling with a winch attached to it, which she would use to travel out of the living room along the small hallway and right across the dining room to the newly installed lift. She would descend in the morning and ascend in the evening. Her sister had moved in to help her until she herself had died from a heart attack quite unexpectedly one afternoon while winching her onto the commode. His mother had swung backwards and forwards suspended over her dying and then dead sister for six hours before the night nurse arrived.

He looked at the winch and tried to imagine his mother there, helpless. Outside, the sun slowly sank on suburbia and the orange fluorescence of the street lights seeped into the room. As he sat in the armchair, his hand rested on the cool smooth surface of a green onyx ashtray sat on the top of the nest of tables beside him. He stroked it gently, enjoying the lack of friction, the cold stone, the smooth dip in the centre and the two short crevices for balancing cigarettes in on either side. He rested his index finger in one of them, pretending it was a fag. He pulled his hand up to his mouth and took a long draw on an imaginary Silk Cut – blue-grey plumes of smoke poured from his mouth and filled the room forming ghostly apparitions of his mother and father and himself as a young boy. Without having to actually get up, he swivelled the chair around so he could open the drawer in the sideboard where his mother had always kept her cigarettes. The drawer was as he expected and remembered. Two packets of Silk Cut, one opened, one waiting to have its cellophane hymen broken. The only new things there were jar upon jar and packet upon packet of medication. He flicked through them, looking for something he might take. He found some temazepam. He flicked through the leaflet that came with the packet. He'd never actually seen it before. He'd always just bought or been given the little pills on their own – no packet required.

Use: Short-term (i.e. 7–10 consecutive days) insomnia therapy. Use for more than 2–3 consecutive weeks requires complete re-evaluation of the patient. Adults, 15–30 mg before retiring. Elderly and debilitated patients: Initial dose before retiring should not exceed 15 mg. Contraindications: Myasthenia gravis, sleep apnea syndrome, previous paradoxical reactions to alcohol and/or sedative medications. Pregnancy, nursing mothers. Precautions: Efficacy not established in patients <18 years of age. Not recommended for use in individuals prone to alcohol or substance abuse. Exercise caution in severely depressed patients, elderly and debilitated patients, impaired renal and/or hepatic function, severe pulmonary insufficiency. Avoid abrupt discontinuation of temazepam. Side effects: Dizziness, lethargy, drowsiness, confusion, euphoria, staggering, ataxia, falling. Infrequent paradoxical reactions (e.g. excitement, stimulation, hyperactivity, hallucinations).

As he read, he pushed six of the little blue tablets through the blister pack and popped them one by one into his mouth, washing them down with water from a glass left on the table by the ashtray. It was a thick-cut glass tumbler with a nice amount of weight to it. It gave him pleasure just holding it. There were six cigarettes left in the packet and as he pulled one out, he noticed there was a red lipstick mark around the tip. Other than that, it was virgin and intact. It was his mother's lipstick, she'd always worn that colour, but he couldn't for the life of him work out why she would have placed this in her mouth only to take it out again and put it back in the packet. He cleared some of his beard out of the way and carefully ran the lipstick end over his lips. He could taste the perfumed wax. He was as close to his mother at that point as he would ever be again or, as he couldn't help feeling, ever really had been. It was one last kiss goodbye.

He took the onyx lighter next to the onyx ashtray and clicked it two or three times before it flamed. He lit his cigarette and sucked down the cancerous fumes into his lungs. He held them there for a few seconds before spewing them forth, back into the room. He flicked the ash onto the flowery carpet, not wanting to spoil the essence of perfection that hung round the ashtray. Then he felt the warmth of the tamazepam kick in, every part of him relaxed and faded. In the failing light of the room and the failing light of his brain it didn't take much for him to start experiencing one of the infrequent paradoxical reactions.

His mother, he noticed, was sat in his father's chair staring at him. Her eyes were looking more through him than at him and she was distant but calm. He liked her like this. He had always felt there was a ball of anger locked up somewhere inside her that was stopping her from being happy and prevented him from ever really communicating with her. But now, there was a wonderful aura around her, beautiful blues and purples were radiating from her, sparks of mauve and pink flicking in and out of her auric field. She was holding something in both hands, something he couldn't quite see, something small. Her fingers were wrapped around it as if protecting something very precious and fragile.

'I missed you, mum.' He said quietly.

'Why am I lying in a box?' She asked.

Driving away from the service station and back on to the M1, he was trying to take in the events of the day. What seemed like a thousand ambulances, police cars and fire engines were heading up the motorway past him. Overhead, he could see police helicopters circling. He turned on the radio to see if he could find out some information about the explosion he had just been in. He had to turn the volume to full before he could hear any discernible voices, and even then they appeared to be talking while swimming underwater in the blood of his punctured eardrums. He turned it off again and ran through the possibilities – a bomb or a gas leak seemed the most likely reasons to him, although he couldn't work out why a toilet on the M1 would be high on the al-Qaeda hit list.

He hadn't noticed the look on the man's face next to him in the café when he bought a coffee. He hadn't noticed the four minders who were walking with him, whispering to him incessantly. He hadn't noticed that they both made their way into the toilets at the same time. He headed for the cubicles on the right and the bomber headed for the cubicles on the left. He hadn't noticed any of this because he had other things on his mind. The day had already been a strange one way before the accidental explosion and the loss of his hearing. It was not every day that he had a body in the boot of his BMW.

He had had a row with his wife over breakfast about something or other. That was par for the course. Bartholomew was running a fever and had thrown up his Calpol, again not totally out

27

of the norm. He had gone through the usual routine of packing his briefcase with various papers and his laptop. He checked his BlackBerry to see if he had forgotten any meetings or appointments. He hadn't. As he left the house, he picked up his bowling ball in its bag ready for the monthly executive bowling networking get-together that night. He opened the boot and placed it in there next to the jack. At this point there was no body in there, it was relatively empty and spacious. He knew this because he couldn't see one in there and as yet he hadn't dragged the corpse off the roadside and with great effort lifted it in, having to rearrange the legs, bending them and laying them flat to make sure he could close the trunk. When he closed the boot this time, it shut easily. He didn't have to push down on it at all, it gently acquiesced to his request for closure and the perfection of German design pleased him.

His usual routine continued for another seventeen minutes. Start the car, drive the car, listen to talkSPORT, head along the back lanes to miss the traffic. The radio started to crackle a bit as reception dodged in and out in the bottom of the country valley. The car took all the corners of the winding road smoothly and with ease. He pressed the radio controls on his steering wheel searching for a clearer channel. This had never happened before on his drive to the office, reception was normally perfect. Radio 1 came on loud and clear, in fact too loud and clear, he must have turned the volume up when flicking through the channels. He hated Radio 1, its cuntish breakfast DJ belched into the microphone, the sound reverberated around his head. He turned the volume down and reached for a CD from the case he kept in the glove compartment. His hand flicked around searching for the black leather wallet containing various assorted types of music, something for every mood. It wasn't there. It had to be there, where would it go? He put his hand further into the compartment's darkness trying to search it out. What he didn't know was that his wife had taken it out of the car the night before, just to piss him off. She'd spent a lot of time recently just fucking with his head. But he didn't know that at the time. He continued to scrabble around and then quickly took his eyes off the road to see where the fucking thing had gone. A millisecond passed. There was a huge bang and, in an instant, he slammed on the brakes and jerked his head up to see what he'd hit. The car skidded and juddered, there was a bumping and the car ran up over something. The screeching tires smoked as it swerved to a halt. The final jerk caused his head to whip back and forth and he just missed smashing his nose across his face on the steering wheel.

The road in front of him was clear. The road behind him wasn't. He got out of the car, his heart pounding, his wrists aching from gripping the steering wheel so tightly. In the shock of the accident he found it difficult to stand up, his legs were jelly. He went to the front of the car, without even glancing back. There was nothing really to see. A small dint in the silver bumper with a little scratch of blue paint on it gave him little indication of the horror. He looked under the car and saw the mangled tangled remains of a bicycle. It looked like the carcass of an expensive mountain bike. On the twisted metal frame, he could just make out the name Claude Butler. There was no sign of the cyclist under the car, and he hoped from the bottom of his nauseous stomach that this was a good sign. He or she had been miraculously thrown clear and was now sitting by the side of the road perhaps banged and bruised but otherwise unhurt. He stood up and walked slowly round the car. About twenty yards back down the lane he saw the crumpled pile of a person. Lying perfectly still, arms and legs jutting out at peculiar angles, not natural at all. He started gulping for air as he walked slowly towards the body. He felt sure he was about to black out. It was worse than he could have imagined. Not only were the legs and arms broken and crushed, as, he assumed, were the ribs and internal organs, but there was blood everywhere. Her tight black cycling shorts were wet glistening in the early morning sun. Her white and yellow t-shirt didn't hide the colour as well, nor did the pale ivory of her badly macerated arms and legs. He was in no doubt that she was dead. Not simply because of her unnatural position and absolute stillness with which she lay there, but because of her lack of a head.

Jill had a thing about sex. She had never really liked it. Not really. And this he found one of the funniest ironies of his life. He had only ever really wanted to marry her because she was so beautiful. All he could think about when he first saw her in a coffee shop on Tottenham Court Road was how much he wanted to fuck her. She had a tight little arse, which she'd somehow wriggled into a skin-tight pencil skirt.

He had watched her for an hour, wondering what it would be like to slowly peel her out of it, trying to picture exactly what underwear she would be wearing, and whether or not the skirt was so tight that it would pull her panties down with it as she squirmed her way to freedom. He wanted to run his fingers over the top her stockings, lick the clasp of her garters and pop them open with his teeth before resting her back on his bed and nuzzling his way up in the dark under her cashmere jumper to discover her breasts held in tightly by her constricting bra. Someone had put Dean Martin on the jukebox and she shook her perfectly formed bum back and forth in front of it. As he remembered that first meeting which unknowingly imprisoned him in a life sentence of unfulfilled desire, he remembered the look of near orgasmic pleasure she had on her face as she swung her hips to 'Volare'. She closed her eyes as she swayed and her pouting lips mouthed the words. He had no idea, as he fell so deeply in love with her, that she would prove to be a cold, manipulating, heartbreaking cheat and liar. As he watched her dance, he didn't have the merest clue that she would sleep with half the town and start a relationship with his business partner that would last for almost their entire married life.

Because of how she was sexually with him, he had often wanted to ask her lovers when they came over to dinner with their wives and sat at his table making polite conversation, eating his food, what it was like for them fucking his wife.

'So tell me, does she suck your cock? Because she won't do that to me. Oh wait, no, there was that time when you said you would do it and then you cleaned my cock with a wet wipe before sucking on it and then said it tasted all chemically so you wouldn't be doing that again? Has she done that with any of you chaps before?'

But he had never said anything of the sort. In fact, he had been more or less inert within his marriage for as long as he could remember. He hated himself as much as he hated his wife, and he hated his wife a lot. He had sometimes thought about poisoning her, especially after September 1983.

In September 1983, he had come home from the office to pick up a legal document he'd forgotten. There was a car in the drive that he recognised as his partner's. He knew what that meant immediately, because sure as fuck Jim hadn't dropped in to pick up the contract as a favour to him. No, the only answer was that somewhere inside, Jim was nuts deep in his wife. His first instinct was to turn his car round and leave, like a kicked puppy whimpering away with his tail between his legs. But he didn't. He quietly crept into the house. Knowing his wife as he did, he knew where they would be. She wouldn't even consider having sex anywhere outside of the bedroom – that was just filthy and wrong. So he silently made his way up the stairs and across the hallway. All his suspicions were confirmed by the sounds of Jim grunting and puffing emanating from their bedroom.

He watched them fucking for ten minutes through the crack in the half-open door. He found he liked watching his wife lying there being fucked by another man. He liked seeing the dead look in her eyes that he had had to watch for so many years. Her head was turned to the side, mainly so Jim wouldn't try to kiss her and smudge her perfect lips. She looked as if she was thinking about something she had to do later that day. She made no noise, not that Jim seemed to mind. He was making enough noise for the both of them. Standing there watching this strange act of necrophilia, he realised there was a difference between himself and Jim. Jim didn't seem to notice or care that he was fucking a corpse. He didn't mind the lifeless eyes staring at the ceiling, the total lack of any reaction to all his hard work, and Jim was certainly working hard. He was red and sweating. The only reaction he noticed on his wife's face during the entire time was when a bead of sweat from Jim's brow had the effrontery to plop from his forehead on to her breasts. A restrained look of horror and disgust came over her. She reached out to the bedside table and pulled a paper tissue from a rose-covered box. She mopped up the offending perspiration. She then took out another and unfolded it on her chest to catch any further unwanted fluid.

He was fascinated by the spectacle in front of him. He was not turned on in the slightest, just mesmerised. It was like watching a wildlife documentary, or more accurately like being out in the field in a hide watching the mating ritual of some male animal whose mate is subdued and silent. Jim shuddered and hammered home his ejaculation and that was the end of it. His wife waited impatiently for him to climb off her. There was nothing more to be seen so he turned round and padded his way downstairs. He went into the kitchen, picked up the papers he needed, had a small glass of cold apple juice from the fridge and then he took his time leaving the house and getting into his car before heading back to the office. He had half-expected one or other of them to come downstairs and find him there, but for some unknown reason neither emerged from the bedroom. His wife was never keen on cuddling after sex and normally went straight into the shower to scrub herself clean. In his experience, she liked to leave the scene of the crime as quickly as possible, often heading for a coffee to remove the nasty taste of intercourse from her mouth.

He did almost nothing about his discovery. If he was honest with himself, he didn't really care that much. Perhaps, if he loved her, he would have felt a modicum of jealousy, but, as it was, it just made him live in hope that one day she would leave him. If anything about the whole thing did get to him, it was more the fact that it was his partner who was shafting him, well him and his wife. Every day he would come into the office smile at him, have lunch with him, chat as if nothing was out of the normal, as if he wasn't in fact fucking his whore of a wife.

The only action he did take was, even by his own standards, somewhat peculiar. His wife's immaculate mouth was her crowning glory, her lips were fleshy, erotic and always perfectly painted with a Chanel lipstick – it was those lips that suckered in her lovers. She offered dreams of pleasure with that mouth that, once caught in her web, would never be fulfilled. That mouth would have to pay. Each night before bed he would head for their en suite bathroom, have a pee, brush his teeth and wash his face. Then each night for a month he would reach into her Louis Vuitton make-up box and take out her deep red lipstick. He removed the lid, twisted the bottom and then slowly and carefully inserted the little dog's dick of a make-up stick up his arse. After ten seconds or so he removed it, took some toilet paper and polished up the smeared gold sleeve, put its cap on and then put it back in its exact position.

He put the lawnmower back in the shed. He opened his biscuit tin full of secrets and took out the only picture he had of Lauren.

Chapter 3

I didn't miss Baby and I wasn't surprised when she didn't come home. Her mother was more concerned about me than she was about her daughter. Neither of us really cared about Baby. She would be fine. She was a survivor. Like a very bad penny, she'd turn up again sometime, somewhere. But I wouldn't be around to see it. Having spent a few days with her I knew the only thing she was in danger of doing was fucking a guy to death and being done for accidental murder.

I had stayed the night at her mum's house watching shit Spanish language game shows all evening. In the morning she made me a breakfast of coffee and eggs and told me Baby had phoned her to tell her she'd fallen in love with a rich gambler and wondered if she could break it to me. I never officially got the marriage annulled, for all I know I'm still married to her, although I don't remember the church ever giving us a marriage license in the first place.

Her mother was sweet and said I was welcome to stay with her for as long as I liked. She told me she could do with a son and that I was as good a one as she could hope for – even if I was English and not Catholic. She wanted me to call her Ma and I had nothing else to do and nowhere else to go so for a few days we played out the game. She took me up and down the strip and showed me the whole of the town. Like my marriage, the whole place was a fantasy, an oasis or more truthfully a mirage in the desert. I loved it. The baking, oven-hot heat. The obscene wealth made from unlucky suckers.The gold and neon of the gambling cathedrals. The strippers and the suntanned beggars. The climate-controlled, permanent twilight of the casinos. The whole city sits there beckoning those who dream of a quick buck like Sodom polished and shined. For every one guy who gets lucky, ten thousand lose everything, if that isn't the perfect metaphor for life, then I don't know what is.

When Ma was working, I just wandered around taking photos of strip bars and drunks. I took photos of people at the drive-in chapels getting married. I took Polaroids and gave them to them as they drove off, only keeping the odd one for myself. A quick developing picture for a quick marriage.

'Hey, Mister.' A kid said walking down the sidewalk. 'What's with your face? You walk funny too, how come?'

In the bright sunshine I could hardly see his face under his Red Sox baseball cap.

'I got attacked by a flesh eating zombie. I was lucky I got away as lightly as I did.' I said.

'Have you looked in a mirror recently? You weren't that lucky.' He said before running off.

At school I'd been bullied a lot because I'd been too pretty or too like a girl, depending on which side of the fence you sat. My mother wouldn't let me cut my hair. It was long, wavy and golden blonde.

'Women would give you money for that, it's criminal to cut it.' She would say to me whenever I protested. It was the Seventies and my mum was a hippy dressed in an accountant's clothes. She dreamt of a freedom for me that she had missed, and the price for her freedom was regular ridicule and beating for me in the playground. I remember getting a kicking for being the only longhaired kid in the school photo.

'You fucking homo, what do you look like? Have you seen what you look like in the picture. Looks like there's a fucking girl in the school.' These were the words I heard before being punched in the face and kicked to the ground. I begged my mum to cut my hair, but she wouldn't have it. Strangely enough when I got old enough to make my own decisions, I kept it long. I only cut it off when I knew what was going to happen. When, as this child had pointed out, considerations of aesthetics were the least of my worries.

'You gonna come with me to see a friend. Maybe you take a picture of her for me.' This was not a question but a statement and I was more than happy to be told what to do, it stopped me wafting around in the parched breeze.

Ma and I got on a bus and headed out for six sweaty hours. She didn't tell me where we were going and, on the journey, she slept most of the way. I took pictures of her sleeping. I took pictures of the desert through the window of the bus and I took pictures of the little girl who kept staring at me through the crack in the seats in front. She spoke in Spanish to her raven-haired mother about me and although I wasn't sure exactly what she was saying, I was pretty certain her mother was telling her not to stare at me. I drank my way through a bath full of water to keep myself hydrated at each truck stop. I pissed half of it out again and splashed water all over my head. The glare of the sun incessantly burning through the coach window made my eyes water and I bought a pair of cheap blue tinted shades. I experimented with using their lenses as a filter on the camera.

When we got off the bus we found ourselves standing outside the vast, high walls of a state penitentiary. Her friend was waiting for us in the visitors' room, sitting there in an orange jumpsuit that glowed out against the white walls behind her. She was beautiful. We chatted for five minutes, before Ma told me to stay and talk some more while she went for coffee. Her friend asked if it was all right for me to take photos of her. She started talking and, twenty minutes later, she stopped. I hadn't said a word. I took close-ups of her hands, of her face and of her tears. I took a Polaroid and gave it to her. She wanted one of me but that wasn't the way it worked, so I had to decline. I wasn't there for that. She talked about her husband's death. She talked about a house burning down. She talked about being reborn in the flames and being swept away by the heat of love. She talked and I clicked away.

Ma came back in, and it was time to go. Her friend wanted to give me a kiss on the cheek and leant forward but was reminded in no uncertain terms, by a guard with a gun, that there was to be no physical contact. I liked her and sort of wished I'd married her and not Baby, but then I wouldn't have Ma as my Ma. I'd have a wife in prison and a wife in prison is perhaps worse than having no wife at all.

She sat in the rocking chair on the porch smoking a cigarette and watched the sun die in glorious Technicolor over the horizon. Her front yard never got fully dark, the whole town being illuminated by the orange glow of the chemical plant that never slept. It pumped out its bile deep into the local water table – babies died of leukaemia, women's teeth fell out and healthy men faded slowly of unspecific fatigue diseases and cancer.

As she smoked, she watched the fireflies appear. When she was a little girl, her grandmother had told her they were fairies from the old country come over to check the family was all right. She said that whenever she had a problem, she could whisper it to them and they'd take care of it. But that was just a story from an old Irish woman who died and left her alone. These were just fireflies and if she wanted any help, they would do jack shit about it. Her tongue flicked around the gap where her tooth used to be up until a week ago. It hadn't fallen out because of the water, or because of a bar brawl, but from a small tap her husband had given her for not bringing him a cold enough beer. The refrigerator had a habit of shorting out and she hadn't noticed until she went to get him a can. It wasn't warm but it wasn't freezing cold like he liked it either. He'd thrown the can along with the foam holder that proudly stated 'World's Biggest Truck Pull' on the outside across the room and slapped her to the floor.

As he stood over her, he reminded her, in his most reasonable of all his violent tones that he'd been away driving for three days without a break; and that the least she could do was provide him with a cold beer when he got home. His dog growled at her from the corner of the room where its blanket lay. Even he was affronted that his master had been so slighted. She knew that the beast would love to be given the word that would allow him to bite her face off.

She hated that dog, that mongrel, flea-ridden, sore-laden, slathering bastard of a dog. No one could guess at the dog's true heritage, it looked like some hellish cross between a pitbull, a German shepherd, a Rottweiler and a bear. Every inch of it was muscle or teeth. He had won it at the end of a night's gambling. The man who owned the dog had been unwilling to give him up and pay his debt, so her husband broke his legs with a pool cue. The dog knew who his new master was and it wasn't the cripple screaming in the dust. He jumped into to the back of their pick-up as if he'd always been in the family. Her man regularly won money making it fight other dogs in the town. It had never been beaten. He'd even let it fight a wolverine once and a rattle snake. The evil hound had ripped both of their throats out and eaten most of the snake for good measure. She knew it would love to tear through her flesh, it wasn't a family dog, it was his dog.

She reached into the cool box by her feet and pulled out a bottle of beer. She twisted the bottle top and drank it down in three large gulps, belched and reached for another. For what she was about to do, she didn't want to drink too much but needed to drink enough to stop her from shaking all over. In years to come, people would ask her why she did it, and why she hadn't just walked away. The police would ask her, psychologists would ask her, strangers she had never met would write and want to know what drove her to it. Wouldn't it have been easier to have just packed a bag and left? After all, he was away a lot of the time driving long haul, she could have been half way across the country by the time he got back from one of his trips, couldn't she?

She didn't answer any of their questions, the most they would get out of her on the subject was a guttural growl. It wasn't because she didn't know why, he only ever left her with ten dollars and how far would she get on that. The reason she didn't answer their questions was simply because it was none of their fucking business. What the fuck did anybody else need to know about why she'd done what she had. They didn't know her. They didn't even really want to know her. She was nothing but a curiosity and knowing the inner workings of her mind during two months one August and September in a backwater in the middle of nowhere wasn't gonna solve the world's problems, it wasn't even going to stop the same thing happening again anywhere else. In fact, if she had thought it would have stopped that kind of thing from happening again, then she definitely wouldn't have said a word, she wouldn't have even grunted.

She had no regrets at all. Not even for a second. He got what he deserved and she got what she deserved and nobody else got hurt, well no one that didn't also deserve what they got, so what the fuck did it have to do with anybody else. She didn't ask them why they married their tight-arsed little wives with the plastic smiles and why they kept filling the world their little scum runt children, did she?

This was going to be a one-shot deal. If she fucked this up, she was as good as dead. She ran through the order of things in her mind over and over to make sure she'd got it sorted in her head. She got up nervously and checked everything was in place. There was a plate of meat on the floor in the living room. There was a two-foot length of two-by-one holding the front door open and there was a baseball bat propped up against the rocking chair. In any other situation and to anyone else, these three things on their own amounted to little but to her all three put together would change everything.

According to the time on her mobile phone, it was one thirty in the morning, the rest of the ramshackle houses on the street were more or less asleep. Four doors down the dirt track, the young guy with the motorbike was playing some old blues records. Some old nigger wailing would be the soundtrack. It was another four beers later before she heard his truck. She stood up, suddenly clear-headed, picked up the baseball bat and stepped across the porch positioning herself behind the wooden strut holding up the porch just to the right of the front door. There were advantages, she thought to herself, of being anorexic.

As he pulled the truck into the driveway, the headlights panned across the scrap of dust where a lawn should have been, illuminating the whole house, everywhere except the shadow in which she was hiding. Her heart was trying to break its way out of her chest with every beat. She heard him pull up, the hydraulic brake hiss, the cab open, he groaned as he climbed down off the rig. She heard the dog jump down after him, it was licking its slathering chops. They walked together across the yard, he was muttering something to himself, she couldn't make out what but even from here, she knew the mood he was in. She smiled to herself, if he thought he'd had a bad day so far, he had no idea that things were about to get a whole lot worse.

As they got to the porch steps, the hound smelled the meat and bounded forward through the open door. She took one step back, hit the timber holding open the door and, as it swung shut, used this movement as the backswing for a home run straight to the side of her husband's head. There was a crunch and the next thing she knew, she was standing over his body.

'The future ain't what it used to be!' She whispered.

He found it hard to take in the fact that her lifeless dead body was being lowered into the ground. Better that than burying her alive, he supposed but either way he didn't like it. He'd spoken to his mother more in the last few days since she'd died than he had in years. He'd grown quite fond of the old lady. She seemed to have aged well, the years revealing a mellower, calmer radiance to her than he'd never noticed when he'd lived with her.

The South London cemetery where the funeral was being held was cold and grey. A fine spray of rain enshrouded the graveyard, it was so dense that it felt like a cloud had descended to gather her up for the transubstantiation. It was the kind of rain that soaks all of a person instantly because there's no room between droplets in which to hide.

He felt bedraggled and out of place. His long hair wet and stuck to his forehead, water dripped from his moustache. He sucked it in, the cold water refreshing his warm mouth. That was about the only bit of him that was warm though, the rest of him was shivering. He hadn't thought to wear an overcoat and his dead father had been a good three inches shorter than him, so the suit he had borrowed from the wardrobe in the spare room failed to cover his extremities. Legs and hands flapped around uncovered like white flat fish gasping for breath. He couldn't find any socks either and now the rain was finding its way easily from his exposed ankles down into his father's shoes, which were now not only tight but sodden as well.

He looked around at the assembled gathering of mourners. There was his dead mother's non-dead sister who had greeted him on the doorstep three days earlier; her husband, whom he imagined was called George; two cleaners who had been paid by the council to come and clean her house once she was chair-bound – although she was convinced they were stealing things – and her half-sister, Dodds, whom he had never met before and who was never spoken of. The only other people there were officials, the priest, the funeral director and his men in charcoal black.

Father O'Leary had given a remarkably good speech in the chapel of rest about his mother's life. He had nearly got her name right, and he knew that she had been a secretary for twenty years working for the electricity board. Other than that he said she was kind, much loved and deeply missed. None of which were true but what was he going to say? That she was mean-spirited, had alienated nearly everyone she had ever met and only six people could be bothered to turn up to her funeral and at least two of them were there to make sure the old witch really was put securely six feet under? Hardly.

As the others listened to these generous words in silent solemnity, he focused his attention on the knocking. It started out softly and then increased to a loud thumping. It was the sound of a fist banging away at a padded silk lining under an oak-look finish sheet of MDF. There was a muffled voice as well. He looked round to see if anyone else had noticed but nobody seemed to have or they were choosing to ignore it. He chose to do the same and besides it became more difficult to hear it the farther into the ground the coffin was lowered and he knew that by the time there was all that soil on top of it, it would be barely audible. The others took handfuls of soil and tossed it into the grave on top of his mother. He took a handful and put it in his father's pocket, the weight of the wet earth felt pleasant. He picked up a second handful and placed it in the other pocket for balance. He threw a third handful onto the gold plaque which read his mother's name and dates.

Father O'Leary looked around at the strangers.

'Would anyone like to say anything?'

There were no takers.

'Steven, how about you? Any final words for your mother?'

He had hardly spoken out loud for years. He coughed to clear the lump he had in his throat.

'I guess.' He whispered. 'I guess.' He repeated a little louder and then a third time now at an audible level, though hardly loudly. 'I guess, I *would* like to say something. My mother doesn't really like being in there.' He pointed down to the coffin. 'And I don't really like her being in there either if I'm honest.'

They all looked at him, some with looks of disdain, others with pity.

'It's okay, I might not like it but I know that's the best place for her. After all she is dead.' He tried to smile reassuringly before he began to speak again.

'You see, I know she's dead, the problem is she doesn't.' He stopped speaking because he wasn't really sure what to say, and now that the words had come out of his mouth, he wasn't even that sure he should have said them. Maybe it was something he should have kept between himself and his mother. Everyone was quite deliberately not looking at him. Everyone except the priest who said softly.

'I'm sorry Steven, what did you mean by that?'

Steven was confused by the question. His head felt cold and wet and the act of trying to think up an answer made him feel a little nauseous. What bit of what he had said hadn't the man understood?

'What did I mean by what?'

'By what you just said, Steven?'

'Which bit of it?'

'All of it.'

'Well, I meant all of it.'

'Yes, but what did you *mean* by it? What did you mean when you said your mother doesn't know she's dead?'

'Just what I said. She doesn't like being in the coffin, because she doesn't realise she's dead. She's not enjoying lying there. That's why she's knocking on the coffin lid. That's why she's shouting. She's quite distressed, I think. But then wouldn't you be if you thought you were being buried alive – even if you were dead.'

The questioner looked at his aunt. She took Steven's hand and led him away. She patted his arm as they walked from the grave through the rows upon rows of other dead mothers and fathers and sisters and brothers and daughters and sons. They reached the car park and she opened the door of her car and ushered him on to the back seat.

'Listen Steven, love, I'm going to have a word with the priest, you know, just to say thank you, that sort of thing. I think George's having a fag but he'll be over soon and we'll drop you home then, all right?'

'All right.' He agreed.

She shut the door and headed off back into the chapel. He watched her until she was swallowed up in the mist and disappeared. He could just make out the silhouette of the chapel's roof. Shivering on the backseat, he considered the fact that somewhere in there was the oven of the crematorium and he thought it might be nice and warm in there. He pictured the men that fed the oven or furnace or whatever it was. It would be so hot that they worked in just their labourer's trousers and were bare-chested, glistening with sweat and muck. In the glare of the fire, they would appear as black shapes smelting bodies, then pouring the remains into a conveyor belt of metal urns. As this picture played across his mind, he became aware of a knocking on the window and he turned to find his mother's half-sister Dodds, tapping on the window. He looked at her and smiled. She was speaking but he couldn't hear what she was saying. He continued to smile as she made some peculiar hand movements, small circular turning motions. He copied them but not really knowing why. Then she reached for the door handle and opened the car door.

'Couldn't you hear me, darlin'? I was saying wind the window down. That way, I don't make the car all wet inside, like I am now.' She had a much stronger South London accent than anyone he knew in the family. She wound down the window for him and then shut the door again.

'That's better. Now, do you know who I am, darlin'?' He stayed silent. Although he knew her name, he knew very little else. The only little bits he had heard over the years were never positive.

'I'm Dodds, your mother's sister. Well half-sister. We had the same mum. Look, I haven't got time to explain everything but, here, take this.'

She reached into her handbag and produced a small ring bound pad of lined paper with a yellow kitten on the front. She scrawled something on a page and then tore it off and gave it to him.

'Don't lose that and don't tell her I gave you it. Now be good. Have yourself a good long bath. That'll do you good. And remember I know what you meant. I'll do what I can for her, you know, to try to lay her to rest, but she was always a stubborn cow, that mother of yours. We'll all pray for her. If you see her in the meantime though, don't be afraid, you're just lucky you can.'

She reached into the car and took the piece of paper she had given him out of his hand, folded it and put it in his top pocket and patted it smooth. She kissed him on his cheek but because she couldn't feel any skin through his thick long beard, she kissed him again on his forehead. He closed his eyes and felt her lips on his eyelids, one then the other. He kept his eyes shut and he heard her click-clack away over the tarmac. When he opened his eyes, George was sitting in the driver's seat.

'What did she want?' He nodded to where Dodds had been. 'Whatever it was, don't tell your aunt about it. Her and her don't see eye to eye, if you know what I mean. Since she joined that Church, they ain't really spoken.'

'She said I should have a bath.' Steven offered.

'Well everyone loves a good bath, lad. Maybe she's not as crazy as they say.' He smiled and winked. Steven copied the wink to see how it would feel.

'OK, I'll have a bath.'

Where her head had been, there was now a hideous red gash pumping blood out on to the road. Great pulses of magenta shot out ten or twelve feet. His stomach lurched.

How could this have happened? He had only taken his eyes off the road for a second, or so he thought, where had she come from? Why hadn't he seen her? How could the head not be there? He tried to think of a logical explanation of how this woman's head had come clean off. She hadn't bounced over the car like they do in road safety adverts; she'd gone under the car. He couldn't work out the mechanics of how this would have happened.

He didn't have all the information. He did not know that Sandra Simpson had been on her knees examining her bicycle for a puncture when he came round the corner. He might not have seen her but she saw him. In a split second, she knew this was the place she would never again leave as a live woman. She tried to dive out of the way but to no avail, her outstretched body was caught up in the wheels and undercarriage of the car. The back right wheel tearing over her neck and sending her head spinning off in a different direction from the rest of her body. It was mercifully quick and she knew very little about it.

He couldn't work any of this out so he stopped thinking about it and became preoccupied by another mystery. Where was the head? He began to walk back up the road looking for it. As he searched, he reached into his pocket for his mobile. He phoned dialled a number he remembered from an advert on television. As he searched for a severed head, he spoke to the lady on the other end whose chirpy efficient voice somehow exaggerated the horror he was surrounded by.

'What town, please?'

'I don't know.' There was no sign of it on the road for as far as he could see, he started to search through the hedgerow.

'I'm sorry, sir? What number are you looking for?'

'I don't know.' What were those beautiful little blue flowers everywhere?

Tiny small beautiful little flowers were scattered all over the place, but there was no head.

'Then how can I help you, sir?'

'I've been involved in accident.'

He knelt down and picked a small posy of the Meadow Cranesbill. When he had eight or nine of them in his hand, he held them up to watch the way the sun played across them changing the colour of their iridescent mauve. He noticed his hand was shaking quite badly.

'Do you want me to put you through to emergency services?' She had a sweet voice, suddenly kind and concerned. When he had not answered her after few seconds, she spoke again.

'Sir, are you all right?'

He thought if he just stared at the flowers for long enough, maybe it would all go away, maybe everything that had happened to him in the last few seconds and minutes would be undone. He would look at this thing of beauty, this small posy of flowers and the whole world would right itself. Time might take pity on him and crank itself backwards to a point before the accident when nothing had happened and nothing had been irrevocably broken.

'Sir? Are you there, sir?' Her voice seemed quite far away now. But it brought him back to his senses for a second and he apologised.

'I'm sorry, what was the question?'

'Shall I put you through to emergency services?'

'Yes, yes, please.'

There was a clicking noise and then a new voice said.

'Which service do you require? Police, fire, ambulance?'

Now he was fully in his body again and no longer looking at the flowers but back at the roadside. There, just three feet away from him, he saw the metallic blue ball that was her cycling helmet. He stepped over to it and rolled it with his foot. The helmet had done its job. Sandra's head was intact and relatively undamaged.

'Which service do you require?' Repeated the voice.

He ran through them quickly in his mind while staring at Sandra's face. Fire was no good, it was too late for an ambulance and the police... the police might not understand. How could he explain this? How could he make it all right? Because of him, a girl was dead. Because of him, her body was lying broken and bleeding by his car and her head was sitting on the verge surrounded by petals and grass here at his feet. He turned his phone off.

With a rising sense of panic, he walked, then ran back to his car. He turned the ignition and pulled away. The bike underneath the car clattered and scratched its way down the road unwilling at first to be released, as if it was somehow clinging on to the murderer with spoked claws. He accelerated and with one final screech, it was free and spinning behind him. As soon as it was liberated from the car, he slammed the brakes. What the fuck was he going to do? He couldn't just drive away. He couldn't just leave this girl there, lying on the road in pieces. He couldn't do it, but every instinct he had told him to flee the scene.

He thought through his life up until this point and everything he had to lose if he stayed, if he was caught. He could lose it all. In one moment of distraction, he could have thrown his life away. That couldn't happen. Then another concern came over him, what if he'd left something at the crash site, something that they could use to find him. Then he'd be in even more trouble because he'd just heartlessly driven away. And the police could track down things now in loads of ways, perhaps he'd left some DNA there, a hair had fallen from his head on to the body as he'd stood over it, or maybe they'd be able to do an analysis of some paint chipped from his car onto the bicycle and then do a match with his tyre marks left in the blood pool. He had to go back and check that he hadn't dropped anything. He had to clean everything up.

He reversed back until he came to the bike and got out of the car. Without thinking about what he was doing, he opened the back door, picked the bike up and after some careful manoeuvring managed to get it on the back seat. A jagged piece of metal from the mudguard sliced through the black leather as he forced it in. Next, he emptied the boot of everything that was in there, the large picnic rug, the emergency petrol can, the litre of windshield washer fluid and his bowling ball bag. He picked up the blanket and walked over to the body. She could barely have been five foot tall and without her head, she was a good deal shorter. Her slender body was easy to wrap up and carry to the waiting metal mouth. Even though she was small, he still had to squash her in diagonally and her legs would not behave as he wanted them to, in the end he had to push the boot shut with great force in order to tightly pack the body down.

He was amazed that in all this time no other car had come past. It was only a matter of time. Now with a sense of purpose and urgency, he hurried back down the road to where the head was. He knelt beside it to pick it up. As he touched it the eyelids flicked open and the mouth suddenly started opening and closing letting out a terrible gasping noise. He fell backwards on to the road in shock and let out a short cry. But almost before it had begun the head ceased its movements and was silent again. Had that really happened? Was it some involuntary final shudder of a dying brain? Had she seen him? He remembered stories he had read in school of the heads of French aristocrats talking and moving in the basket after the guillotine. As he looked at the girl's face now, it was as if it had never moved, not even during her lifetime; it looked utterly inanimate. He couldn't bring himself to touch it again, but he couldn't leave it here. He walked back to the car, took his bowling ball from its bag and placed it on the passenger seat and returned to the head. He scooped it into it the leather satchel. Blood leaked all over the handle and through the seams but this could be cleaned later, he supposed.

He zipped it up and began picking up any bits of broken glass from the girl's bike lamp he could see. He was worried about the blood – there was a lot of it, not only in his car and on the bag but all over the road. He put the head in the passenger's footwell and then tried to wash as much of it away as he could with the wiper fluid. It was certainly diluting but not disappearing. Finally, he took the green plastic can of petrol and poured it all over the blood patch where the body had laid and on the long thin streak of blood where it had pumped out of her neck.

He leant down with his zippo and ran his thumb back over the serrated wheel which created the spark which in turn ignited the lighter fuel and, more quickly than he had expected, lit the petrol on the road. The already evaporating petrol had made a gas cloud above the road which enveloped his hand only momentarily but long enough for him to lose all the hairs on it. He jumped back. The road was alight. The flames were higher and more impressive than he had thought they would be. They might attract the very attention he was seeking to avoid. Thankfully they began to die down almost as quickly as they had blossomed. The tarmac looked black and scorched. He was in his car and away before the fire was out.

As he brought his mobile up to his face, he could smell the sticky blood under a mask of gasoline on his hands.

'Hi, Cynthia. I think I'm going to be late today, something's come up. Could you rearrange my morning's appointments? Thanks.'

His shed gave him great pleasure. It was a place he could retreat to away from the world and all its expectations. It was his place. His wife never came in here. He kept it padlocked and secret. There was little room in here and he liked that, he liked the feeling of being constricted. When things were getting on top of him and he needed to get away from everything and everyone, he would crawl under the work bench pull a blanket over himself and lie there in the dark, dank warmth, his head resting on his gardener's kneel pad. Nobody knew he did this. He would sometimes lie there for three or four hours. Gradually he would calm down, become drowsy and eventually fall asleep.

It was not that he was ever particularly happy in the shed. It was more an absence of criticism, self-loathing and hatred. The shed was his place to come for peace and nothingness, and that was as near to contentment as he got.

Sitting in it now, he looked around him at all the bits and pieces – bits and pieces of a lost or wasted life. There were balls of twine that would never be unwound; secateurs which could as easily have cut through his wife's fingers as they cut through the barbed rose stems; two cans of WD40, the magic oil that seems to fix any fault; packets of seeds which would always remain sealed and unseeded; slug pellets; a small fridge with four cans of lager unopened; an old badminton set messily bundled up; a box of tools he'd inherited from his father; a fan heater for the winter and his biscuit tin which held the only evidence of his secret life, the other him, the other life he'd led, the one that had kept him sane.

He picked up a tatty old shuttlecock and, like a medium performing psychometry, he shut his eyes and let it give up its past. Images came slowly at first but then faster and faster, flooding into his mind's eye in the flickering bleached colours of an old cinefilm. He saw his two sons fighting with the net trying to untangle it and erect it in the centre of the lawn. The bamboo sticks, which acted as poles, had to be driven deep into the lawn and when their little weak boys' arms were unable to thrust them far enough into the ground to make the net stable, they came running over to him, to his shed, from where he'd been watching them through the plastic window. Once it was up, he would have to sit and umpire the match. He was always at pains to be impartial – always trying to keep any possible conflicts down to a minimum.

Then he was asked to roll back his sleeves, take off his shoes and socks, feel the wonderful cool grass under his feet and then, having also rolled up his trouser legs, he would play both of them until a champion had been found. The hot summer day would quickly make him sweat, the rivulets running down his back making his shirt stick to him cold and clammy. He would go into the house and make them ham sandwiches and homemade lemonade from a recipe his mother had left him. They would sit and laugh eating and drinking until the light breeze of early evening would take the sting out of the day's heat. Occasionally, all three of them would re-build the brick barbecue and they'd cook themselves sausages and sit closer and closer to each other as the cold night air swirled in.

His wife was rarely there. Her theory was that, as he was hardly there during the week, he should look after the boys at the weekend while she was out with her friends. He enjoyed his time with them, and what she had thought of as a kind of punishment for him had become one of the true pleasures of his life. When she realised this, she sent the boys away to boarding school during term time and abroad on trips for most of their holidays. They travelled all over the world, from Egypt to the Inca trail, but not because they were there to experience and learn but because their mother wanted them away from him, because he loved them.

He opened his eyes and reached for the bottle of Jack Daniels hiding unsuccessfully in a large grey leather gardening glove behind a mute decoy duck. He had been given it one Christmas by his partner, with a tag around its neck that read 'Happy shooting. Quack, quack, bang, bang.' He had wanted to shoot him in the face. He unscrewed the lid and took a long deep swig. It burnt pleasantly on its way down. He swigged again and again. He liked a drink. His wife, however, was the archetypal 'lady that lunches' alcoholic that drinks wine with her lunch, has a 'little something' around teatime and then moves on to more wine and spirits as the night goes on. As she had got older and her beauty faded, she drank more and more. It was as if each emptied bottle was sucking up her youth and prettiness drop by drop. The more bitter she was about it, the more she drank and the quicker she aged.

He drank more the older he got but he rarely got drunk, he preferred to be stoned. This was only part of his life that he kept away from his wife, not because she would be horrified by his mild addiction to drugs, although she undoubtedly would be, but because it was a bit of him that he wanted for himself, it was one of the many things he did to define himself away from her and her children and his job and the boring house and his dead life.

On the shelf, on its own, was his father's shotgun wrapped in a tartan cloth with a piece of string around it. His father had bought it when it was new over ninety years before, it was a thing of beauty then and it was still a thing of beauty now. A double-barrelled Holland and Holland twelve bore with scrolled push-forward underlever, two wonderfully engraved cocking hammers and two exquisite thirty inch Damascus barrels. The thousands of folds in the metal gave it its strength and its beautiful dark marbling. He loved running his hands over the oak stock, smooth and polished. He loved the smell of the oil in the barrels that kept it from rusting.

When he inherited the gun, he joined a gun club, which was what his partner's cryptic message on his decoy duck had referred to. He hadn't lasted there very long, not because he didn't enjoy the shooting but because he didn't like the whole gun 'set'. As it happened, they were nowhere near as annoying or as obnoxious as the golfing fraternity, but he was never one for joining something or belonging. The actual shooting was fun, there was something about the kick of the weapon, the loud rumbling crack of the shot, the smell of the gunpowder smoking from the discarded cartridges, which took him out of himself for brief moments. He was a surprisingly good shot and won the novices' trophy in the club's annual 'Christmas Clay Pigeon Shoot' competition. But shooting clays was different from shooting a living thing.

One night he took the gun from its locked metal cabinet in the dining room, strolled out on to the back lawn and shot the fox that had been raiding their bins for the last six months. It was a good shot, it was dark and the animal was at the far end of the lawn in the flowerbeds, skirting its way to or from its home. He loosened first one barrel and, then swiftly after, the second. The fox was lifted off its feet by the force of the impact. He put the gun on the patio table and walked slowly down towards it. It was lying on its side panting desperately. When it saw him approach, it made a slight attempt to move or escape but yelped in pain and lay still again gasping for air. Its eyes were full of panic and wild bewilderment. There was blood on its hind legs and across its stomach; it was probably dying slowly from internal bleeding. He knelt down by it and reached out to stroke its head. It snapped round, its razor sharp teeth just catching his index finger. He stood up, took a handkerchief from his pocket and wrapped it around his wound. Then he walked over to the shed, unlocked it, took up a spade and returned to the beast. He raised the tool above his head, paused for the briefest of moments and then, with one swift blow, killed it.

He dug a small shallow grave and buried it by the azaleas. He never returned to the club after that. The gun had remained in the gun cabinet locked up ever since, well, until two weeks ago when he had taken it out, wrapped it in an old picnic rug and brought it down to the shed. He had also taken a few cartridges from his ammo box and placed them in the biscuit tin. He put the shuttlecock down and reached up for the gun and began to unwrap it one final time.

Chapter 4

I stayed with Ma for one more night. To say thank you for all her kindness, I took her out to dinner at Taco Bell. We laughed a lot and sang along to the three-piece mariachi band but, half way through the meal, I got one of my headaches and had to go throw up. It was a shame to waste such great fajitas but there was nothing I could do about it. I took a picture of the toilet before I flushed it away. I wasn't sure that was a picture I actually wanted but I took it anyway. We went straight back home.

Ma was lovely and made a bed up for me in front of the telly and kept bringing me long cold cokes until she needed to sleep. The painful stabbing somewhere behind my temple had shaken me up and got me wired, so I spent all night awake riding the adrenalin and anxiety. There was a channel that had a 'Who Wants to be a Millionaire?' marathon playing, so I watched it until my eyes were sore. I fucked up on all the sport questions. Babe Ruth was the only answer I gave whenever a baseball question came up as he was the only player I had ever heard of. Over the whole night, it was right twice, which wasn't bad.

Ma made pancakes for breakfast and told me that, maybe, I should go home. She looked worried and concerned, but I think she just didn't want me to be the kind of son I was becoming. She really wanted one that could carry her groceries in from the car for her or one that would have a place with a pool that she could come and swim in on her days off. It was time for me to go home anyway.

I had bought the ticket to the States simply because I had never been there and wanted to. I had done a lot of that kind of thing recently. The truth was though that I wasn't even sure where home was. I didn't feel like any place was particularly homely. Perhaps, I thought, I would just head back to England before going away again. I was definitely in the mood for running away to try and find myself, but I had been running for a while and there was no sign of me yet.

Ma opened up one of the kitchen drawers and pulled out a crumpled letter. I could see from where I was that the drawer was packed with similar letters all stuffed in the same blue envelopes. By the way they looked, all worn and crumpled, I guessed that she had read each of them over and over again. This was what she did when she was alone at night.

'I am going to do something for you, and you will do something for me, yes?'

'Ma, if I can do it I will, I promise.'

'You are a good son.'

She went to stroke my head and then thought better of it.

Along with the letter she had in her hand was a picture of a woman.

'This is my sister. She lives in England. In London. You go and see her. She will give you a good meal. She's a fine cook. You go there. And you carry her my love. You make sure she has that. I want her to know that I love her. So, you take a picture of me, okay? You take a picture of me that shows how much I love her and miss her and when you get there, you give it to her and then you must take a picture of her for me. And that picture has to show me how she really is. You capture her in that camera of yours and you send her back to Ma. You can do that for me?'

I promised her that I would try. She had only had one picture of her sister since she had been in England and it was a poor blurred thing. I knew I could do better than that. I spent the morning with Ma following her around as she got ready to go to work and then walked with her all the way, clicking off shot after shot. I caught her many ways in many lights but what I really caught was how I loved her. She was kind, generous and loving and that's what I tried to transfer onto my memory card. I couldn't capture the way she loved her sister, but I could capture the way she had made me feel, the way she had opened her heart to me, a perfect stranger.

When we got to her work, she gave me a set of keys to go back and pick up my clothes and stuff before I headed off for the airport. I kissed her and she held my head for a second, her hands on my cheeks.

'If we don't see each other again...' Her eyes began to tear up. 'I want you to know it would have been nice to have you as a proper son-in-law. My daughter didn't deserve someone as nice as you. Be well, my son.' And then she was gone.

I got a cab to the airport and waited around all day for a flight to take me back to London. On the flight, I felt pressure building up in my head and I hated it. It wasn't excruciatingly painful, it was just unusual and uncomfortable. I tried watching a movie to distract myself but, for some reason, the more I tried to concentrate on the small screen embedded in the headrest in front, the more I lost the vision from the peripheries of my sight. It looked like the screen was at the end of a long tunnel. In the end I gave up and tried to persuade an airhostess to leave me a bag full of mini vodka bottles. She assured me that that was strictly against company policy. I told her about my illness and she left the bottles. Two minutes later she returned with three Valium as well.

'I didn't give you these, all right.' She said looking pityingly at my face and head.

They went down very smoothly with the vodka. And before I really knew it, I was drifting and floating and lost in the songs I grew up with.

When we landed, all I had with me were three cameras, a canvas bag of dirty clothes, a manila envelope full of Polaroids and my laptop. The man at customs assured me the film would be fine and unaffected by the X-ray machine. He wouldn't let me take his photo. As I walked off, I turned on the mobile phone that I hadn't used in the two months I'd bummed round the US. I turned on its camera and took a picture of him anyway while pretending to text someone.

She let the baseball bat fall to the ground and spat on him.

'You ain't never gonna fuck me again! You ain't never gonna hit me again! You ain't never gonna take the belt to me again! You ain't never gonna do nothin' again, you piece of shit.'

She kicked him hard with enough force to break a rib, but as he was already out cold he gave no outward sign of new pain.

She walked across the porch and peered through the window to see whether or not the poisoned meat had affected the dog yet. It was vomiting all over the floor and after each wretch it backed away from its own puke as if somehow trying to escape the torture in its guts. Its legs were shaking and as she watched, they gave way and with a final bout of squealing and whining, it hit the wooden floorboards. Its eyes half closed as everything started to shut down. She opened the door and walked in, if it had any strength left t all, it would have jumped for her throat but it just lay there its tongue lolling out, foamy saliva bubbling from its throat.

'Now, who's the Daddy? It ain't that piece of shit out there, is it, you cock-sucking hound.' She crowed.

She propped the door open, grabbed her husband by his boots and began dragged his carcass into the house.

'You're mighty heavy for a skinny fuck.' She grunted.

It was harder going than she had imagined. She pulled him in stops and starts right across the living room, through the dog's sick and down the hallway to the top of the cellar steps. She dropped his legs and caught her breath for a second. Her armpits were dripping with sweat and her hair was stuck to the perspiration on her forehead. She lifted up the front of her t-shirt and mopped her brow with it before stepping over him and back out to the cool box. She needed a beer.

The dog's eyes were now completely closed and, in his deep comatose state, only the shallow rising and falling of his ribs gave away any sign of life. She threw the bottle top at him and got no reaction when it bounced off his head. She chugged the beer down in one and then got back to the job in hand. As she hauled him down the stairs, his head thumped and bumped on every step. His baseball cap came off and rolled down to her feet. She paused to pick it up. Before she put it on she noticed the once-greasy soiled white material inside the hat now appeared black with blood. Down and down she dragged him. The wound on the side of his head left a fat smudged trail marking the line of his unconscious journey.

In order to get him into the cage, she had to get in first and then pull him into it with her. It was the first time she had actually stood inside, looking out through the bars. She felt no remorse as she looked down at the evil sack of shit.

'Welcome home, hon.'

She opened the tool chest under the stairwell and brought out the set of handcuffs she had stolen from Max's bedroom. She cuffed his ankles together. She made sure they were nice and tight. If he made any sudden move, they would dig into his skin and cut him, she liked that idea a lot. Before finally locking him in, she fetched a small, sturdy three-legged stool, an old dog blanket and a pillow, and placed them against the back wall. Then it was time. She locked him in. He was on one side, she was on the other and there was no going back.

She fell to the ground and began to sob. Years of pain and mental torture were now behind her. Emotions she'd held back behind a giant dam now came crashing over her in waves. As the tears ripped out of her, she grunted and scratched at the floor until her nails bled. She threw herself around and beat at her breast until she was exhausted and slept.

However, her subconscious wouldn't let her sleep for too long. The images that played through her dreams were confused and distorted. At one point, she was bound and gagged and being fucked from behind by someone she couldn't see. In another scenario she was being punched repeatedly by a man who then set his dogs on her. She woke with a start.

The solitary dim light bulb directly above her illuminated the room bleakly in sepia tones, casting long shadows and creating dark corners. She looked straight at the cage to check he was still there. He was. She had no idea how long she'd been out but she had the feeling it had been minutes rather than hours. There was no sign of him stirring. She got up and checked the padlocks were secure. She rattled the cage pulling vigorously at it to see if it was really as strong as she wanted. It was well and truly bolted to the wall and floor and was going nowhere. She had a mixture of feelings as she watched him – fear, elation, hatred, guilt and panic. All of them combined gave her a sense of rushing, as if she was on speed. She needed to calm down. She walked slowly up the stairs looking back with every step to see if he was moving, picturing him suddenly jumping up and easily pushing the door open. It didn't happen. He was more dead than alive.

In the kitchen, she made herself a large flask of black coffee and took two Valium and three Prozac with a glass of brackish water. Alert but chilled-out was the required outcome.

She carried her rocking chair downstairs with the coffee canteen balanced on a soft pink cushion on its seat. Then she began her vigil, waiting to see if he'd regain consciousness.

The hours crawled by and her mind wandered. She thought through the events that had led her to this. She thought about all the things she had planned for her new life from this point onwards. But as the hours rolled by, she became obsessed with just looking at his motionless body. Why wasn't he waking up? She replayed the swing that had nearly taken his head off. She hadn't wanted there to be any chance that he would not be knocked-out cold. Anything less would have been potentially lethal for her. Animals when wounded were at their most dangerous. For this reason, she had held nothing back. Her little league coach would have been proud of her. If her husband's head had been a baseball, she'd have hit it out of the park. But had it been too much? Had she not simply knocked him out for long enough to get him incarcerated but in fact knocked him into the big sleep? She couldn't have killed him. She just couldn't have. He had gone down like a sack of wrenches. If the blow hadn't killed him, perhaps something else had. His head had smashed heavily into the doorframe as he collapsed.

She hadn't thought about killing him. Well, of course, she had, a million times, but in the scenarios she had planned out for months, it always involved him being alive. The cage was fairly redundant if he was already fucking dead. Maybe she would just bury him there and leave. She felt cheated and angry, as if by dying he had managed to fuck her over yet again. Even in death, he was still a pain in the arse. She became more and more convinced as the night went on that he was dead. She had inadvertently become a murderer. Twice she picked up a broom and, holding it by its brush, prodded him with the extended handle trying to provoke some sign of life. There was no response. Wherever she poked him, his limp body simply folded around the wooden pointer in her hand.

She sat back down and poured herself a coffee. She sipped it, trying to think straight. The only way she could tell if he was alive would be to go into there and feel for a pulse. If he *was* breathing, she couldn't see it or hear it from outside. There was no other option other than to open it up and actually feel his heart pumping or not as she suspected would be the case. But what if he was just playing possum, playing a waiting game, waiting to strike as soon as she came within inches of him. She'd have to risk it. Besides, she figured he wasn't clever enough to come up with a plan like that anyway. She unlocked the first padlock but before she undid the second, she tried one final prod with the broom. He twitched. In her shock, she staggered away from the cage and then dropped the lock, sending it scudding across the floor. In a mad panic, she scrabbled to find it. He was coming around, slowly shaking his head. Without taking her eyes off him her hands found what they were looking for and she sprang to her feet and ran to the cage door. She needed to secure it before he got to his feet.

He drove through the windy back lanes of Sussex with the body of a decapitated woman in the boot of his car, her bike on the backseat and her head in a bowling ball bag on the front passenger seat. The hedgerows flashed by as he drove faster and faster away from the accident. He needed time to sort through everything that had happened. He needed time to try to work out why he had thought in a moment of blind panic that taking the body with him was the only logical solution to his current predicament. It now seemed like the most stupid thing he had ever done.

He turned on the radio and flicked through the channels, this time keeping his eyes on the road, until he found something that soothed him. Classical music Handel filled up a void that had appeared where he used to be. The very essence of everything he thought he was and could be had changed, he had lost himself. His body mechanically manoeuvred the car left, right, stop, go. He needed straight roads and distance, so he headed for the nearest motorway and, before he knew it, he was driving North on the M25 circling London. As he drove, he began to formulate a course of action. He had stuff he had to do before he could enter back into his normal life again.

Just past Northampton, he pulled off and headed for small and smaller roads, losing himself in a way he hoped to lose the bike. He needed to get that out of the car. It was conspicuous and the easiest thing to ditch. When he'd not seen a house for a couple of miles, he turned the car down what looked to be a disused track heading into some woods. A mile further down, he parked and got out. There was no sign of anyone, this place was as far off the beaten track as he could hope to find. He took the bent-and-buckled frame out of the car and began to carry it deep into the wood. He stumbled and tripped, his shiny black loafers were ill-suited to the terrain. Mud and leaves flicked up and into the turn-ups at the bottom of his charcoal suit trousers.

Two hundred yards in, he found a huge crater in the woodland with sheer banks on three sides. Standing on the edge, he looked down at the thirty-foot drop below him. Roots were poking through the sandy walls showing where the trees' search for water had ended unsuccessfully in that direction. At the bottom of this hollow was a massive pile of the detritus of modern life. There were washing machines, clotheshorses, boxes of mouldy magazines, a rusting fly-mo, filthy festering clothes, oil cans, tires, and three or four bicycles. Here and there, he could see places where practising arsonists had tried to set things alight, charred black patches had once blazed here but never with enough consuming heat to catch the entire sodden fly tip. This unexpected find was at first unnerving and worrying. It was obviously not the unfrequented spot he had taken it for and he scanned the woods around him for anyone he had not seen in his preoccupation. He was alone. He wondered how on earth so many large heavy white goods had made it this far into the woods but concluded that perhaps he had found the long route through the trees to it. In fact, he could now see two distinct paths to his left and right that looked well trodden. He had stumbled a scratchy new path of his own creation. Then it occurred to him that as long as he was quick and not spotted, this might actually be the perfect place to dispose of a trashed bike. No one would find its presence here in the least bit suspicious.

Speed, he told himself, was of the essence, so he tossed it on top of the rubbish below him. He looked at it lying in the middle of the shit and crap and it looked too clean and new. Although it was obviously twisted and broken, its paintwork showed no signs of wear and tear apart from the scratches where it had been dragged under the car. If all the other objects had one thing in common, it was that that they all looked old and knackered – even the things that had obviously been added in the last few days were ancient examples of tumble dryers or washing-up bowls. He walked round the perimeter of the tip and as soon as he could find a pathway, he scrambled and slid his way down, descending into the pit. Still worried about being seen, he pulled his way as quickly as he could up the mass, his feet sank into the wet stinking compost of rotting waste. It filled him with a feeling of disgust and he realised he may have overreacted, he couldn't imagine many people would climb this fetid pile to recover a twisted wreck, however shiny it was, but he wanted it to be buried, to disappear as if it had never been. After a considerable struggle, he reached it and immediately started pushing it deep into the mass of the mound which happily, albeit slowly, accepted it. When it would go no further, he covered it with boxes and leaves and other bikes and old shoes and whatever came to hand.

Before it was gone forever, he noticed that under the bike's seat, there was a small black zipped pouch. He squeezed it and could tell it was full of something. A quick examination of the contents found it contained a purse and a notebook. He unclipped it, shoved it in his pocket and completed his task of camouflage. Job done, he ran back through the woods to his car and drove away.

As far as he could tell no one had seen him and no one would ever find the bike, not here, not over a hundred miles away from the accident. This bit of history had been erased. Even if it was found there by some kids, there would be no way it would be linked to the events of the morning. It had successfully become just another bike some thoughtless dad had backed over in a driveway or some such thing.

He was filthy. His hands were covered in a layer of mud, which in turn covered gasoline and blood. There was evidence of his activities under his nails, on his clothes, in his hair. He needed to get cleaned up and was desperate for a coffee and a cigarette. He found his way back to the motorway and headed for Watford Gap service station. He would wash, perhaps buy some new clothes, eat, start smoking again and think for a while.

If there was anyone more surprised than his aunt by his mother's will, it was Steven himself. She had left everything to him. The house, her savings, the car, the whole lot, everything was his. She had not been a wealthy woman, so it was hardly like winning the lottery but it meant he was more or less set up for the rest of his life, if his dealers didn't find him again and manage to persuade him that what he really needed to do was shoot it all into his veins or snort it up his nose. His aunt and Uncle George had sought legal advice to see if there was any way of overturning the will. There wasn't. He never saw them again. In fact, she would make George drive a mile out of their way rather than go past the road where he lived in the house she thought should have been hers.

The day after the funeral Mae came over. Mae was his new next-door neighbour and his mother's old one. They had fallen out eight years before over a dispute about where she could put her bins and they had never spoken again.

When the bell rang, he was in the middle of gathering all his mother's clothes together and taking them into the back garden.

'Hello, dear. It's Steven, isn't it?'

He nodded.

'Sorry to hear about your mother. Although I suppose she told you that we didn't always see eye to eye.'

He looked at her blankly. His mother had never spoke to him about an old lady that might come and stand on his doorstep.

'It's Mae, dear. I'm Mae.' Seeing no hint of recognition coming over his face, she continued. 'From number seven… You know, love, next door. I'm your neighbour.'

'Oh.' He said.

He hadn't spoken since George had dropped him off and this guttural sound of acceptance loosened some spittle in his throat and he coughed.

'Well, the thing is. Your Mum, God bless her, wouldn't let me keep my bin over there, on the communal driveway. Said it was unsightly. She made me keep it out back and bring it round to the front on bin day. Well, I'm not as young as I was and my back gives me some trouble. And I was wondering whether you'd mind if I kept the bin there.'

She pointed to a spot between the two houses.

'That way the bin men can get to it and put it back there themselves and I don't have to do any of the lifting.'

'Okay'. Steven managed.

That was it, with that the feud was healed. Two syllables, more or less whispered from his mouth had put an end to all the bad blood. She invited herself into the house and spent the morning with him, bagging up all his mother's stuff. She took them over to her house She said she would take them down to the charity shop the next day but over the coming days, he would often see her walk past the house dressed as his mother. He thought it was an act of kindness she was doing for him, trying to make the loss less painful by pretending to be his mum. She needn't have bothered but he didn't want to take away the pleasure this act of charity obviously gave her, so he never mentioned it. Before she left, she asked him if he needed anything or if there was anything she could do for him.

'I don't like shopping.' He said hoarsely.

He reached into his father's big grey cardigan pocket and brought out an old brown window-envelope. Mae could clearly see the Queen's head peering through it. It was full of large denomination notes.

'Would you like me to get you something, love? I'm going up the shops this afternoon. I'm sure I could pick you up some bits and pieces.'

'I found this upstairs.' Steven was pushing the envelope towards Mae. 'It was hidden behind the mirror frame of my mother's dresser. It fell out as I moved it. I don't like mirrors.'

She opened it and looked at the wad of fifty pound notes inside.

'My word! There must be…'

'Three thousand four hundred and fifty pounds.'

'I've never seen this much money before in my whole life. What was your mother doing with all this lying around the place? She must have been crazier than I thought. No offence, love. Now you take this straight down the bank, you hear. Right this minute. I mean, what if you got burgled or something?'

'I want you to have it.'

She didn't understand what he was talking about. She looked anew at this strange bearded man in front of her. He was what she would have called 'away with the fairies'. His quiet voice reached her from wherever he was.

'What do you mean, you want me to have it?'

'I want you to have it.' He took her hands and wrapped them around the envelope making her hold it.

'But…'

'As I said, I don't like shopping.'

He walked her to the door with her new-found fortune in her hand and just as she hadn't spoken to his mother for the last few years of her life, she would also never speak to her neighbour's son for the rest of her life. However, a deal had been struck, a bargain had been made. Every Monday morning, he would open the door and find a plastic bag of food. Every week, he would have three cans of beans, a loaf of bread, some butter, a litre of milk, a pack of economy sausages, three apples and a tangerine. Every other week, he'd get tea bags and a small packet of porridge oats. Once a month, he'd get sugar, toilet paper, soap, jam and washing powder. Occasionally, there would be would be odd extras – a bar of chocolate, a four-pack of beer, a mango, a foot scraper. There was no rhyme or reason to them that he could see, but they were better than any presents anyone had ever given him.

Although he didn't speak to her again, he did like hearing her sing. She would always sing the same small refrain from a hymn he didn't know, when she was hanging out her washing, throwing bread to the birds, feeding her cat, walking down his path to drop off the shopping, it was always the same song and the same words.

'Jesus' blood never failed me yet, Jesus' blood never failed me yet. This one thing I know, for he loves me so.'

In Mae's third plastic bag, he found a bottle of Radox bubble bath. Its thick blue liquid looked like Royal blood bottled for the masses. The word 'bath' reminded him of Aunt Dodd's advice. He climbed the stairs, taking off his clothes as he went. By the last stair, he was completely naked. He entered the bathroom, put the plug in the bath, unscrewed the cap, let a big gloop of it fall and splat onto the enamel and turned on the taps. Steam filled the room and misted up the windows obscuring his view of the back garden. With his index finger he wrote the words 'bath time' in the condensation and then climbed into the hot bath. He didn't get out of it for the next two years.

Lauren had come to work at the offices as a temp. She was there more or less to do the work that his personal secretary should have been doing but for some reason couldn't manage. Maybe it was her age or her worsening alcoholism brought on by her husband's death of cancer two years before, either way he had a choice. Fire her and hire someone new or keep her and hire someone new who could pick up the pieces. The way he saw it, the law practise was doing fine, he had enough money to not really worry anymore and Jean had been through enough shit over the last few years to not have to face losing her job as well. Besides, if he got someone new in to help out, maybe she would buck her ideas up. As it turned out, it didn't quite work like that. She just got lazier and lazier and her drinking became more overt and she gradually faded into nothing over the next ten years and died a broken woman.

Lauren wasn't the best looking woman he'd ever seen but she was by no means the ugliest. She, like most of the population, was somewhere in that middle ground. In her thirties, she had what he thought of as being the quintessentially English female shape, that is to say, like a pear. Her breasts were rounded but small, her bottom and thighs were large but not overly so and her legs tapered down to thin ankles. Her hair was a dark unnatural maroon cut in a bob. All this he noticed when she entered his office for the first time to take instructions on what he would require of her. Her white shirt and black pencil skirt were as they should have been. When he looked back on her attire later to see if there had been any hint of her other life, it was perhaps only in the shoes, which were black and just a little higher-heeled than his average secretary, and her stockings which were immaculate and expensive with an exquisite black seam running perfectly down the backs of her legs.

She was efficient and attentive but apart from that, he hardly noticed her presence in the office. She only worked two days a week and six months went by without him saying much more than thank you for his morning coffee. She had taken over organising the coffee because, on her two days, Jean decided to do nothing at all. She was in many ways the perfect secretary; she anticipated his needs in such a way that he had little or no knowledge that she'd actually done anything. In fact, so inconspicuous was she that he didn't recognise her the first time he saw her with her clothes off.

One Friday night on his way home from the office, he picked up a local paper at a petrol station. He had no desire to go home. There was no one waiting for him. His wife was out and the boys were away at school. He sat in the car before pulling away, flicking through the pages looking for the cinema times. He lost himself regularly at the movies. There was nothing he fancied seeing, so he continued to look through the adverts. Three minutes later, he was phoning an unfamiliar telephone number. Twenty minutes later, he was sitting in the lounge of a flat he didn't know, talking to a woman he'd never met before with his heart pounding and adrenalin fairly crippling him.

'The young lady'll be with you in just a few minutes.' She said.

She reminded him of one of the Monty Python team dressed as an old lady.

'Can I get you anything, dear? Tea, coffee and cold drink perhaps? We have beer or wine.'

He felt vulnerable and uncomfortable enough without having to make small talk and when he had made the decision to come here, this was the last thing he pictured doing. He had no idea of the etiquette of this kind of transaction and he suddenly thought that he had put himself in a ridiculous position. Why would he, a prominent lawyer in a small town, visit a prostitute so close to home? Admittedly, he had had the common sense to travel to another town but it was only five miles away and this suddenly felt like a prime way to find himself being extorted or blackmailed or mugged even. What if there was something in the drink she was offering him that knocked him out? What if they tried to steal his wallet? How could he go to the police about it? He made up his mind to leave while he still could.

'No, I won't thank you. Actually, I think I should... you see, I really haven't much time. I thought this would take a lot less time. Or rather, I thought I wouldn't have to wait. I'm really sorry if I've wasted any of your time but I think, on reflection, its better if I just go.'

He stood up to leave and heard a noise in the corridor outside the living room. A door had been opened. He could make out two voices, one was a low speaking man, the other a confident well-spoken woman.

'You see!' The maid said, 'She's finished. She'll be able to see you in a second. Please take a seat and I'll just freshen the room up a bit before you go in. It really won't take a sec.'

As she closed the door behind her and left him alone in the living room with a slightly out of focus porn film playing on the TV screen, he heard her talking to the woman outside. He was straining to make out the words but nothing was clearly audible. Then he heard one door open and then another. He could hear a toilet being flushed, the sounds of aerosol being sprayed and a shower running. After the longest minute, the maid was there again at the doorway. She was smiling broadly and ushered him through to a back bedroom.

'Come on through.'

He followed.

He found himself in a pink bedroom with a white wrought-iron bed. A wicker chair stood in the corner and on a small bedside cabinet a radio played quiet classical music, next to it was an assortment of sex toys, condoms, talcs and oils.

'The young lady won't be long, she's just freshening up. Make yourself comfortable.' She left him again in yet another strange room that smelled of air freshener and candles.

Should he take his clothes off? How was all this meant to work? He sat down on the wicker chair and then stood up again. He was shaking. A grown man and shaking like a leaf. He took his jacket off and left it there. He checked his watch. It told him it was six forty-five. He'd already been in the flat twenty minutes. By now, he should have been in his car driving home. That had been the plan.

She didn't come in until six forty-eight. She had long blonde hair and was wearing a black see-through negligee underneath which he could see a black lace bra and matching panties, with stockings and high hi-heels. She was instantly attractive and arousing. And a different type of anxiety came over him, a performance one, the nerves that come with desire.

'Oh! Hello.' She said sounding a little surprised and nervous herself, which reassured him a little.

'Hello.' He replied, now feeling that, with her between him and the door, there was no chance of backing out, although looking at her soft flesh, he now no longer wanted to.

'Well, what can I do for you?'

He hadn't really thought this through enough. This question confused him and he obviously showed it on his face because she started to list prices and options for him to choose from.

'A straight massage is forty pounds. A massage with hand relief is sixty pounds. Half an hour full sex or a blow job is eighty pounds or you can have an hour for a hundred and forty pounds. I don't do 'A' levels or water sports.'

So this is what it felt like to visit a hooker. It was all somewhat clinical and matter-of-fact. In some ways, he was grateful to her that she was so efficient and workman-like in her approach as it took the pressure off him. But what did he actually want and why had he come there? He already had an erection but at the same time he felt guilty and disgusted at himself.

'I think maybe just the massage?'

'Is that with relief or without? And would you like me topless?'

'I'm not really sure. Can I decide as we go?' His anxiety was apparent in the quivering of his voice.

'Not really, no.' There was a bluntness to this answer that took him aback a bit and made him realise this really was a monetary transaction and not a first date where you could just see how it develops.

'It's just you have to pay me before, and if I don't know what you want, I can't tell you what it will cost.' She sounded slightly more tender this time as she explained the reason.

'Of course, of course. Well, erm, how would it be if I paid for it with it, but if I decide not to have that, you can keep the money. Would that be acceptable?'

'I suppose. So that's sixty pounds, please.' As she said this, she opened the door in the front of the bedside cabinet and pulled out a fresh towel, which she laid out on the bed. She took the money from his quivering hands. 'If you'd like to pop your clothes off, I'll be back in a moment.' And like her maid before her, she left the room.

He stripped quickly, not wanting to be discovered in the act of undressing. He laid himself down on his front. The towel smelled strongly of washing powder which eased his mind; he had worried that this might be a soiled towel and he would have found that too repulsive for words.

With his head to the side, he watched her legs walk in the room and then behind him where he could hear her removing what few clothes she was wearing. He wanted to turn round and watch her, but felt this was rude, so kept his eyes to the side and examined the radiator three feet away. It was much like any other radiator. He was comforted by its normality. It was an ordinary radiator, behind an ordinary table on top of which stood an ordinary lamp, it was an ordinary clean towel under him. Everything was ordinary except the extraordinary exchange.

She climbed on to the bed and straddled his legs, sitting just below his arse. She offered him a choice of oil or talc. He let her decide. She went for powder and as she reached forward over him to get it from the bedside table, he felt her soft warm breasts gently touch his back for a second and then they were gone. She powdered his back and then, with long sweeping movements, she began. It wasn't like the massage his osteopath gave him for his squash injury. For a start, his osteopath wasn't naked and straddling him on a bed. But there was a quality to the massage that was different. It was arousing but unlike the intimate massage a lover might give. It was somehow sensual and yet lifeless at the same time. All the moves were right, the pressure was accurate, all the places touched were correct but he knew the intentions were solely motivated by money or at best the desire to do a good job.

She didn't say anything and made very little noise. He was disinclined to enter into any small talk and, in that way, he found it a little like a visit to the hairdressers. He sort of felt he should say something just to avoid being rude but couldn't really think of anything beyond banal pleasantries. There was also the added pressure of not actually being able to ask her about her life because that might be rude and he certainly didn't want to give anything away about himself to her. After ten minutes or so, she climbed off him.

'Would you like to roll over now? Have we decided yet what we'd like?'

He didn't want to roll over. He was torn, conflicting emotions and desires were all vying for headspace. He wanted to leave and yet his cock also told him that he wanted to cum. But he would be too embarrassed to turn over now. He would be embarrassed by having to show himself to her, and also by having to see her, even though he did want to stare at her nakedness with every fibre of his body. He reluctantly rolled over. There she was on her knees next to him. She still had her pants and stockings on. He'd felt them on his legs as she massaged him. Her pink nipples were more beautiful than he could have imagined and this sight instantly made him fully hard. She had that white, pale, almost translucent skin that many English women have, that looks like marble, complete with just visible hints of blue veins. He wanted to touch her but had no idea if this was allowed.

'It looks like he'd like you to get your full money's worth,' she said with a laugh in her voice referring to his now twitching member.

It was then that he saw her for the first time, then that he realised who she really was under that long blonde wig. There was more make-up on her than he'd ever seen before, and she'd never worn that shade of red lipstick to work but it was undoubtedly her.

'Lauren?' He asked but it was a question he already knew the answer to.

'Mr Gregory.' She said as if answering him on the telecom in the office.

'Considering the circumstances, please call me, Peter – or Pete.'

'Hello, Peter.' She said as if being introduced to him for the first time at a party. 'So, what would you like?'

Chapter 5

England felt especially cold and wet after the dry arid heat of Las Vegas. I knew I was back though when I saw a blonde eight or nine-year-old boy, holding his podgy little baby brother, shout out at the top of his voice across the airport lounge.

'Oi mum, fatso wants a boob!'

To me, that one phrase more or less summed up England. Fatso wants a boob. Good for fatso. As I headed down towards the tube at Heathrow, I weighed up where I wanted to go. There was nothing waiting for me anywhere. I could go back to the small Midlands' town in which I'd grown up. That would mean watching the same faces I'd known all my life looking at me like I was a stranger, or, I could go somewhere where I *was* a stranger and try and find someone who wouldn't treat me like one. I opted for door number two.

The only contact I had in London was just a name, address and phone number on the piece of paper that Ma had given me.

I noticed there was a one-hour photo-developing 'studio' just by the entrance to the underground and decided to get the pictures of Ma developed. Perhaps I could exchange the photos for a bed for the night.

While I waited for them to be done, I sat on my suitcase. I took a few Polaroids of the typical airport limbo-land.

An airhostess came up to me and asked if I would take a picture for her of her friend and her daughter. She didn't want to be in the picture herself. I snapped away and gave it to her and she put it in her wallet.

'Can you take another?' The mother said.

So I clicked off one more. She gave it to her daughter.

'Now any time you want me, you can look at this, okay? It means we're always together, just like we're always together in this picture. You know you'll be fine with your father. He loves you more than anything and if you change your mind you can always come back.'

I took one more photo for my own collection as they walked off towards the departure gates, and watched it develop as they disappeared.

When the guy at the counter called me in, I went over and picked up the envelope full of snaps. On the tube I flicked through them, taking out two or three of the nicest ones of Ma. I headed for South London.

I phoned Ma's sister Rosa when I got to Eltham. When I got no answer, I decided to phone my doctor.

'The professor is busy at the moment.' His secretary said.

I could hear a whispered voice in the background asking who it was, then he came to the phone.

'Sorry, Jack. You know what it's like. Lots of patients always wanting stuff. Just wanted a little time for a coffee. How are you? Where are you?'

I told him I was back in the country and he sounded genuinely pleased. He sounded even more pleased when I told him I was in London.

'That's marvellous. So when are you coming in to see me?'

'I don't know, I hadn't really planned anything yet. I only landed a few hours ago.'

'It's just that it would be good to catch up. I'd like to check on your progress. Did you do what you wanted to? Did you find that man you were looking for?'

'I did, yes.' I wished I hadn't phoned him. 'Anyway I must go; I've got some things to do.'

'Come and see me tomorrow, Jack. How about that? I'll clear some space in the diary, say around one?'

'I won't wait too long. I won't be around all those sick people. If you're late I'll go, okay?' I hated his waiting room. Life was short enough without wasting it sitting around waiting to be told you've got no time to waste.

'Of course, Jack, I understand. I'll make sure I'm free when you arrive.'

'I mean, I don't want you putting anybody else out or anything. I don't want anyone else shuffled and put back. I just wanted you to know that I can't sit around waiting, that's all.'

'Of course, I understand. I'll see you at one.'

There was still no answer when I phoned Ma's sister again, so, as I had nowhere to go, I did what I always do in that situation. I headed for the nearest cinema. I asked which film had the least gunfire or loud music. The kind twelve-year-old behind the counter told me that he didn't actually know, he looked as if he didn't know anything about any fucking thing. He was slow in his movements and his sloping forehead showed all the signs of South London in-breeding of generations of sub-humans. I chose the artiest film they had showing and snuggled down to sleep for a couple of hours. It was described as a complex dark comedy examining what it means to be in love and that smacked to me of something that would have little in it to disturb my sleep. I was the only person in the whole theatre apart from an old man who shuffled in hoping for enough nudity and sex to be able to have a wank to. About half way through the movie, I woke up briefly to turn over in my seat and saw him humping his fist two rows ahead of me. Either that or he was shaking up his bottle of coke a lot for the thrill of it fizzing over. When I awoke again during the closing credits, he'd gone.

I phoned Rosa and this time she answered.

'My sister called me this morning and told me all about you. A lost sheep travelling in the wilderness. I was at church this afternoon, I'm sorry.'

'I have a picture of her that she wanted me to give to you.'

'Well, come round now.' She gave me directions and I was on her doorstep within ten minutes.

She sat on the stairs, a Miller Lite in hand, watching him. For the last hour, he'd been groaning and rolling around in the cage but hadn't as yet actually opened his eyes or shown any true signs of consciousness. All she knew for certain was that he wasn't dead. The beer tasted strange in her mouth, nothing tasted or felt like it had. She needed the alcohol to quench the dryness in her throat, but it didn't seem to help. Her mouth felt dry and full of cotton.

Bored of waiting, she left him for ten minutes to drag his dog out of the house and into the backyard where she chained it up to a large iron spike. Its dead weight felt heavier than her husband had, but then she figured there was more muscle on the dog. Like her husband, it might well be dead or on its way out; she had given it a load of poison in a highly unscientific way. She didn't really care if the mutt lived or died but if it did live, she had plans for it.

Back in the cellar, her waiting was over. His eyes slowly flipped open. He looked drunk or stoned. He tried to push himself up to a sitting position but slumped back to the ground. He tried again and only succeeded in rolling himself over onto his back. He spluttered as if his throat was filling with blood or vomit and he was struggling to keep his airways open. Watching him floundering around inside his man-cage, he reminded her of two things. She remembered seeing a newborn foal on her uncle's farm, the newness of its legs and the weakness of its muscles made it wobble and fight desperately to find its feet. The other animal was her fish. She had owned an angel fish in a tank a friend had given her when she'd been working at the Taco Bell. It was the only real belonging she'd brought into the relationship. It was only small but she kept it clean and the fish was the only thing of beauty in the entire county as far as she could make out. One day, when she'd forgotten to fill the truck up with gas because a pipe had burst, her husband had come home and quite coldly and calmly put his hand in the tank, pulled out the fish and thrown it on to the floor. It lay there flapping and arching its back, drowning in air. When she had reached down to save it and cupped it in her hands, he picked up the tank.

'And where do you think you're gonna put that now?' He smirked.

He dropped it to the floor and it smashed into thousand pieces, spilling water and shards of glass all over the living room floor.

'Now just stand there! Don't move, you hear!' He shouted at her.

He had signalled to the dog whose hackles were up and whose fangs were bared. He kept her there holding it for five minutes until the fish had stopped moving its gills and was well and truly dead. He walked her over to the waste-disposal unit and watched with pleasure as she placed it carefully in before, he turned on the grinder. Now he was the fish and she would be the one watching and grinding.

He was obviously having difficulty catching his breath and although she wanted him to suffer, she didn't like watching this gasping. It made her anxious and conscious of her own breathing. It made her feel like she was gasping with him.

'Turn on your side you dumb fuck, or you'll die right there, I reckon.' She shouted at the cage.

His head turned, trying to work out where the voice had come from. He was disorientated and bleeding, no different from any other late night in from the bar she thought. He'd fucked her in worse states. On some level, he must have been aware of things because he managed to roll himself on to his side and his breathing eased a little. His eyes closed and he drifted into a comatose state again. She went back upstairs for a nap in the lazy boy in front of late-night Jerry.

She had not slept long when she heard the shouting.

'Help! Help! Come down here you cunt and let me out! Help! Help!'

It was the desperate cry of a desperate man and it made her smile. She was, however, worried it would travel to neighbouring houses, although she figured on the cellar insulating most of the noise. Even so, she needed for him to shut up. She got up, picked up a cattle prod from the kitchen table, the one she had stolen from Hank's car, and went down to the cellar.

'Now you'd better settle on down.' She said to him in a firm and controlled tone. 'You just quieten on down a bit, you hear.'

'Have you lost your fucking mind?' He screamed at her, spitting as he did. 'Now you open this here door and take off these fucking cuffs or I'm gonna gut you like a fish, you got that.'

The stupidity of the man never failed to surprise her.

'Now you just listen to yoursel' for a moment. I think that knock to the head done loosened something. Now why do you think I would let you out if I thought you were gonna try and gut me like a fish? That to me sounds like the talk of a man who wants to spend a good deal of his time, maybe even the rest of his life, down here. Don't you think?'

There was red madness in his eyes, which flashed so brightly that for a second she felt scared despite her words. And when he spoke next time, it was a low rumble that chilled her with its intensity.

'You're gonna open this here door, and let me out of this fuckin' cage, because if you do it right now, maybe I won't kill you. Maybe, I'll just take my knife to you a bit, 'cos you know you deserve to be punished for this. You know the good Lord wants you to pay for what you've done tonight. But you let me out right now and I'll go easy on you.'

It was really only then that she realised he was never coming out of that cage again, well not alive at least. If he could get anywhere near her, he would shred her. She walked towards the cage slowly.

'You're right.' She said, looking sad and hangdog. 'I know I done wrong by you. But you drive me crazy. I just wanted you to know what it feels like. I'm so sorry. I see now, its madness. You're right to punish me, I deserve it. I should get down on me knees and pray for the Lord to forgive, and for you too. You're a good man, only doing right by me.'

He was standing close to the bars now, leaning against them for support. He wiped some blood from his forehead and smiled as she slowly came closer.

'That was some hit you gave me. You know that.'

There was relief in his voice, even a slight laugh. He was back in control and within seconds, he would be free and she would be a bloody mess. Bones would be broken for this. He would slice her face. He played through each blow in his head.

'You plumb near tore my head right off.'

'I'm sorry, really I am.'

She looked almost on the verge of tears, he could tell she was afraid of what her punishment was but knew that she had to take it. She stopped a couple of feet from the cage, turned round and walked over to the crawl space under the stairs. She scrabbled around for a few seconds, then came out holding his large hunting knife in her right hand. His eyes fixed on it. He didn't see the electric baton she held in her other hand down by her left leg.

'What you doing with that?' He asked.

She gripped the handle hard until her knuckles turned white.

'Don't you want this? Ain't this what I deserve?'

He couldn't tell from her tone how this was going to play out.

'I'm frightened to give this to you. I know you'll do me harm. I know I done wrong but I don't think I can take it if you use this on me again.'

He held his hand through the bars of the cage, palm open.

'Now you be a good girl, and give that to me right now. You don't want to do anything even more stupid. You unlock these padlocks and all, and maybe I won't be so hard on you. Maybe I'll just give you what you oughta get and no more.'

She nodded and as she feigned handing over the weapon, she raised her other hand, pressed a button and released a huge charge into his outstretched arm. He shot off his feet and fell to the floor. Snarling, she ran at the cage and gave him another hit through the bars. His slumped body shook and spasmed.

'You got to be crazier than you look if you ever think I'm gonna let you outta there you motherfucker.' She screamed at him. 'You ain't ever touching me again, you understand me! You're gonna learn some things, and there ain't nothing the good Lord can do to help you now, pray all you like, 'cos I'm going to hell for this and I don't give a fuck who knows it. You see, me an' Him ain't real close. And I figure He ain't been there that much for me so I ain't gonna pay no attention no more. The Lord ain't here in this room, he ain't here in my heart, and if He does punish me it'll be long after I've done finished with you, you miserable sack o' shit.'

He knew then that she meant to kill him. He began howling and hollering and screaming at the top of his lungs, while she just laughed.

'Oh, hush up now! I said, hush the fuck up!' She shouted over his cries. But he wouldn't be quiet, so she went over to the big old stereo she'd brought and blasted out Supertramp to cover his screams. The sickly-sweet harmonies she loved, but had been unable to listen to whenever he had been in, filled the cellar, burst up the stairs, leapt through the rest of the house, out of the grates in the walls and drifted over the whole neighbourhood. If anyone could hear him shouting underneath the decibels of MOR, they would just take it for another all-night row. No one ever called the police – no one wanted to make her husband angry by doing that. Even if there'd been a gun shot, no one would have done anything about it.

The glorious lush sounds of 'Breakfast in America' drowned him into insignificant submission. She sang along, happy for once.

He sat in the service station café, looking down at the Big Breakfast in front of him, not sure he could even take a mouthful. The egg was swimming in clear hot grease, its yolk was solid and artificially yellow. He doubted if even the staff knew how many hours or days it had been sliding around on the hot plate. The sausages were crispy, dry and grey. The bacon was fatty and flaccid. The fluorescent beans had a crust. When he tried to cut through the fried bread it cracked into small pieces of superheated asbestos dust. He managed to put a forkful into his mouth. He chewed and chewed, to help him swallow he slurped his extra strong tea to compensate for his lack of saliva.

As he ate, he began to calm down and to convince himself that he was in control of the situation. Things were not as bleak as they seemed. All he needed to do was dispose of the body, head and purse, then get on with his life as if nothing had ever happened. It was going to be a grim day to say the least, but on the other side of it, if he was clever and careful, lay a normal life just waiting to be reclaimed. Sure, he'd made some bad decisions and he knew that if the situation ever came up again, he would do things differently, but here he was and if he just held it together, things would be all right.

He'd left Sandra in the car, but had brought her little black cycling pouch with him. He unzipped it and tipped the contents out on to the plastic coated tabletop. He pushed the items around with his fingertips. His mobile rang.

'All right, Dickface! So come on then, where the fuck are you, you skiving wanker? You'd better not be knobbing that Teresa from the conference last week, you dirty bastard.' Dan let out a tiger growl.

Dan was his best friend and had been ever since school. They'd gone to uni together, they'd joined the same company and they played in the same squash league, which was really an excuse to go drinking once a week and have time away from 'the little ladies'. If there was anyone in the world he could confess to, it was Dan – if he'd stop talking long enough to let him speak.

'Come on, you little horny puppy, what are you doing? Don't give me any of your old shit. What are you up to that's so important you couldn't do it with me. I could do with a day out of this fuckhole and there you are, swanning off without me. You've not pissed off to Amsterdam again without me, have you? Christ, that was a weekend!'

They had gone on a stag night to Amsterdam two years earlier. Both of them had been unfaithful with hookers, both of them got stoned, both had the best time of their lives. Now the word 'Amsterdam' was synonymous with pleasure and freedom, it was the promised land of milk, dope and honey.

'Dan, I need to talk to you.' As he said these words they caught in his throat and his eyes welled up.

'You all right, mate? What's up?'

'I need to talk to you… Something's happened.'

As he spoke, he unzipped the purse and found inside a picture of a smiling beautiful woman being hugged by a beautiful smiling blonde girl. Tears began to run down his face and onto the remainder of his breakfast.

'You sound like shit, mate, what's up? You okay? Where are you? Everything all right at home?' There was a large pause where neither man spoke and the only sound was that of a soft sobbing. 'Where are you? Just tell me and I'll come and get you.'

'I'm... I'm... fuck I don't know, Dan... I'm somewhere on the M1.'

'What the Hell are you doing up there?'

'I've done something. Something stupid.'

'What? Look, just get yourself down here. Meet at me the Bowlplex tonight? Do you think you can do that? We'll skip out early? Just come back, it can't be that bad, mate. I'll make sure it's all right.'

'Okay. Okay. I'll be there.' He hung up on Dan and looked down at the two faces looking up at him and tried to dry his eyes.

'Are you all right?' A voice said from somewhere above him. It belonged to the soon-to-be Martyr.

'I'm fine, I'm sorry.' Like all Englishmen, he hated causing a scene.

'They are very beautiful.' The bearded man said pointing at the photo. 'Your wife and child?' He had the slightest of accents hidden beneath a very upper class clipped pronunciation.

'Yes, they are. My wife and... my daughter.'

'You are a very lucky man, I hope the sorrow you are feeling passes soon.' With that, he walked off towards the toilets.

He put the purse, the two keys, the notebook, the lip-gloss, the biro and twenty-three pence back into the pouch and followed the man. He needed a pee and to wash his face in some cold healing water. Three minutes later, the bomb went off and in an instant the man with the beard evaporated.

He knew he was injured but couldn't risk being taken to the hospital or being questioned by the police. After all just twenty yards away, his car had a decapitated head in it and a boot-full of body. He had to calmly get in the car and slip away from the swarming emergency services.

He drove South towards home. It was no good though. He couldn't go back with the body in his car. He had to get rid of it and he had to make a good job of it. She must never be found. If he was ever to have a moment of peace he had to make her disappear so completely, so irrevocably, that it would seem as if she had never existed. To do this he needed things and fate was on his side. As he sped along he caught sight of a large billboard on the side of the motorway proclaiming the opening of a huge garden centre just two miles from the next exit.

He picked up a spade, a pair of heavy-duty gloves and some black plastic sheeting and placed them in his trolley. He had never done anything like this before, what other stuff would he need?

He wandered up and down the aisles scanning the endless shelves. He thought he could take advantage of the free wifi in the on-site café for inspiration but was worried he'd be spied tapping 'What tools do you need to hide a dead body?' into Google and caught that way. He was sure there were all sorts of chemicals in the shop that he could use to help speed decomposition but he hadn't got a clue which ones they might be.

Just as he'd done for the bike, he lost himself down country lanes until he found himself in another wood. This was obviously a managed woodland and where the last one had been light and airy, full of oaks, ash and birch, this was a forest of dark dense pine. This was no place to walk for fun. This was a woodland waiting to be harvested for its wood. The ground beneath his feet felt spongy from the years of matted pine needles that had choked and killed any green growth below. He took the spade and wandered until he found the perfect spot. The carpet of mulch made the digging easy at the start and it was two and a half feet down before he struck solid earth. He kept digging down another two foot or so. It wasn't a particularly evenly-dug grave. It was wider at one end than the other and shallower nearer the base of the tree he'd chosen to bury her by because the thick roots made it too hard going. But it would do and after all, without her head, how would she be able to tell if it wasn't perfectly executed anyway?

Back at the car, he was overwhelmed by the smell when he popped the trunk. It had continued leaking for a long time by the look of things and he was glad he'd bought the plastic sheeting. He laid it on the floor behind the car and tried to get her out of the car in one smooth movement but failed. The sticky slippy blood made it difficult to get a clean hold and any dignity he had been hoping to afford the body was lost; he struggled to get a strong grip with the thick gloves but after a minute or so had to abandon them. Naked from the wrist down he grappled with the corpse until it was clear of the car, then dropped it with a wet thud.

The blood was no longer vibrant, it was darker and stuck like thick glue all over him. His hands were so covered, they were almost webbed.

He parcelled her up in the sheet and straining slightly, lifted the home-made body bag on to his shoulder. After he'd scrambled back through the cracking lower branches of a hundred or so trees, he eased her down as elegantly as he could. He looked for a moment at this unique sight. He took a mental snapshot of the pit and its content, the only person he'd ever killed and buried, then began to fill in the hole. When it was done he used the loose mulch to cover newly turned soil. With great care, he smoothed out the spot with a layer of dry top needles. He took a branch and used it to scrub out his tracks as he walked backwards out of the wood in a way he'd once seen an Indian brave do in an old black-and-white cowboy movie when he was a kid. The brave didn't hit his head on as many things as he did while making his retreat. Things were always harder than they looked in films.

Back in the car, he drove away with only a head in a bowling bag and a black pouch left to dispose of. He turned the radio on for some soothing music but had to turn it up so loudly to hear it that he worried he might draw attention to himself in traffic. Ever since the explosion, he now realised, he had been more or less completely deaf with only a high-pitched squealing ringing for company. That and his own internal monologue that seemed to be chatting away to itself incessantly. It had been a busy day and there was a lot to talk to himself about; lots of questions but few answers.

His dreaming state overlapped his waking one so much that he no longer knew which was which. He didn't go anywhere in his dreams anymore. His little cell brought everything to him, a vortex sucking in all existence, shaping it, distorting it and then spewing it out again, for his eyes only. This small bathroom, this tiny white-tiled world could contain within it an entire universe.

When he woke up, he would climb out of bed, have a slice of toast and then run the bath. He would sit in it all day until it got dark and then he would climb out, make himself a small supper and then head for bed. While he was submerged for those eight to nine hours, his mind skipped in and out of consciousness and took him to a place he came to know as the 'Between'. It was neither here nor there. It was a form of conscious hallucination. He was creating these vivid worlds and he could manipulate them to some degree. He couldn't turn them on and off at will though, they were far more powerful than mere daydreaming; they had their own intentions and sometimes he was unsure whether or not he was creating them or whether the house itself had its own psyche with which he was interacting.

From his vantage point lying in the bath, anything might happen. One morning, a huge lake appeared on the floor. It slowly seeped up through the black-and-white linoleum. The walls effortlessly moved back to make space for its ever-expanding presence. Gliding far into the distance, they stretched and moved to accommodate the new visitor. The sun's reflected rays danced on the ceiling, creating strange symbols that he couldn't decipher. Sat in his tiny bath boat bobbing up and down, he was set adrift. He watched the lake lapping his iron and enamel vessel. He could have paddled in it, or even gone for a swim but he was worried that if he got out of the bath, he might not be able to find it again or that it might sink and he would be left stranded in the Between. The bath was the portal between worlds.

Occasionally he would poke his head over the side and look deep down into the waters. He kept expecting to see something swimming, a fish or eel or something. But as far as he could tell, this was a dead pool. He drifted on this mind-made ocean for a long time, the slow rising and falling of the tides causing gentle waves pushing him this way and that. He enjoyed the day very much, and as the sun set in the bathroom and, quite by coincidence, outside the house as well, the last ebb-tide of the day occurred and the walls slowly ever so slowly began to return to their normal positions and the water drained back through the floor or out under the door. By the time he decided he was ready for some dinner, the bathroom was more or less back to normal, even the bath mat had dried out.

The bathroom had many seasons as well, but these were more in tune with his emotions than with those of the actual world. When he was in a thoughtful, slightly melancholic mood, the bathroom would spend much of its time filling itself with autumnal leaves of brown, red, and gold. They'd start in a pile on the floor, at rest, in peace. Then a slight breeze would come from under the door, blowing like a whisper from God's mouth, catching a few of the top leaves, lifting them for a second before depositing them again safely and relieved. Then the wind picked up, the top leaves headed for the ceiling, then the next layer headed skyward followed by the next, then the next.

As the wind became ever more ferocious, even the wet leaves at the bottom of the stack got peeled from the linoleum, leaving only wet fingerprints to show they had once been there. Although the Room started the dance, he was in charge of the music, he conducted the rhythm. The beats and pauses were all immaculate. By merely opening his mind, he could control the symphony of motion. He took it through various movements but it always ended with him weeping, overcome by loss. This was the underlying theme; it was a ballet of sorrow. The leaves would fly into shapes and sculptures of those he'd loved; his mother, his wife, his child – all of whom had now disappeared forever. When the pain got too much to bear, he would calm it all down. The leaves drifted once more to the floor and were swept away by invisible hands, taken to a distant bonfire and burnt; only a trace of the smoke reached him on the wet, cold, misty early-evening air.

Once, when he was feeling so low that he could hear the voices in the rest of the house crying and moaning as if every pipe, every floorboard, every brick in every wall was in mourning and he could no longer stand it, the Room stepped in to help him through. His tears were filling up the bath to overflowing when he felt the snow. First landing on his nose, then his hands. As soon as it touched his skin, it melted, vanished and was gone. But what started out as the odd flake soon became a heavy soft floating downpour of cleansing white beauty. And as the room filled with drifts and a dazzling frozen carpet, all the sounds from outside became muffled in the way only snow can soak up the world's noise. Eventually, there was silence. He caught flakes on his tongue and it brought a smile back to his face. In the freezing bathroom the heat of his bath steamed gently like a hot spring in the wastes of the Northern Territories in the heart of winter.

One evening he climbed out of the bath and reached for a towel to dry down his wrinkled skin. As he patted his face, he decided it was time for the beard to go. Opening the bathroom cabinet, he looked for something that might help remove it. There, amongst his mother's haemorrhoid cream, cotton buds, plasters and Vaseline, he found a small pair of scissors and his father's cut-throat razor. His beard now reached half-way down his naked chest. He started to cut it back. When it was down to long stubble, he began shaving with soap, hot water and the cut-throat. He had never shaved with a proper old-fashioned razor before, in fact, he hadn't actually shaved at all for the last five or six years, it all felt very alien and as if he was reclaiming some innocence, re-birthing his face. The slightest slip with the razor held at the wrong angle and his face was nicked and bleeding. The wounds poured forth drops of blood that fell into the full basin and mushroomed into crimson clouds.

Bit by bit, like piecing a puzzle together, his face came into view. And then with one final splash he wiped off the soap foam and pulled his hair back into a ponytail so he could see himself again. He'd been hiding away behind the beard and the pain for a lifetime. He was surprised how little he had changed, he was a bit older but that was fine, what was more shocking was that all the things he'd done hadn't shown themselves indelibly tattooed into the creases and crow's feet. He should be pockmarked and scarred but his skin was remarkably smooth and fresh, and apart from three small bleeding slashes it was perfect. He recognised himself again. What's more, he was a nice looking man, and perhaps had even been beautiful earlier in his life. He started to cry for his years lost in the wilderness. Tears fell from his eyes bouncing off his cheeks in arcs of silver light. As each tear hit the floor, the Room turned them into a flower. On impact, a different coloured blossom sprang to life. Some blue, some white, crimson reds, exquisite yellows. They bloomed in front of his eyes. He cried into every corner of the Room until it was full and the sweet perfume cleansed him. He lay on the floor and slept on a pillow of sweet soft petals.

When he awoke next morning, they were gone but their smell had permeated his skin and remained with him, soothing him for days.

He had well and truly fallen into the bottle of Jack Daniels. He could feel its wonderful warmth. On the workbench in front of him he had four sheets of pristine white writing paper, four immaculate envelopes and his Mont Blanc fountain pen. He pretty much hated all the possessions he'd amassed for no good reason over the years, all except this pen. His wife's main hobby was spending money and she did it with a skill that was almost preternatural. She would avoid Sales like the plague. As she had told him many times over the years,

'Why would we want things in our house that people wouldn't buy at full price.'

Her taste was eclectic; she would buy whatever was currently in fashion with the fashionable people she read about in endless magazines. On the rare occasions when he told her she couldn't buy some thing because it was just too expensive, she would throw a pouting tantrum. No one had ever said no to her it appeared. He knew what she really wanted to say to him at times like that.

'If you can't afford it, then what the fuck am I doing here with you.'

But she had enough dignity not to speak. She would simply not buy whichever large item it was, be it a huge stone thousand-year old Buddha just discovered and imported from India or a new painting 'by the next-Picasso', she would go and spend an equivalent amount on new clothes from Harvey Nichols or Armani and simply not tell him. The first he would know about it was when the credit card bills arrived at the door. He didn't bother to challenge her on the subject anymore. It simply wasn't worth it. She would shout and storm around breaking things and these would all have to be replaced often doubling the bill. It made him sick to think of the money they had spent over the years and in his eyes wasted, and not just to keep up with the Joneses, but to show the Joneses what they couldn't afford. He earned a lot of money by any standards but he wasn't in the kind of league that she would have liked to be in; upper middle class was a good couple of rungs down from where she saw herself financially and socially. Over the years they'd moved four times and each time to a bigger house and each time she used this as an excuse to fill the rooms with more and more stuff, and when the rooms were full she'd start throwing the stuff out to make way for new more expensive things. To her, working on the house and her personal stash of belongings was a bit like painting the Forth Bridge – once you get to one end of the house you have to start all over again. He wanted to cut her hands off to stop her habit of reaching for her credit card, but he suspected that no sooner had he hacked them off she'd enter the house wearing a pair of Prada prosthetics.

Perhaps aversion therapy was the solution. Over a period of a month, he'd chop off a finger every time she made a new and pointless purchase, making her really weigh up how much she actually 'needed' something.

'But we need one!' She repeated over and over – her consumer mantra.

'How much do we really need it?' He could say wielding his small Yakuza blade, holding her hands to the table with outstretched fingers awaiting the chop.

The Mont Blanc was one of the few exceptions to his almost Buddhist philosophy of non-attachment to objects. It was simple and beautifully crafted, both elegant and perfectly designed for its one particular job – that of writing. It felt smooth in his hand, with a weight that constantly reminded him of its presence with an understated balanced ergonomic splendour. Lauren had given it to him and perhaps this somehow added to the way he felt about it. She had only ever given him one present during the time they had been acquainted, but he valued this gift more than anything his wife had given him over countless birthdays, Christmases and anniversaries.

Looking at the blank pieces of paper in front of him, he wasn't really sure how to start them. In many ways these letters would define him. He wanted to clearly express the reason for what he was about to do, in a way that wouldn't or couldn't be distorted by the police or psychologists in years to come. As he could never speak of these things again himself, these words in dark blue ink on stark white paper would be there always as a testament to answer the question – why?

He had writer's block. He couldn't think of a way to start a letter of this magnitude. There were four letters to be written to four entirely different people who knew him as four totally different men. He put the pen down for a second to think and picked up the gun.

As he placed the cartridges in the cocked barrels, he looked to see if her car was back. From where the shed was positioned, he could just make out enough of the drive past the house to see if the car was there or not. It wasn't. This meant he still had a little time. He looked at the gold brass circles sitting in the black barrels. He snapped the shotgun shut, cocked it and put it back down on the bench near the window. He picked up the pen and began writing.

'It's beautiful, I don't know what to say. Thank you.'

'It's my pleasure. I just thought you needed a nice pen and I saw it in a shop window and bought it for you, no big deal really.'

She was standing in his office on her last day. After he had put his clothes on, she had told him that she thought it was best if she left the company.

'But there's no need for that really. Honestly, I'm sure we can work round this.'

'No,' she said. 'I think it would only feel weird in the long run, for you more than me. Funnily enough, this isn't the first time it's happened.'

Then he said one of the most stupid things he'd said in a long time.

'But what will you do for money?'

She stood there in her underwear in front of him.

'Peter, this is what I do for money. Haven't you ever wondered how I manage to afford the car I drive?'

He had never seen her either driving to work or away from it, so he had no idea what kind of car she drove.

'What do you drive?'

'I drive a Porsche, a brand new Porsche.'

'Oh, right. I guess you could have had a rich husband.'

She smiled at this. 'Believe me, I could have had and still could many times over if I wanted to, but I like my independence too much for that.'

'So why do you work for us? If it's not for the money, that is? Surely you can't do it for the love of the work?'

She buttoned up her shirt, pulled up her skirt and sat down on a chair crossing her legs. He was amazed that he had never noticed how attractive she was. Every part of her exuded sex and sensuality, she radiated it.

'I do it for the tax man.'

'Eh? I'm sorry, I don't understand.'

'I do a day job three days a week so I have something legitimate to put through my books. That way I can keep the money I make from here for myself. That way I can have the life that I want, without having to give away a penny of the money I've earned from sucking cock. It's a good living. Luckily I also enjoy working at your place. The people are nice and it gets me off my back for a few hours.' She laughed.

She was not a woman to change her mind so he accepted her letter of resignation. It was a simple well-crafted formal note simply saying that 'due to a change of circumstances I will no longer be able to continue working for the company.' She agreed to work out four weeks' notice in order to train up a new PA and to show her how to do all the things that Jean no longer would.

Chapter 6

Rosa listened as I told her the short version.

One Tuesday morning I blacked out. One Wednesday morning I was wheeled in for tests. One Friday morning I was told I was dying.

I was sent home and the pictures of the inside of my head were sent on a quest to find a doctor who could help. They bounced around the country until they landed on the Professor's desk. He looked at the scans and didn't immediately send them on or put them in the lost souls pile. He wanted to meet me. He wanted to get to know me.

I took the train down to London and we chatted in his office and then went for a walk along the South Bank. He avoided talking about the procedure for a long time. He talked about books we both liked, paintings in galleries we'd both seen. He laughed easily and said I reminded him of himself when he was a young man. We sat on a bench looking out over the Thames on a bright crisp morning and he gave me a choice. I had two options as he saw it. I could leave that day, go home and be dead within three months or I could let him try something. He wanted to try a piece of kit that he had only just received; it had a new way of showing precise images of places inside the head that had been invisible before. It was all new territory.

I had a reasonable chance of survival. But until he was in there, he couldn't say how successful the operation would be. He was, however, convinced that my condition would kill me in the long run. It was only a matter of time. What he was offering me was a painful and dangerous schlock horror slicing up which might kill me or might blind me or, best case scenario, might offer me another few years of life. This would also be followed by radiation that would burn through my head destroying and cooking the flesh it touched and penetrated, and this in turn would be followed by the slow leaking of poisonous chemotherapy into my veins, bag after bag of clear vomit-inducing liquid agony. How could I resist?

His assistant gave me the idea of photography.

'Have you videoed yourself? For your loved ones?'

This junior doctor had a wonderful bluntness that I found refreshing.

'I videoed my father before he died and I can now watch it back whenever I want. It's a lovely thing to have.'

'I have no one to watch a video of me.' I said.

My bluntness matched his and he left. But it got me thinking about images captured on film, memories pressed onto celluloid or on a less romantic memory card. The person who'd most want to see images of the way I was before the operation was me. I had no intention of dying on the operating table but when I came round, I would no longer be the person I was before. I would look different. I would be different.

I bought myself a Cannon EOS, a little Nikon Coolpix and uprgraded my iPhone to one with video and a better camera. I also bought a few disposable cameras with real film, for those times when I couldn't recharge the others. The night before the operation, I spent a long time taking self-portraits as best I could. Firstly of me as I was and had been for as long as I could remember. I asked one nurse to take photos of me cutting off my own long hair, and another to capture the final step as I shaved the rest of it off with a shaver. I took close-ups of the drugs they gave me and as I drifted off under their influence, I asked the night nurse to take some of me sleeping. The compact digital travelled with my sleepy sedated body down to surgery with a note for the Prof to take pictures at every stage of the operation as he could and for the jpegs to be disposed of if I failed to recover from the operation.

He made an incision inside my mouth from ear to ear and peeled my face off. The loose detached skin, which I used for everything from kissing my first love to expressing the pain I felt when she left me, was clamped by the ears away from my skull. I had been de-gloved. A manual surgical saw and a small circular electric saw cut through the bone and the surgeon's hands were placed inside me to lift my brain out of the way so the machine could enter the passageways of the sinuses deep within my head. For twelve hours, they meticulously excavated and uncovered nerve endings and veins that had been consumed by the hungry cancer. They scraped it back to the bone wherever possible, and when they had cut and sliced as much of it away as they could without killing me, they began the lengthy process of reconstruction.

There had been a slight complication they had not foreseen, and they had had to make a long incision from the side of my nose to my forehead. This, they assured me, would leave only a barely noticeable scar. The larger slice across the top of my head, which made me look like the victim of a botched Native American scalping, would be a deeper scar, one they hoped would be hidden when my hair grew back. They had stapled and stitched me together and, most importantly, they had brought me back from the edge of darkness. I had cheated death, for a short period of time at least. When I came round, I was unaware of the pain, I was only aware of being alive and able to see. Tears flowed out of my bruised eyes. Everything looked very beautiful. I wanted to capture all of it.

'Jack,' the Prof said. 'It was a good operation. However, we couldn't get it all. There's still a good amount inside you unfortunately. It was somewhat more advanced than we had thought. You're quite lucky to have been as well as you have been for so long. The radiotherapy and chemotherapy may slow its re-growth but, as I said before, this will be the thing that gets you, my boy. It was multi-site, very nasty really.'

'So what can I expect?'

'A normal life for a while. Then I would expect blindness first. There was a large amount of it around your optic nerve which we could only tinker with. After that, you will slowly fade away.'

'Thank you. Thanks for the honesty.'

That was how it was after the treatment ended. I had some time, not long but nobody could tell me how long.

Rosa listened and I talked. Then she let me take the pictures of her to send to Ma.

When exhaustion finally overtook him, he stopped screaming. She was relieved because it was starting to fuck her off in a big way. He had tried to trick her a couple of times by going quiet and waiting for her to turn down the music before beginning his wailing again. On the second time he did it, she shocked him again with the cattle prod and pulled out his hunting knife, running it across the bars. That seemed to do the trick and the mixture of concussion, fear and physical tiredness all combined eventually to quieten him down.

The same could not be said for his hound though. By the next morning it had thrown up all the meat and by the look of his perky demeanour most of the poison as well. He was pulling at his chain, growling, barking and howling for freedom. She watched its struggle from the kitchen window. She knew that with its persistence and unearthly strength, it would work its way free. The stake buried some three feet into the ground was already beginning to move. The brute was more than capable of dragging a five-foot-long heavy iron bar with it as it chewed its way through the door to get to back its master straight through her. It looked hungry as well. It would take a great chunk of her for its breakfast given the chance. It was also in danger of bringing the neighbours over. Their dogs were already barking in sympathy; it needed to shut the fuck up.

She opened the back door and its ears went back, it snarled and leapt forward, snapping back when the chain reached its full length. It jumped again and again. She sat on the back steps staring it down. It hated her every bit as much as she hated it. She had never really liked animals, flee-ridden, biting bastards. All they had ever done was remind her of how we were no different from them. They got hungry, they'd eat or kill. They got thirsty, they drank from any puddle or bowl. They got horny, they'd fuck anything they could get their cocks in.

She knew a woman on the street who regularly got fucked by her dog, she said it had started out as an experiment to see if it would lick paste off her pussy, the damn thing was so good at it, she couldn't buy enough paste to keep her or it satisfied. The local Seven Eleven had to order in more especially for her. Eventually she thought she'd let the thing try fucking her, as its prick was always hard, angry and red whenever it was going down on her. She knelt down on all fours and let it take her from behind. It fucked her fast and furious. Two months later her husband got his marching orders.

'When your dog can fuck you better than your man, what's the point of keeping him around messin' up the place?'

There would be no loving with this angry mutt though. She couldn't even stroke it without it going for her. She stared into its dark eyes and down into its black heart. It quieted down a bit and became still, a low growl coming from it the only sound that it was still communicating its hatred.

'Now you and I had better make a deal. I know you ain't pleased with what I done, and I ain't mighty pleased with you still bein' alive, so I guess we're even. Now the way I see it, you got two choices. Either you shut up right now and think of yourself as my dog, or I guess we're gonna fall out even more, and I ain't gonna be the loser in that fight. I ain't gonna lose out ever again, and definitely not to a stupid fuckin' hound. So what's it gonna be? I'm going inside to get myself a beer. You think on it. When I come back out, I'll expect a decision.'

As she turned to go back into the house, the dog lay down placing its head on its paws, its breath making small clouds of dust from the dry dirt yard.

'You wan' a drink'. She called downstairs. 'It's gonna be a hot one.'

There was no reply.

'Suit yoursel' but I ain' offerin' again today. Last chance. You want somethin' to drink?'

There was a muffled groaning noise from down in the pit which she took to be a 'yes'. She filled a plastic bucket with some water and emptied half a bag of ice into it. She threw a small kid's beaker into it – one of her friend's brats had left there weeks before – and took it down to him. He was lying on the floor at the back of the cage next to the wall. She was still wary of approaching the cage but he looked docile enough at the moment. She placed the bucket in front of the cage. It was too big to go through the bars, but he could scoop himself out some water as and when he wanted.

'Now that's to last you all day. I ain't fetching and carrying for you no more. You do what you like with it, drink it all now in one go, knock it over and throw it all away or ration yourself and make it last, makes no difference to me.'

She placed a second bucket beside it, this one was empty.

'This one's for you to pee in.'

She left him and went back upstairs. She shut the door on him and rested on the lazy boy drinking a beer in peace for once. Neither dog, nor man made any sound. Perhaps they were finally adjusting to the new regime.

She stretched as she got up and opened the door to the back yard. Without even a second's hesitation, the dog jumped as high and hard as it could ripping the stake out of the ground, howling as it leapt forward. She slammed the door in its face and, as she walked back through the house, she could hear it tearing with claw and tooth at the flimsy door. It would only be a matter of seconds before it was through and at her. In one smooth move she took up her husband's hunting rifle from where she had hidden it behind the living room door, she pulled back the bolt, slid one of the three bullets she had in her jeans pocket into the barrel and slid the bolt closed. She knelt down where she was and shouldered the gun so that she could see clearly along the gun's sites. One of the chipboard panels at the bottom of the door was torn aside by the dog. No sooner could she see its ugly head than she took a shot. It was short, sharp and clinical. There was a loud crack and the dog's head exploded. She blew the jaw and part of the skull clean off. It fell to the ground out of her view. She reloaded and stepped quickly through the house. She kicked open the door and put another bullet into its twitching body, then four seconds later another one through what was left of its head.

Teeth and blood and bone and muscle were smashed together. The smell of cordite and torn flesh filled the air. She shut the door on the mess and walked back into the house.

'I killed your dog.' She shouted down to her husband.

She threw the gun down onto the sofa as she walked past it and grabbed her keys. She needed some more beer and some industrial bleach to wash away the dog's blood and brains that was all over the white peeling boarding on the back of the house. Cleanliness was next to godliness after all.

Down in the cellar he heard the gun shots, heard her shout down telling him that she had killed his dog and then had heard her drive away. He pulled himself to his feet and cursed the dog for not ripping her throat out. He pulled on the bars that made up the door, he yanked the padlocks hoping one of them would give, but as much as the thing rattled nothing was giving, nothing was moving. He shook the whole cage with all the strength he could muster. He shook it until he ran out of breath. He screamed and shouted for help, but no one came or heard. She had cranked the television volume up full blast before leaving and chances were, from where he was, with all the earth for insulation no one would hear him. He tried one last time to shake the cage, giving it one last almighty push. This time something did give, just by the tiniest amount, but he felt it. He pushed again and again examining the cage to find its weak spot. It was there on the right hand side near the top where it touched the wall; the bolt had slipped just a fraction of an inch. There were still more than enough bolts to hold the cage securely in place, but it gave him hope. He shook the whole thing again with renewed strength. When he stopped, he re-examined the loose bolt but, as far as he could see, he had made no difference. But it was a start and in time it would become his one fixation. He needed to get the cage off the wall and, however long it took, he'd do it. Then he'd rip her to pieces. He needed his strength and so he needed to behave whenever she was around, that seemed like the only way forward, although he knew himself well enough to know that he and his temper were different beasts inhabiting the same body and he had little control over his fellow body guest.

She came back twenty minutes later and went straight down into the hole, finding him drinking from the baby cup. He looked calmer. She put this down to a sense of mourning for the dog, or if not that a sense of fear that he might be next on the list.

The Bathroom played with him for a year or so. It gave him anything he needed to heal and to think. He started to see clearly again, clearer in fact than he had ever seen before.

'Jesus' blood never failed me yet...' was the only real sound from the outside that ever entered this space. And when it did, he found the Bathroom would slowly turn into a chapel of rest. His mother's coffin was there, laid out beneath a stained glass window of Christ on the cross. White-silver glass nails pierced through his hands and feet. He wept for the lost souls and welcomed others back to the fold. Was he lost or was he being welcomed?

He lay in the bath, arms outstretched over the sides, having a water crucifixion himself. Jesus wasn't smiling. His eyes looked down on the small pews that now filled the bathroom as if he knew they were all empty and wept for the lack of interest. From his watery coffin he stared up at the Lord and the small red spear wound in his side winked at him. It winked and then wept small rubies of ecstatic pain. Sunlight hit the window, and all of a sudden he was swimming in red and blue, it seeped through him exquisitely. Lying there in the colour vibrations, he could hear Him speak slowly about the plans he had for the future and the things people now needed to know. The smell of the place entered him. It was the smell of centuries of guilt, service and mourning. Further back there was wealth and greed and further back still and all but faded the unmistakable scent of a martyr's blood and a crowned king's death.

He'd been forgiven, he'd been given redemption. This long baptism had truly cleansed him; not just his body but his soul, and more than that, he'd been given a gift, he could feel it surging through his body. His hands were burning to heal.

His mother sat up in her open coffin and smiled.

'Well? How does it feel? What was it like to be touched by Him? You are a very lucky little boy. You know that?'

The chapel slowly faded and his mother was the only thing left to show any indication that this epiphany had happened to him. She was sitting by him now on an old kitchen chair. She picked up a bottle of shampoo and began to soap up his hair.

'I think I just feel calmer, like I can switch off all the noises now.'

'How do you mean?'

'The thoughts generated by just one person are almost infinite in magnitude. Like radio waves transmitting on all frequencies. It's been difficult for me to switch them off, to not listen. But in here everything is quiet and still. I think the walls are made from some special material that keeps thoughts out. I have often wondered whether, if I had a radio in here, it would be able to pick anything up. I am fairly sure it would just pick up the background static of space.'

'And?'

'And I think that because it's so quiet in here it gave Him a space to come in and speak to me.'

'And what did He say to you?'

'Nothing and everything.'

'Come on tell your mummy, there's a good boy.'

She pushed his head under the water and massaged the suds away. He came up for air and smiled at her.

'He gave me a message, but it's not for you mum, sorry. But I do love you, more than you'll ever know.'

She looked sad. He smiled at her gently to reassure her.

'But why can't you tell me, baby boy?'

'Because mum, he said it was a gift for the living, not for the dead.'

She looked down at him and started to sob gently. She put her head in her hands and was quietly inconsolable.

'Please tell mummy, please tell mummy, please tell mummy. There's a good boy, be my little baby boy and tell me.'

He stood up and let the water drip from him and return to its main body in the bath. His hair bedraggled over his face. He stepped out and stood naked and glistening in front of his mother's chair.

'Your baby's all grown up mum. I can't tell you what He said, 'cos it's not for you, but He did give me something else, something for you. Now look at me mum and I don't want you to be afraid.'

His mother looked up at him through tear-blurred eyes and saw him hold his arms out to his side. His palms were flat facing the ceiling. He shut his eyes and slightly tilted his head to the left. As her vision began to clear, she could see something around his hands. At first it looked like a barely perceptible heat mirage around them, but before her very eyes a light blue flame began to lick round both hands. It started as a gentle small glow but grew to be a fire that rose upwards almost as far as the ceiling. When the room could no longer contain the flames, he opened his eyes. They reflected nothing of the inferno, only deep peace and love for her.

'I think this is where it all begins. This won't hurt, I promise. Shut your eyes if you're frightened, it will only take a second. Good bye, mum.'

In one smooth movement, he brought his hands down on to his mother's shoulder and she was instantly consumed. She didn't shut her eyes, she held his gaze for those final seconds, then she was no longer there and he never saw her again. No sooner had she disappeared than the flames were gone and he felt suddenly exhausted and drained, it was all he could do to make it back into the bath and gently let the water replenish him.

The Bathroom went quiet on him and showed him very little in the way of visions after that. It was waiting for him to see the sign that he had been told would come. He had no idea what form it would take but it would be soon, he knew that, and all he needed was absolute peace to prepare him for the next stage. He needed to find a peace to take with him wherever he went and in the face of whatever would come up.

He only had to wait another three days.

When he opened the door Monday morning, he found that there was no bag and no food. The only thing he could see was the flashing blue light on the top of the ambulance outside Mae's house next door. He walked down the path in nothing but a pair of ill-fitting jeans. He stood by the gate and watched as they brought a black body bag on a trolley out. It looked small and insignificant, the two men carrying her showed no sign of strain on their faces, this was no heavy burden. A third man came out of the cab of the ambulance having finished a conversation on the radio and approached him.

'All right, mate. Bit chilly to be dressed like that, isn't it? You'll catch your death.'

Steven looked up at the white clouded sky and realised by the chill breeze and the lack of leaves on the trees that it must be somewhere near winter.

'Thank you. I saw your lights and thought I'd see what was going on.'

'Did you know her?' The uniformed man flicked his head towards the back of the ambulance where Mae was being placed. 'The old lady, did you know her well?'

Steven wasn't sure how to answer this so he paused for a second before finally saying.

'She used to sing to me and bring me food.'

'Well I'm afraid she won't be doing any of that anymore, we got a phone call from someone saying they were worried about her. We found her sitting in her chair downstairs in the living room, peaceful as you like, like she was just taking a nap. Ain't that a nice way to go. We should all be so lucky, I tell you. My mate over there reckons she died sometime over the weekend or maybe even on Friday.'

Steven had a sudden urge.

'Could I just say goodbye, do you think?'

'What do you mean?'

'Could I just look in on her one more time. Just to kind of say goodbye.'

Although he obviously wasn't entirely happy with the idea, he let Steven climb up into the back of the van and left him alone for a minute or so with the old bagged lady.

Steven quietly began singing 'Jesus Blood' and gently unzipped the bag. Mae looked up at him with bright shining eyes.

'Hello, I just wanted to thank you for being so kind to me and I guess I just wanted you to know that everything is going to be all right.'

He placed his hand on her forehead and felt the cold skin gently warm with the heat radiating from him.

'There's nothing to be frightened of, nobody's waiting to judge you, they're only waiting to hold you. It's truly wonderful. Now sleep and when you wake, you'll be new again, and laughing like you remember laughing when you were a child.'

He placed his hand on her mouth and she kissed it.

'Thank you.' She whispered, then she shut her eyes and he slowly zipped her back inside.

As he stepped down out of the van, the shortest and youngest ambulance man winked at him.

'Were you just singing to her in there, mate? Did she join in?'

Steven smiled. 'Only on the chorus.'

'All right, what do you want to talk about?' Lauren asked perplexed.

'I'm not really sure. I think, I thought we could just chat for a bit?

'OK, where would you like to start?'

'I…I thought maybe you could start.'

'Oh, well, let's see. I guess you don't want to talk about work, so how about the weather. I suppose we all like talking about the weather. The weather?'

'No, that wasn't what I meant really.'

'What did you mean then?'

'I guess, I wanted to talk about, the start?'

'The start?'

'Yes, how it started?'

'How what started?'

'This, all of this?'

'What this flat? I saw it in a local paper and it seemed to suit what I needed so I took out the lease. Turns out the guy who owns the place owns a few flats in the area and a couple of them are used for this as well. I pay him more than the going rate and he seems happy about it, and the neighbours don't seem to mind, if they even realise.'

'No I didn't mean about this, I meant about it...'

'About it? I'm not sure I follow you.'

'I'm sorry I'm not making myself very clear am I? I mean how 'it' started?'

'Well as far as I can tell, 'it's' always been around. Isn't that why people say it's the second oldest pro...'

'No, I meant for you. How did you get into it?'

'Oh I see, I'm sorry I was being obtuse. Why do you think I would want to talk about that?'

'But I thought...'

'What did you think?'

'I thought...'

'Money doesn't buy everything, Peter. You said you wanted to pay to talk to me for an hour.

But you didn't say what you wanted to talk about. I thought you wanted me to talk dirty to you. I thought you wanted me to tell you about me sitting on another girl's face with her tongue deep inside my pussy. I thought you wanted me to tell you what it's like being fucked by two guys, one in my arse, one in my cunt. I thought you wanted images to wank to.'

'No, that isn't what I want.' Peter said shocked at her language.

'I've never actually had someone come in here who wants to talk. I've seen that on films, where a guy gives over money and says he wants to talk, and then goes on about how his wife doesn't understand him and shit like that, but I've never actually had one before. Do you want to tell me about your wife?'

'God, no.'

'Then what? Why do you want to know how I started in this line of work? What do you want to know? Do you want to save me, Peter? Do you want to psychoanalyse me?' She was smiling and mocking him slightly and he could tell he had angered her by his question.

'No, it's not that…'

'Cos, I have to be honest, Peter, I have a perfectly good psychologist that I go to and I pay him almost as much as you just paid me to talk about that kind of stuff. Not that I go there for that. I go there for other things. I was getting panic attacks.'

'As I said, it's not that kind of thing. I don't want to judge you, or save you or anything like that.'

'You see, Peter, I think that's the problem. I've had some men who think that when they give me money, they're actually buying me and they can ask me to do whatever they like or get me to tell them anything they like. It's not like that. I provide a service, a range of products if you like. You come in, you pay for what's on offer and that's what you get. You don't have carte blanche to use me in any way you'd like just because you've given me eighty pounds. Someone doesn't go into HMV, ask the assistant for a CD, pay the money for it and then say "and now I'm gonna fuck you up the arse". Quite rightly the person behind the counter would be offended. More than I would probably, but it does piss me off. So when you said you wanted "to chat", that didn't mean that you were buying an open entry into my life. I don't have to tell you anything about why I do this. I wasn't abused as a kid, I'm not a crack addict trying to pay for my addiction. I'm not an Eastern European illegal immigrant trying to get cash the only way she can, most of which she has to give to her Mafiosi pimp. I'm not going to fit into any box you want to put me into. So I tell you what, let's ask you some questions. Why have you come here? How many times have you been to a prostitute? Why aren't you getting this from your wife?'

'You're the first one I've ever been to.' He said uncomfortably.

'Of course I am.'

'You are but there's no reason for you to believe me. I wasn't really sure why I came to see you the first time. I didn't actually think it through. I just got in the car and came here. But I've thought about it a lot since. Of course I have and the fact that you knew me scared me more than you can imagine. And the fear is still with me. My heart is racing right now.'

'Then why come back?'

'Because I think maybe you can do something for me.'

'Well, that's what I do.'

'I want to hire you.'

'What do you mean? As an escort?'

'I suppose. I have come to realise that I have been dying for a long time.'

'Are you ill?'

'No not actually ill, I just mean I've been dying inside slowly. I've been weak and pathetic and because of that I'm bitter and miserable, and I want to stop that if I can.'

'But how can I help you?'

'I don't want you to pity me or look down on me for a start. I don't want you to see me as just another sad loser who comes in here because he can't get it anywhere else, or someone whose wife won't sleep with him.'

She looked at him straight in the eyes. 'Will she fuck you?'

'No.' He said ashamed. 'But that's not what I wanted to talk about.'

'Why *do* you want to talk? If you're not getting fucked by your wife and you come here to get some, what's the problem? I don't have a problem with that. That sounds very understandable to me. In fact, I think it's fine. Rather than leave her, you go and find your sex somewhere else and stay in the marriage. That's fine isn't it? You must love her a lot not to leave her.'

'No, I don't. I want to kill her.' It was the first time he'd actually said this out loud. He'd thought about it for years. He'd sat and murmured away in his head about the ways he could murder her and not be caught. He'd even thought about whether or not he even minded if he got caught. His life was meaningless anyway and would it be any less meaningless spent lying in prison? But he'd never actually said it out loud to someone else before.

'Why don't you then?' She asked neutrally. He had expected surprise or shock from her but not such a matter-of-fact response. Perhaps she was trying to test him.

'I have two boys. I don't want their lives to be affected by it. Not that their lives would change if she wasn't around or if I wasn't either, come to think of it.'

She started to undo her dressing gown. 'Why do you say that?'

He watched as her body emerged from the silk. She was wearing purple underwear and her skin looked soft and smooth.

'Because, she keeps them away. They're at a boarding school. And she's always booking them off on adventure holidays and the like during their breaks. I spend no time with them.' He knew that this made him sound pathetic. He had let his wife completely control his life.

She walked across the room to her wardrobe and took out some jeans and a pink jumper. She obviously intended to get dressed if they weren't going to have sex.

'Could I change my mind?'

She turned round to look at him with a quizzical expression. 'About what?'

'I don't think I do want to talk. I think I'd rather have sex.'

She smiled and put her clothes back into the wardrobe.

At home he showered himself, scrubbing every inch of himself to get her smell off him, paranoid that his wife would be able to tell, would smell his guilt. He put his clothes in the washing machine. She was out. She was always out. He wondered if she was out being fucked by his partner or whether she really was out with her friends playing bridge like she said.

He was confused about his visit to Lauren. Straight after, he had felt relieved and strong, as if he had broken something that had held him back for years. But as he drove back towards his house and his life, he began to feel regret and self-loathing in equal measures. Had his life gone so terribly wrong that he had to resort to going to hookers for sex? He argued with himself that it wasn't about that, and that he had nothing to feel bad about. He was not doing this out of desperation but because he wanted to do it. He was also baffled by the fact that he felt guilty about breaking his marriage vows. His wife was regularly making a cuckold of him and she seemed not only to not feel any guilt but seemed to positively revel in it.

He felt sick to his stomach. He was angry and lost. He was shaking when he lit a cigar and poured himself a scotch.

The phone rang but he was unable to pick it up. He didn't want to speak to anyone, he was too afraid he might cry or blurt out everything that he had done to whoever was on the other end. The caller display told him it was his wife's mobile phone. He definitely didn't want to speak to her. He sipped, then gulped the whiskey back. He waited for a minute after the ringing had stopped and then picked up the phone and checked to see if she had left a message. She had.

'I'm staying over at Ali's tonight. We're going to play late, and I've had a little to drink. I'll see you tomorrow evening. And don't forget we have dinner with the Redfields at the Plum House tomorrow. Ciao.'

He hated the way she said 'ciao'. He hated her. He poured himself another large tumbler-full of scotch and picked up his car keys. Ali was his wife's sister and she lived on the other side of town. Fifteen minutes later he was knocking on her door. The lights in the house took a while to turn on and Ali opened the door rubbing the sleep from her eyes.

'Hello, Peter.' There was surprise in her voice. 'Is everything okay? It's one in the morning.'

'Is she here?' He said sipping away at the glass which hadn't left his hand throughout the whole drive.

'Who? Is who here?' She was too tired to lie.

'My wife.'

'No, she… I don't know where she is… She was… I mean…' He was touched by her attempt at loyalty but her floundering, stumbling speech was all the answer he needed.

'It's okay, her car's not here. I guess I've just missed her, she'll probably be at home before me.'

'That's right, Peter. She's probably on her way home.' Ali looked relieved that he had given her a lifeline out of the situation.

'Sorry to wake you.' He finished his drink and tossed the glass into the hedges to the side of the garden.

That was when he decided that he would kill her. That was the precise moment that he knew he didn't care what happened any longer. All he wanted was her dead.

'What's that all over your trousers? What do you look like? What happened to you today?'

He could just about hear her, but he could tell she was upset more from her expression than by the tone in her voice, which came through to him in muffled glimpses. She reached towards his face and stroked his cheek. When she took her hand away, there was blood on it. He reached up and felt the wet trail leading down from his right ear.

'What's happened? Are you all right?

'I was involved in an accident.'

She looked out through the open door to the car, expecting to see the extensive damage that must have been incurred for him to look like this. There was a small dent in the bumper but nothing as significant as she'd feared.

'It wasn't a car accident.' He said looking at the blood on his hand. 'It was some kind of explosion. I was in a service station that blew up.'

'What, the one on the M1? That's been all over the news. They think it's al Qaeda. What on earth were you doing there? Are you okay?'

She came towards him to hug him but he stepped away from the embrace and started to climb the stairs. She was calling something after him but he couldn't make out what it was. Everything was swimming and all of a sudden he thought he might pass out. With every step he climbed, he felt weaker and he was covered in cold clammy sweat. He stumbled into the bathroom and locked the door behind him.

He leaned against the sink unit for support and looked at himself in the mirror. He was in a lot worse state than he thought. Not only was his face scratched and bruised, but under the warm light which normally made everyone look like they had a tan, he looked whiter than white, almost transparent. There were dark blue patches under his eyes. Those weren't the eyes he'd had that morning before he'd left. In fact he didn't recognise the face in front of him at all. He sank to the floor and lay there quietly for a few minutes just trying to breathe. The cold tiles pressing on his cheek caused a shiver to run down him that he couldn't control or stop. He shook and shook.

Lying where he was, he peeled of his clothes and wanted them to disappear as they came off him wet and incriminating, but they lay there in a small messy pile. He pulled himself into the power shower and turned it full blast. The blood from his head turned a light pink as it diluted in the water and circled its way down the plughole. As the steam rose around him, it clouded everything and he wondered if he could stay in there forever and never have to face anything else again.

He turned the hot up until it was stinging him, but it didn't seem to go deep enough to touch the ice in his core. The hairs on his legs were glistening and smooth against his skin. The blood that had run off them was his and hers mixed, entangled and joined like they would be from now on. He thought of Lady Macbeth and the speck of blood that all the oceans in the world could not wash away. Now he understood the tattoo that the blood of the innocent leaves; it's invisible, unable to be scoured or bleached away. He wanted to tear at his skin, to pull it off, to rip his own flesh away, peel away anything that had ever come in contact with the agony of the mistake.

There was a knocking at the door. He was unaware how long it had been going on for but it was a loud thudding now, suggesting it had once been a quiet tapping.

'Do you want me to call the doctor? I think you should be looked at?'

'No!' He screamed; the sound reverberating around the little cubicle. 'No,' he repeated more quietly. 'I'm fine, really I am. I just need a little time, I think. May be an Aspirin. I'm okay. I'm okay. I'm okay.' He said this over and over and over again getting quieter and quieter and slipping once again, being pulled by gravity, this time into the shower tray where he sat hunched, water falling into his mouth as he cried.

When he came downstairs an hour later, she was feeding Bartholomew. He was sitting in his pyjamas having fish fingers shovelled into him. She was making what he assumed were train noises, as the spoon headed for his mouth. The food entered the tunnel and was consumed. She turned to look at him.

'You're not going out, are you?'

He was dressed in his bowling shirt and a pair of jeans. His hair was slicked back; he was clean-shaven and smelling of aftershave.

'It's bowling night. I have to.'

She looked incredulously at him. 'You're in no shape for that. Stay in tonight and I'll cook you something nice and we'll snuggle up and watch a DVD and then you can get an early night. I don't think you realise what you've been through. I think you're in some kind of shock.'

He went over to the fridge and pulled out a can of diet coke which he downed in one gulping swallow. He belched and Bartholomew laughed.

'That's the first time he's laughed all day,' she said smiling at her little boy, and kissing him on the cheek, then giving him a noogy. 'His ears have been really bad today. Haven't they little man?'

'Did you take him to the doctor?'

'Yeah, he said it was an infection. He gave me those drops to clear it up and said we should just give him Calpol to keep the pain down for the next couple of days.'

He picked up the small brown medicine bottle and unscrewed the small lid with its nipple top. He squeezed it and sucked up some of the clear fluid into the pippet and turned his head letting the dropper drip the medicine into his ears. It stung and was freezing.

'See Barty, I've taken the medicine as well. Now we're both all better.'

Without a goodbye or even a backward glance, he walked out of the kitchen, picked up the suitcase that he'd quietly placed in the hallway and walked out of the house leaving the door open. He was aware that his wife had followed him and watched him leave calling after him but he didn't look back.

He was back in the car. Back in the bubble. She was waiting for him in her little bag. He stroked the faux leather side of it where he imagined her cheek to be and then drove off to the bowling alley.

Chapter 7

The Prof looked genuinely happy to see me. There was no one in his waiting room, which was unusual. I had the feeling he had cancelled some people despite my protestations that he shouldn't. He bounced out of his office taking his white coat off as he did and threw it at his secretary in a playful way.

'Come on, let me buy you a coffee. We'll go for one of our walks, eh?'

It was colder out than during our early summer walks. When he'd purchased drinks from the coffee shop in the foyer, we headed for the river again using the cardboard cups as hand warmers. Every time I looked at the Prof since the operation, I found my eyes being drawn down towards his hands. It was hard to believe that those hands had been inside my head. He had touched parts of me that I hadn't.

He told me about his holiday with his family to the South of France and then as we leant over the railings and looked across to the Houses of Parliament, he asked me about my trip.

'So you said you found your guy?'

I took a picture of him with my camera before answering his question.

'Did he let you take a photo of him? Or did he think you were trying to steal his soul?' The Prof had a grin on his face as he said this.

'Well, no he didn't mind. Neither of them did actually.'

'Neither of them?'

'I tried a couple of things.'

He looked intrigued and wanted me to elaborate. He was fascinated by the lengths his patients would go to avoid dying.

'I found a voodoo guy in New Orleans and then I found an American Indian healer in Nevada.'

We continued walking along the embankment. He wanted to hear the story. He wanted to know what they did exactly. He wanted to know how it made me feel. If I felt I was cured. If I thought it had been worth it.

The guy in New Orleans had been easy to find. I had read a report in a paper that there was this man who claimed to cure all sorts of things with a modern form of voodoo. He had hundreds of people willing to testify to his bona fide credentials as a healer. I tracked him down through his website to a small shop in downtown New Orleans. I phoned him up and he said it was all quite simple. All I had to do was get on a plane, pay him some money and he would cure me. He said he would combine voodoo rituals with some herbal medicine he knew and finally, if it was required, he could perform psychic surgery. But he would assess me when I arrived.

I sold my house to get the cash. After all, if I was going to die anyway, what was the point in owning a house. The guy wanted ten thousand dollars for the treatment and told me it would take a week of various ceremonies to cure such a terrible illness. I participated in five rituals in the end and ate loads of herb parcels he made up for me and drank some bitter tasting drinks. These rituals either took place in the basement of his house amid the smell of dark incense and burning candles or out in a forest just outside the city. A large congregation of people dancing and drumming and drinking attended these outdoor events.

During the fifth and final ritual, he placed his hands on my head and made a small incision into my scar with a razor blade. He fished around with his fingers under the skin before pulling out a small piece of bloody something, which he immediately cast into the fire.

I liked him a lot. He was funny and so certain of his abilities. He was a perfect con man. I knew from our first meeting that he would be unable to help me and that the only power he actually had was for those who believed in him. I didn't. But if I was dying anyway, all I wanted to do with my last days was experience those worlds out there that are hidden from us all. The dark worlds that exist around us all the time. The beautiful layers of darkness that lie just underneath society's skin. Knowing I was going to die had removed a lot of the fear I have lived with that had kept me safe and comfortable. The pictures I took there were fantastic.

Next I moved on to Nevada and found an old Indian guy who said he would be happy to try an old healing ceremony he knew. This was a much less expensive and briefer affair. Although I felt a lot more pain.

I had to fast for two days only being allowed to drink water. He then took me out to the edge of the desert to a little plot of land that he owned where he lived in a caravan with three wild mutts. We built a sweat lodge together. We got naked. He did a thing called smudging around me, which was basically burning a small bundle of sage or something around me to cleanse my aura. We then went into the sweat lodge and he took me on a journey through my subconscious. In and out we went, being super-heated by the burning fire inside and then suddenly frozen by the numbing bitterness of the desert night. I thought I might die that night.

After five minutes in the dry black heat of the lodge, my head was pounding and I could hear the blood pulsing through my ears like the loose-skinned drum he had beaten outside for hours on end. In the darkness of this small round tent made from bent branches and skins, I cried and shouted. After hours of this cycle I saw the stars for the first time, the sparkling lights around my peripheral vision, which were the first signs of the next stage of my illness. I passed out.

When I woke up, I was in a nasty, sweaty hotel room miles away on another reservation. I don't really know what happened, but I think my guide had freaked out when he found me unconscious and thought his best bet was to leave me to die somewhere away from him. I didn't try to find him again, instead I blew a load of cash at the casino and got married.

That was more or less the story of the trip.

We made our way back to his office and he did the normal series of tests. He touched my face with a small piece of cotton wool and I had to tell him when I could feel it. He tested my sight. He looked up my nose, down my throat and tested my co-ordination and hearing.

When he was finished, he looked sad for the first time that day.

'Jack, I think this is it. It's come back a lot quicker than I had hoped. We can scan you just to check. But I'm pretty sure we'll find that it's grown back. And there's really not much we can do. I think maybe we're looking at...'

I stopped him before he could finish the sentence. I didn't and still don't want to know the prognosis. I declined the kind offer of more hours spent inside huge claustrophobic metal coffins designed to give me a picture of the path of my death.

At the store, she'd bought a large can of vegetable oil. She fished around in the kitchen cabinet and dragged out the turkey fryer. She hadn't fired it up in while. She took it out on to the back yard and plugged it in through the kitchen window. It began to hum quietly in anticipation of the flesh to come.

His hunting knife was razor sharp and made quick work of the dog. She took its hide down to the back fence and pinned it out like she'd seen her husband do with any number of deerskins or racoons before curing them. Its skinned body looked naked and smaller than she'd expected. She gutted it and placed the foul smelling intestines in the brown paper bag the oil had come in. She folded over the top and threw it down the garden. If she didn't remember to put it in the garbage can later, something would come and eat it up in the middle of the night. She started her butchery with the back legs which appeared to have the most meat on them. She cut them off at the hip joint and then cut the paws off from the knee knuckle. The ribs and back had little to offer except some small bits and pieces. She removed what was left of the head, although this took a lot of work to get through the spine at the top of the neck. Next she got to work on the front legs and with some careful dicing and slicing, the dissection was done. It was hardly clinical but is served its purpose. The bits were small enough to drop into the fryer, so she opened the lid and popped them in one by one, watching the golden liquid bubble around them.

Just twenty minues later and, hey presto, crispy dog dinner-time. With a cleaver she hacked the bits into smaller unrecognisable pieces and covered them in hot chilli sauce. As a final touch she opened up a packet of tortilla chips and poured them over the mess. Some fell to the floor and, for the first time, she realised the dog had been good for one thing at least, it was better than any vacuum cleaner.

'Food.' She said. 'Move to the back of the cage.' He moved. 'This is all you're getting for today, so enjoy it.'

She sat on the stairs and watched him ravenously start into the spicy fried dog. He was ripping bits off and swallowing them without chewing, leaving a pile of dog bones on the plate. Within five minutes he'd eaten the whole lot and was drinking heavily from the water bucket to quench the burning in his mouth.

'You shot my dog?' He asked after a few minutes, wiping the water and grease away from his stubbled lips.

'Yep. And you just ate it.' She said this with little expression and in truth it had given her little pleasure to do it.

'Tasted good.' He said and took his cock out and peed into his bucket. 'It was a dumb fucking critter anyway. It should have bitten your face clean off.'

'But then you'd have died down here, locked in there. Or did you think, Lassie would have run to the neighbours and brought them back to save you. "What's that you say, boy? You pa's stuck down a well? No? He's trapped in a cage in a cellar? Well, hell, let's set him free then." That dog didn't have the brains God gave him. He'd have come down here and just sat by you til' you both died. Dumb crackers both of you.'

He laughed. As far as he could remember, this was the funniest thing she'd ever said. He reached through the bars grabbed the piss bucket and, before she could move, threw the contents over her.

'You fed me my dog, you fucking whore!'

He began screaming at her again and smashing himself against the bars.

'I'm gonna get outta here and I'm gonna fuck you up. I'm gonna fuck you up so much you'll wish you were dead.'

She stood up and left him there to snarl and growl on his own. Upstairs, she peeled off her clothes and stepped into the shower. It wasn't the first time he'd pissed on her, but this time there would be consequences.

She scrubbed her skin and hair until she was sore. She could still smell his musk on her. It made her wretch.

She put on an old t-shirt and a pair of shorts and went back downstairs. She grabbed the portable television from her room and carried it down to the basement. She plugged it in and wired the camcorder into it.

'I'm off out now. I won't be back for a while, that's if I come back at all. You shouldn't have done what you did, you son of a bitch. But I'll learn you.'

She picked up the piss bucket and placed it out of his reach on the other side of the cellar.

'From now on you have only one bucket. And that's got the water in you need. You can drink it all and then piss in it, or you could just piss in it and drink that as well. It don't matter to me. You can just shit where you like, you filthy fucking animal.'

She turned back to the camcorder and turned its function onto the play mode. Then she flicked through the channels until she found the one tuned in to the video she wanted to leave him with.

'I don't want you to get bored, so I made you a home video. And it'll explain where I am as well. Now you be good, you hear.'

With that she stepped out of the way of the screen and left the cellar and the house. He heard the pick-up start up and drive away.

'That's right, you like that don't you.' A man's voice was saying from the television.

The camera was being held in someone's hand looking downwards at his wife whose head was bobbing backwards and forwards on a large cock. This was only the start, over the next hour and half, he saw or heard when he couldn't face looking at the screen man after man fucking his wife every way conceivable. And every time there she was staring blankly down the camera lens looking straight at him leaving him in no doubt that she had done this especially for this purpose. The rage inside him knew no release and the pains in his chest that grew after man after man and friend after friend put their cock in her pussy, her mouth, her arse, made him think he was having a heart attack. When the video finally finished, it clicked itself off automatically and a bright blue blank screen illuminated the cellar. And as night drew on, it was the only source of light in the entire room.

He pressed and pulled and yanked the cage every five minutes or so until he was exhausted and then he would take a break before starting again. His shoulders ached from pushing against the steel and his hands were blistered from the tearing grip he'd had on the bars. Eventually he had loosened three bolts before he lay down to sleep.

Steven looked at the number on the yellowed piece of paper and looked at the phone. He had been walking around the house for hours since he'd said goodbye to Mae. It was obvious to him that this was the sign he'd been told to look out for. He also knew it was time to leave because the house refused to speak to him anymore; it was empty like the discarded shell of a snail. He had been told that when it was time to leave this would happen. But what was he to do? Where was he to go? The only link he now had with the outside world was the number Dodds had pressed into his hand after the funeral. But he had no way of knowing if this number was still active or not, or even if she was still alive, she had looked old then, perhaps she had passed away as well. He felt sure though that he would have known if this had happened. He was sure she would have come to visit him if she had been on the Other Side.

He wasn't sure what to say, so he paced up and down looking from the paper in his hand to the phone and back.

He picked up the receiver and dialled.

'Hello, Doris here, can I help you?'

'Is that Dodds? Aunty Dodds?' He had never heard her full name, so this threw him and he wasn't certain that this was in fact the right woman.

'Steven is that you? Is that you, lovely boy?'

'Yes.'

An hour later he was sitting across from her drinking tea from a cup and saucer. She looked older than she had two years before but there was still something in her eyes, some sparkle that had lost none of its brightness.

'I had a bath like you said.' He said.

'What for two years?' She laughed. 'That was a long one, eh? You must be all wrinkled like a prune.' She hadn't really thought he'd been in there all that time.

'Yes, it was a long time, but I had a lot of things to think about. And sometimes my skin would get sore, but I used Vaseline and it seemed to heal any redness.'

She stared at him as they talked but often he felt she wasn't actually looking at him but around him as if there were tiny fairies circling him that she was watching flit here and there. Sometimes she would smile as if responding to something other than the things he'd said or done.

She told him that he had better stay with her for a while. He had no reason to disagree.

On that first afternoon she walked with him down to the local shops and bought him a whole new wardrobe from various charity shops. She also took him to an old-fashioned barbers who shaved him with a cut-throat razor and hot towels and didn't nick him once. As for his hair, it was all cut off and shaved right back to a Number Two. There was nowhere to hide now.

Here he was, in striped shirts, brown corduroy trousers and loafers. He enjoyed being dressed by someone else. The whole process was free of decisions.

Everywhere he went everybody knew Dodds and smiled at her, nodded to her or even came out of their way to cross the road to say hello.

'This is my nephew, Steven. That's right, Lal's boy. He's going to be staying with me for a while. You'll be seeing him around I'm sure. Of course you'll see him at the church.'

On the first night at her house, just after dinner, she turned to him after a long period of silence.

'You know that you were sent to me, don't you? You know that I was waiting for you?' There was a look of genuine excitement in her eyes. 'He told me you'd be coming. I had hoped it would be sooner, but now you're here, that's the most important thing.'

Steven liked the dark green leather sofa he was sitting on, being swallowed by. It squeaked when he moved.

'I think I know what you mean.'

'You hear the voices, don't you?' This was somewhere between a question and a statement. 'What do they tell you? Do they tell you to do things? Do they give you messages?'

He paused unsure of how much he should disclose.

'I do hear voices sometimes, yes.'

'And?'

'And I don't always know who they are from. Sometimes I do. And sometimes I think I can talk to those who have just died. But it makes me...'

Dodds was rocking backwards and forwards with joy at hearing him speak about this for the first time.

'It makes you scared?'

He thought about this carefully and wasn't sure that that was the sensation he felt. It was something else, something more like anxiety.

'I'm not scared exactly. I simply worry that it's just my brain playing games with me. I worry that if I listen to what they say too much that I'm giving in to some kind of madness. So I try to block them out whenever I can.'

Dodd's face was like an actors' handbook of useful expressions; she showed concern, happiness, fear, disappointment and worry all within milliseconds of each other.

'And can you stop them? Can you control them? Do you ever see anything?'

Steven stood up and continued talking as he paced up and down on the flower-patterned carpet. The movement seemed to help him clear his thoughts.

'I can't stop them, but I can ignore them. They sort of drift off into the background, but they're always there, hundreds of them whispering and chattering. But when He comes, I can't ignore him. If He comes, everything else stops. If He wants to tell me something, there's no way I can do anything about it. I have to relax and let Him come through. If I fight it, my whole body shakes until I fall over, like having a fit, but if I just relax, it's easier. It's almost like He comes into me when He tells me things. As for if I see things? Sometimes. Sometimes I see these things flickering in my peripheral vision. Sometimes they come and talk to me as clearly as I can see you. When He comes I can't see anything other than Him.'

'Who is "He", Steven?' She asked dipping a ginger biscuit in to her tea.

'Him.' Steven said pointing to the crucifix hanging on the wall above the gas fire, with its fake flames licking away. Neither of them spoke for a time.

'Do you think I'm mad, Dodds? I'm worried that I might be mad.'

'We're all a little bit mad, Steven. That's what makes us all different. Some of us are just more different. But no, dear, I don't think you're mad. If you were mad you wouldn't know it, would you? I think perhaps you have a gift, and this is what I was told to look for.'

'Told by whom?'

She smiled at him and tapped a finger against her temple.

'Them, of course.'

It was the start.

He sat outside the bowling alley for some minutes wondering whether or not to go in. He wanted to see Dan, so, eventually plucked up enough courage to get out of the car and walk through the sliding doors into the brightly lit Bowplex.

The sound of bowling hit him as soon as he crossed the threshold. There is no other place that has that sound – the sound of heavy rolling balls gliding down highly polished lanes, smashing into wooden pins with a jangling series of impacts all rolled into the one noise of a strike. It smelled as well of sweaty feet covered by air freshener and heavy-duty carpet detergent.

Dan was walking up to him while he was acclimatising himself. He flinched when Dan's hand slapped down on his shoulder.

'Whoa there, steady boy. Bit jumpy today, aren't we?'

He couldn't think of what his normal reply would be on a normal day so he just shrugged and made some non-committal noise somewhere deep down in his throat.

'You're keen tonight. All ready to go, I see. Couldn't wait, eh?'

It took him a second to realise what Dan was referring to. He was holding his blue marbled bowling ball in one hand and its bag in the other. He obviously thought he had taken the ball out in his eagerness to get on with the game.

'Listen, you okay? I was worried about you earlier, that call was a bit fucking weird. What's going on? Trouble at home?'

Looking at Dan's fake concern, he didn't want to tell him anything about his day. He wouldn't understand. So he told him what he knew he wanted to hear.

'Yeah, just a row, nothing too bad though, sorry about that. I blew it all out of proportion. I'm fine; we're fine, honestly. Listen, I'm not feeling that great though tonight so I think I might just…'

'You might just what?' Dan laughed and put his arm round him leading him further into the venue and further away from the door.

'You might just go and get yourself a pair of shoes and drink some beer and let Uncle Dan show you how to play this damn game. Seriously, it'll be good for you. And anyway you know how the Head feels about bowling night, the team that works together plays together.'

Their boss was obsessed with two things: hitting targets and bowling, and this was his gift to the staff. Once a month he paid for this bonding bowling session. It wasn't compulsory but all his team came. He had had shirts printed up with the company logo on the back and the moto 'Play To Win' embroidered on the front pocket. They had been imported especially for them all the way from 'Milwaukee in the Good Old US of A', he announced when he unpacked the box and tossed ten shirts out across the boardroom table at an end-of-month pep talk. His one had a special inscription on the front which read 'Who's the Daddy? I'm the Daddy.' A phrase he would shout out every time he hit a strike. He'd then shoot them all with imaginary pistols. It was difficult to keep laughing at the same joke month after month.

'Here, I'll take this. You go and get your shoes. Hey, what's this?'

Before he knew it, Dan had taken his bowling bag off him and was taken aback by its weight having thought it was empty.

'You got yourself another ball? Fucking hell, that's keen. You're arse kissing more than usual. Is there some promotion coming up that I haven't heard of?'

He snatched the bag back and held it close to his chest, protecting it.

'It's just a spare. Nothing special.'

'A spare? What do you think is going to happen to that?' He was pointing at the blue ball in his other hand. 'When did you last see a bowling ball break?'

'My mother got it for me, all right. For my birthday.'

'But that was weeks ago.'

'It had to be handmade. Now can we leave it?' He was a little more aggressive than he needed to be, so Dan took the hint and started walking off towards the lanes.

'We're on lane three, I'll sign you in, you grumpy fucker.'

After sliding his feet into somebody else's shoes, he went over and started bowling badly, much to the delight of the rest of his work colleagues. He was usually the only one in the firm that could give their boss a run for his money and this gave the two men a close bond, forged from competition. But today, he was a fuckwit like the others. Every other ball he bowled scuttered off into the gutter and the ones that did make it down the lane all the way seemed to be drawn to one side or the other picking off only one or two pins. After three games, he had come seventh, eighth and ninth.

He guttered the first ball of the fourth game and a collective cheer of derision went up from all watching. He stood by the open mouth of the ball-return waiting for his to come back, trying to ignore the cat-calls and whistles from behind him. He dried his hand on the small fan on the top of the machine and stared down at the ten pristine reminders of his failure waiting like soldiers to be shot down. He was so focused on blocking everything out in his attempt to keep it together that he almost missed Dan's voice.

'Fuck me. It must that ball of yours. Perhaps you're right after all, perhaps you do need that spare one. Here, pass it over, let's see how does with his mummy's ball.'

He swung round just in time to see Jane from accounts pass the little bag over, Dan's fingers were already on the zipper.

'No! Stop!' He shouted.

It was loud enough and desperate enough to stop Dan from moving and anyone else in the group from talking. They all stared at him. He tried to lighten the tense moment but was shaking and was sure they could all see the white panic that had come over him.

'Leave it out, Dan. Put it down. It's just a bad patch, no need for a new ball. Look, you'll see I'll get a strike now. Go on, put it down.'

Dan put the ball down underneath the moulded plastic chair nearest him. This over-reaction had been noticed by everyone, his boss looked especially concerned by the sudden break in bonhomie. He turned away from them and picked up his ball, which had rolled home to him during the aching awkwardness. He blew on his fingers, picked it up and stood perfectly still looking straight down the alley. He needed to get this one. The weight of the ball started to make his arm shudder and he knew he had to move, had to release it but he was frozen. Then it broke and he took five steps forward, back swing, bent legs, lean forward, and it was gone. He stayed in the release position watching it as it flew away from him towards the pins. Without intending to he had placed a good deal of spin on the ball and after the agony of watching it head towards the gutter again, it began to turn and struck the pack just fractionally off centre. Every single one of them was blasted into the back gully. He stood up and turned round. There was the slightest of pauses before the eruption of enthusiastic screaming and yells.

'Now that's more like it! Come on!' Dan shouted running over to him and giving him a big bear hug.

'Nice bouncebackability.' His boss said winking at him. 'You see, guys, that's the kind of thing we need in this firm. People who can dig deep when they need to and pull out a strike.'

'What the fuck was all that about?' Dan whispered into his ear before he letting him go from the tight embrace.

'Sorry.' He whispered back.

He didn't stay for the usual beers because something had caught his attention. Some small drops of blood fell from the seam at the bottom of the bag when he picked it up. He threw a paper napkin over them, smeared it as he wiped it up and then held the towel under the bag. It was time to get out of there.

He drove round for hours, driving down to the coast and then back through various back roads and twisting lanes. He had no idea where to go. He had made his mind up never to go home again, but hadn't worked out where in fact he would now be staying.

'I can't think straight. Where shall we stay tonight?'

There was no reply. It was two-thirty when he eventually passed the roadside motel and pulled in. He booked a room and took a walk over to the large petrol station attached to it. He wandered around the shop gathering supplies – chocolate bars, coke, biscuits, crisps, pasties and a cheese and pickle sandwich. He passed a freezer cabinet with a small selection of ice cream and frozen meals and opened the door allowing a cold cloud of air to escape. He reached in and pulled out three bags of ice cubes from the bottom, then thought for a second and grabbed the last three bags as well.

'Got enough ice, mate?' The young, over-confident spotty youth behind the counter said sarcastically.

'I don't know.' He answered honestly.

He picked her up from the car along with his heavy suitcase and struggled his way over to his room. He began to strip and once naked, he picked up the bag and carried it into the bathroom. He put it in the bottom of the shower and pulled the showerhead off its hook and down into the tray. Kneeling on the cold tiles outside, he reached over and unzipped the bag. The smell hit him. It was overpowering. He coughed and gagged. Blood, rusty iron and death. He grabbed her head by the hair and pulled it from the bag, coagulating blood had stuck it to the bottom of the bag and he had to give it a firm pull to bring it free. There was the sound of suction reversing.

Her vital fluids were smeared all over her. Her hair was a matted mess. However, as he held her up, he noticed that only the occasional drop fell from her. She must be nearly drained he thought. He turned on the tap and tested the water with his hand, in the same way a hairdresser might at the basin, before he began to wash her face and hair. Firstly he washed the bag out. Small flecks of her flesh washed away down the plug with the mass of pink diluted blood. When it was as clean as he could get it, he swivelled around and balanced it carefully upside down with the top open on the heated towel rail. Then he turned back and ever so carefully began to clean her up. Firstly, he shampooed her hair until it was free of any clots or matted knots. Then he went over the face and severed neck with a small face cloth that had been sitting by the sink. Finally, he opened one of the small bottles of conditioner provided by the hotel and slowly massaged it into her hair. He was sure she would have loved this when she was alive. He pictured her lying in a steaming bath full of bubbles with him behind her slowly pressing his fingers into her scalp; she would have purred like a giant cat.

When she was clean, he lifted her up carefully and placed her on the side of the sink where he dried her with a white towel. Although it was hard to tell because it was still damp, but her hair looked darker than it had in the picture. In the picture she had been tanned and now her alabaster skin made everything about her look different. No less beautiful, just like a fine sculptured version of the real woman. He carried her on a towel into the bedroom and laid her gently on the bed. He opened the mini bar and emptied it on the floor. He took the bags of ice out of the carrier bag and lined the walls of the small fridge with them; it only took five of the bags as it turned out. He placed her carefully in the centre of it. He broke open two mini bottles of gin and tore open the last ice bag. As he drank from a plastic glass, he sat cross-legged in front of her, her mesmeric face gently illuminated by the internal light diffused through her ice halo. When he finished his drink, he leaned forward to kiss her cold forehead and closed the door to let her get some sleep. He curled up on the floor for the night so he could be close to her.

If his wife's sister had told her about his visit the night before she certainly didn't show it when he got back from work. He had caught her lying once again and yet she seemed supremely confident, even radiant.

When he came in, he could hear the television on upstairs in the bedroom turned up loud enough so that she could hear it above the sound of her hair dryer. He made himself a scotch on the rocks and went up to see her. She was looking at herself in the mirror of her antique dressing table as she blow-dried her hair. Her fingers ran through it as she scrunched and volumised like a professional. Her beauty regime took up a lot of her life, and even though she was past her first bloom, she was still a fine-looking woman who spent a lot of time and money making herself look as good as she did.

He undid his tie and took his drink into the en suite. He compared and contrasted the two of them. She was tanned, fit and firm, he was pale grey, lined and exhausted. He was tired with life and consumed by bitterness that he wanted cut out of him like cancer. The hair dryer was turned off and he could hear from the distorted way she spoke that she was applying her lipstick while she spoke to him.

'We have to be there at eight.'

She had spent the previous night fucking her lover and had been found out and the first words she said were 'We have to be there at eight.' He didn't respond, he just kept staring at himself. His eyes were full of tiny red lines making them look like a fractured pieces of glass. He stuck out his tongue and was vaguely disgusted by its brown-coated appearance. The sides of his tongue were fluted. He had been grinding his teeth a lot and chewing on the edges of it. He had an ulcer that pained him whenever it caught on a tooth or when he ate. He took out his tooth brush and started brushing his tongue to see if he could scrub it clean, to see if he could do anything to remove the stains which had taken him over.

'What are you wearing tonight? Everyone's dressing up. Don't let me down. That dark blue jacket would be good.' She sneered through to him.

He showered and dressed in the blue jacket, shirt and trousers he found waiting for him on the bed. She was nowhere to be seen, although he knew exactly where she would be, she would be drinking vodka in the kitchen as she always did before they went out.

'It adds a shine to my eyes and a rosiness to my cheeks.' He had heard her say many times. In his experience, however, it added the potential for her to be drunk before they actually got anywhere and that was about all.

In the car on the way they didn't speak and her overly made-up face looked like a marble sculpture next to him. As soon as the front door was opened to them, she came to life again. A smile cracked across her face and she lit up with vodka radiance.

'Darling you look simply wonderful.' She said to the hostess, already laughing at some anticipated later joke.

As they entered the house, she turned to him and whispered menacingly to him.

'Don't embarrass me tonight.'

Like most nights, he watched the proceedings unfold in front of him. Ten of their friends were all there to celebrate another fortieth. For a good eighteen months he had been forced to celebrate this rite of passage with nearly everyone on the circuit. He was a few years older than his wife and most of them were her friends.

When he had turned forty-eight earlier in the year, he had celebrated it by taking the boys out for the day in London. They went to see

Chelsea play football, ate burgers, went on the London Eye and then to see a musical. It was one of the happiest days of his life. He hadn't been surrounded by the insincerity and the fawning that now immersed him. She'd had a bridge contest, or so she had said, at the time. It had suited him and the boys that way.

As he looked round at everyone, he realised he had nothing in common with any of them. Some of them he'd been having dinner with for over a decade but never really got any further than a relationship based on social status. He listened to the men talk about golf, squash, cars and work. About the ups and downs of the market and the occasional reference, with a wink and a nod, to someone's sexy eighteen-year-old au pair. He hated them and their gruesome banality. The women seemed occupied with clothes, hair, gossip and the occasional reference to how bad their husbands all were in bed. He wasn't sure what he wanted them to be like or to talk about but with every smug guffaw that exploded from them, he wanted them, more and more, to all die a sickening, painful death. The only time he was tempted to enter a conversation was when quite out of the blue the question of immigration came up.

'God, please don't start on politics.' His wife had bellowed. 'Don't start Peter off. He'll only go on about the marches during his student days. Champagne socialism is so boring.'

The fat rugby player to his left chirped up.

'All I'm saying is, I'm with Ali G. Let all the sexy young ones in and turn all the ugly mingers back. I mean if we've got to support their sponging arses, we might as well be able to lust after them a bit.'

There was a small round of applause and a lot of laughing. Peter tried to work out what would happen if all of them were to die right that second. Would it make any difference to the world? Maybe their children might miss them but in the long run, he thought, they might actually do better without their vacuous, small-minded parents. His bitter lemon sorbet tasted too sweet to him.

There was only one couple sitting at the table that he had not met before and so had no predisposition of hatred towards them at the start of the evening. He should have realised, though, that by the very fact of their having been invited to the party, they were 'those' kind of people.

They had only just moved into the town.

'We moved down from London because we fancied a change of pace. You know we've done the whole London thing, and we thought it might be nice for Tanya and Kieran to have a bit of country-living in their teens. Get them away from some of the more undesirable influences up in town.'

She said this while taking out a small plastic bag of cocaine from her handbag. She flicked it and shook it to make sure all the coke was at the bottom and wasn't going to fly out the minute she opened it. She then took out a small mirror and laid it on the table. She chopped out a couple of lines and then with a rolled-up twenty pound note took a good long hard snort. Coffee and coke was a new thing for this crowd. But no one seemed to bat an eyelid. Either they were too English to say anything or this had become more of a norm than he had realised. Rubbing her nose and sniffing profusely, she offered the mirror around. His wife was the first one to take up the offer. There was no way from the efficient way she did it that this was her first time. There was obviously more that he didn't know about her. If the vodka hadn't given her eyes a sparkle, this certainly did.

When everyone moved into the living room, his wife made her way to their CD collection. As Beyonce sang she danced with the coke woman. She entwined herself around her new plaything grinding in time to the rhythm. Joints were skinned up and he slowly watched them all smoke or drink themselves into oblivion with his wife at the epicentre of the mind-quake. He got up when his wife's lips brushed across the stranger's mouth. As the two of them began to kiss deeply, he made his way out into the hall and once he had recovered his jacket and keys, he was in the car and away.

When he woke up the next morning, she was lying next to him, her make-up was smeared across her face and there was lipstick on her neck that didn't match the one on her lips. He cancelled work intending to go to Lauren's but when he phoned, she told him she was booked all day but that he could make an appointment for the next day. He said he'd leave it. Instead, he drove down to Brighton and reading through the local advertiser for prostitutes over a coffee in Starbucks, he saw an advert which read:

'Fantasy Rooms, Brighton Parlour, must be seen to be believed. Themed rooms from hospital, office and fetish. Nurse Leela, PC Tess, Mistress Elizabeth and Secretary Anthea. Can't be missed. No extra charge for themes.' He phoned the number and got an address.

The girl who answered the door could have been no older than twenty. She was wearing a white shirt whose buttons were bursting open revealing her black bra underneath. Her short pencil skirt didn't reach far enough down her legs to hide the top of her stockings and the garter she was wearing. Her heels were black six-inch nails. This was Secretary Anthea. He was led into a clean Ikea-decorated magnolia living room and was introduced to each of the girls and talked through all the possible activities of which he could partake in this particular establishment. This was nothing like his experience with Lauren. This was altogether less intimate, this was only about sex.

For two hundred pounds, he got to 'party' with Mistress Elizabeth and Secretary Anthea. Over the next two hours, he was spanked and tied up, he watched them lick, suck and fuck each other with dildos. They had a selection of drugs in a small tin first-aid box which he was invited to try. He had slipped so far there seemed no point in stopping now, so he accepted whatever they recommended and paid accordingly. They gave him Viagra to keep him hard, poppers to get him high and to relax his arse so he could receive the butt plug they fucked him with. Lastly, and for another hundred pounds, they all snorted lines of coke. He wanted to know what it was like; he wanted to know what it was all like. At times his heart raced, at times he was scared, at times he thought he was going to have a panic attack and at times he reached areas of euphoria he had no ideas he was capable of. Wafting backwards and forwards on clouds of amyl nitrate and cocaine, he was blissfully far away from himself.

All three of them lay on the bed for the last hour interwoven over one another, sweaty and smelling of cum, chemicals and lube.

He walked along the seafront for an hour after the session trying to process what he had just done and what it meant. He had no regrets. He felt released and alive. The sharp sea air blew straight through him. He was entering new worlds and had tried something he had no idea even existed, or that it was so readily available, only one quick phonecall away. Besides, what had he got to lose, really? His life was rapidly going nowhere. The worst that he figured could happen was that he could be found out and uncovered; he might have to leave the job he hated, the wife he despised and a life that had cheated and fucked him over. He wanted something to frighten him and wake him up, something that would cut through the flab of his life like a surgeon's knife.

He was so alienated from himself he couldn't even remember how he'd got into this spineless state. He felt like he had been in a coma for years. As his head gradually began to clear from the drugs, he drove back to work and stayed late, not working, just sketching images in a note pad of Anthea and Elizabeth, two girls who had fucked him for money.

He made a brief shortlist of ways to kill his wife. He took the pad outside and burnt it in a metal bin before he went home for the evening via a sex shop to buy some more small phials of amyl.

Chapter 8

Rosa told me I could stay with her for a few days until I found myself somewhere to live. She was worried about me. She and Ma were like two peas in a pod. They shared the same heart, the same sweet nature.

She was a religious lady and would like me to walk her to her church each day. I'd drop her off at the service and drift around the area taking photos until she came out, then walk her home.

On one such occasion I sat on a bench and was watching leaves slowly falling from a large beech tree when a car pulled up in the side street I was on, and the man inside sat in the car dialling a number on his mobile phone. Getting no answer he turned it off and looked agitated. He was watching the doorway of a Victorian house on the other side of the road. It was a huge house which looked as if it had been split into flats. There was music playing inside his car but from where I was sitting I couldn't make out what it was.

On the plane on the way back from the States, my inner ears had been excruciatingly painful, unable to cope with the change in air pressure. I couldn't clear them and ever since then, all sound seemed muffled. I hadn't told the Prof about that, I probably should have.

The guy in the car phoned again, looking up at the house as he did so. He was obviously trying to contact someone inside. He sat there for a long time. Sometimes phoning, sometimes just staring at the house, sometimes sniffing at a small bottle he had in his lap. I took several pictures of him. As I got up to walk away, he got out of his car and crossed over the road. He pressed one of the buzzers and stood facing the door. I took a shot of him from behind and went back to Rosa.

The church was emptying as I came round the corner. Rosa saw me and asked me if I would be good enough to wait for a few minutes while she went and had a chat with someone. I said 'of course' and she walked off towards a local café with a tall man.

I wandered into the church to take some photos. I shot off a load of Polaroids before a kindly elderly lady came up and asked me what I was doing. I told her I was waiting for Rosa and she said I could take as many pictures as I liked in that case. I gave her one of the pictures to watch develop as I walked around taking snaps of chairs, bibles, the plain cross on the back wall and the view from the main hall through the back door into a kitchen. After five minutes or so, I made my way out and found the old woman waiting for me on the steps.

'I'm sorry dear, but this one doesn't appear to have worked.' She said.

I looked at the picture in her hand and sure enough, it was just a blurred fog of colours. We sat and watched the remaining pictures develop and none of them had any clear images on them at all. I looked at the camera and noticed the slot where the film cartridge had been placed was slightly open. It obviously hadn't clicked into place properly.

'I think light got into the camera by accident and spoiled the film, or it's just a dud batch. It's happened to me before with old film stock. It's an old camera anyway. I inherited it from my Nan who bought it when they first came out. I'm lucky it's worked this long. Sorry about that.' I said.

The old lady didn't look disappointed at all.

'I like the colours though, don't you?'

When Rosa came back, she looked happier and calmer than she had done on the way to Church that morning, when something had clearly been worrying her.

She cooked a Mexican meal that night and told me her whole life story. Like everybody's, it was sad in parts and lovely in others and painful at certain times. She told me everything and I caught most of the moods of her story on film. There would be some photos here to send to Ma certainly. But as she spoke, the stars began to appear again, small shimmering pricks of light at first. My eyes flicked round to get a better look at them but they avoided closer inspection by always staying to the outer limits of what I could see. I needn't have bothered straining my eyes because after ten minutes or so, they crept to the front of my vision but I still couldn't actually focus in on them. They were elusive tiny explosions speckling their way across my sight.

As Rosa carried on talking, I sat myself down in a chair and tried to breathe slowly and regularly. For the first time I couldn't see anything at all. I sat there with my eyes wide open seeing nothing but visual fireworks. I turned my head in the direction of Rosa's voice. At some point I think she drifted into Spanish, but my mind was elsewhere. I was trying to work out what to do if I could never see again. My balance had totally gone as well and if I hadn't been sitting, I would have had trouble working out which way was up. My breathing became a little more laboured as panic began to set in but by the time Rosa finished her story and offered me a tea, I was able to see shadows of light and dark again and by the time she approached me with the mug of hot liquid, I was able to judge where it was, enough to take it from her. Colours looked less bright and the whole world had lost some of its vividness but at least I could see, for now.

She had been drinking heavily in the bar and went out back to throw up before coming in again to drink more. She had played pool, she had danced to the jukebox, she had laughed and sung at the top of her voice. It had been one of the best nights she could remember but then there wasn't a lot of competition.

She had been on her own for most of the night and had enjoyed it like that, just her and Pat, the old boy behind the counter. When Susie came in, they'd played around a little and drunk some more but by the time Hank arrived, she was well and truly wasted and wanted to go home.

'What you gonna have?' he asked her.

He'd obviously been drinking somewhere else before he'd got there because, even in her state, she could tell he was half cut.

'Thanks Hank, but I think I'm gonna head off home, it's been a long one.'

'What you suddenly got yourself a job you have to get up for in the morning?' He laughed.

'No, but it's kind of late already.'

'Course you ain't got no job, who'd hire you?' He was on top of her and in her face, sounding angry but grinning. 'Now you gonna play nice and have a drink with me and Bobby.'

Bobby was his sometimes wife. Sometimes she was and sometimes she wasn't. Sometimes he hit her and sometimes she hit him. Sometimes she went back to live with her mamma and sometimes she came back to him. She was a tiny little woman but she was hard as nails and had a mouth on her that Satan would have been proud of.

'You thinking you're too good for us, you little slut.' Bobby, it appeared, was more drunk than Hank. 'What you got to be so snooty about. You ain't no better than nothing. All Hank did was ask you if you wanted a drink.'

Hank she thought she could handle, but Bobby was a different propostion altogether. She had just made up her mind to have a beer with them to avoid any bad feelings. Susie came over from the pool table where she had been playing some big black guy that neither of them had met before. He had been leaning over behind her while she aimed her shots and she'd been grinding herself back against his huge cock, which was having trouble keeping itself inside his tight jeans.

'Hank. Bobby.' She said by way of greeting.

'Susie.' Bobby said in disgruntled acknowledgement. She had always hated Susie. Susie was pretty, single and happy most of the time. That made her unpopular with most of the women in town.

'I thought you were heading off, hon.' She said.

'I was but Hank and Bobby here said maybe I should have another drink.'

Susie shook her head.

'Nah, you'd better run along, I reckons. You got stuff to do in the morning and all. And you're gonna have trouble driving the truck as it is tonight.'

'I think she looks okay to me. Anyway, what's it gotta do with you, Susie? Why don't you go back to your nigger?' Bobby slurred.

There was only the slightest of pauses before the pool cue in Susie's hand swung backwards and then forwards again, shattering Bobby's cheek bone. Hank jumped on Susie and the black guy with the dick jumped on him. As bar brawls went it was fairly tame and it ended when Pat clicked the hammer back on his Colt .45 and pointed it around the room at everyone. Although all four of them were cut and bleeding, there was little permanent damage, except for the fact that one side of Bobby's face was a little flatter than the other.

In the middle of the scuffle she'd slunk out the back way and headed back home leaving the in-breds to their fighting.

She didn't want to go downstairs. She wanted him to die. She reached into the fridge in the living room for a beer and was just deciding whether or not to take him one down or just head for bed, when she saw the lights outside as a car pulled up. The huge staggering silhouette that climbed out of it and zigzagged its way up the path to the house could be no one other than Hank. Apparently, there was unfinished business.

He banged on the door.

'Go away, Hank. I'm off to bed.'

'Open up this fucking door, or so help me I'll knock it down.'

She shouted back to him. 'You'll wake him up. Go on home with you, you're drunk.'

'He ain't in!' Hank shouted back and then belched.

'What makes you say that?'

'His truck ain't here, and you ain't never allowed out drinking if he's around.'

She had taken her husband's truck out to the highway and parked it in one of the giant truckers' pit stops and then hitched back home to keep suspicion down. She had left the cab open and the keys in it and was perfectly convinced that it would have been stolen by now, its plate changed and if no one reported it stolen, it had as good as disappeared. But now Hank had managed to put two and two together in his pea brain and come up with the wrong four.

'Well, he might be back real soon. Come on, Hank, leave it tonight. Go on home to Bobby.

'Bobby's spending the night in the hospital.'

His heavy boot kicked the door open with great ease and he stumbled in.

'Besides, I wanna see me the bear, or whatever it is you got down there.'

He was rubbing his greasy belly under his t-shirt as he came towards her.

'And maybe I might be wanting some more of what we started the other day.'

He was actually slathering at the mouth. He wiped away his anticipation on his sleeve. His enormous hands were filthy, the nails black with axle grease and grime. Two days ago she'd have fucked anything in her attempt to catch something to give to her dear husband, but now she didn't need anything or anyone and she had found a whole new world of self-esteem that came with taking back control of her life. Hank wouldn't be putting his hands on her again, and she felt disgusted that he ever had. She wanted him out of her house but he was a big man with sex on his mind. He began to unfasten his belt.

'Hank, come on, let's not get into this.'

'What's got into you? Not me that's for sure. Why you being like this? Come on. Come over here.'

He reached out his hands towards her and licked his fat drooling lips. He was trying as best he could to seduce her. She knew he had already exhausted any finesse he had and the next step would be violent and angry.

'Hank,' she said, trying to buy herself some time as she scanned the room looking for something to defend herself with.

'You looking mighty purty.' He said lasciviously.

He was pretty much on top of her now and as she felt the wall behind her she knew there was nowhere else to retreat to.

Tim Arthur

'Your mouth looks…' But before he could finish whatever filth he was going to say, he heard a sound from below that stopped him.

'What's that noise?' He was punchy from the drink and this made him sway his head round trying to locate the source of the noise.

'Hank, come on, let's get you back into your truck.' She risked taking him by the arm and trying to lead him out of the house.

He wasn't quite as punchy as she'd thought. Before she could do anything about it, he grabbed her arm, turned her around and twisted it behind her. His fat belly was now pressed into her back and he leaned over her shoulder and took a long slow lick up her cheek.

Then he heard the noise again, only this time he could make out a word or two.

'Hey! Hey you up there!'

Hank threw her to the floor and walked down the hall towards the door to the cellar. As he opened it, he could hear the calls from downstairs more clearly.

He turned to say, 'Hey, that ain't no bear down there!'

But he only got as far as 'Hey that ain't…' when she jumped at his face with her nails, he lost his footing and tumbled down the stairs into the cellar with a series of bone-crunching thuds.

The adrenalin was suddenly under control again and she ran into the kitchen, found the large bread knife and started down after him to finish the job. Descending in to the blue light of the pit, she could just make out that Hank was trying to get up. She could also see from the strange angle of his leg that it looked as if he'd broken something. He was trying to clear his head and deal with the fulgurating pain and the surroundings all at the same time. It was asking a lot of his small brain. He saw her coming for him and almost at the same time saw the cage inhabited.

'What the fuck? You fucking crazy cunt! What the fuck have you done?'

He began to back away from her and the knife in her hand. He dragged himself across to the cage and looked in at her husband who quite casually got up from the small stool and hobbled towards him. He reached through the bars, grabbed Hank's head and pulled his amazed face towards him slowly at first as if moving in for a kiss and then, with a quick snap over the last inches, smashed it against the iron bars.

As Hank slid to the floor, his head was still being held and two strong thumbs were gouged into his eyes, blinding him, then a knife stabbed him three times in the back, the third strike finding his heart.

'Shouldn't have fucked my wife, Hank. That just ain't right.'

When he woke up, he was shivering. The early morning cold had crept into the room just as the first rays of the sun had. In the weak half-light, he sat on the end of the bed rubbing his eyes trying to rub himself into consciousness. The events of yesterday had taken their toll on his body, every muscle ached, his shoulders were stiff and there was already a vice-like grip on his head. His sinuses were dried out and burning after a night in the artificial air-con of the hotel. These places had pumped round the same old bacteria infested air since they'd opened in the Seventies.

In the shower he soaked himself for a hot steamy twenty minutes. While he tried to loosen up his knotted torso, his big toe scrubbed away at the last of the dried blood that had galvanised itself to the enamel around the plug hole. It flaked off easily and then dissolved quickly, circling its way down the pipes below.

He dried himself thoroughly and shaved perfectly, brushed his teeth, applied deodorant and aftershave, pumped his small moisturiser dispenser and massaged the blue cooling balm into his face. He put on an immaculate white shirt and his best suit. He tidied the room and packed all his belongings away. The last thing he did was to open the mini-fridge.

'Morning. So does the light go off when the door's shut? I know, I know of course it does.' He laughed and lifted her by her towel cushion, now a light pink from the slow release of the rest her blood, and placed her on the bed. He took one of the defrosted but still chilly bags of ice from inside and put it in the bottom of the bowling bag he'd retrieved from the bathroom.

He brushed her hair before placing her on a clean hand towel. Her hair was definitely darker than in the picture and he thought she looked a little older as well. No doubt the sun that had given her the rich tan had also bleached her hair, perhaps after a long summer on some Greek Island. It was possible that she had once dyed her hair, but she didn't seem to him like the kind of woman who would have done that.

He balled up the soiled towel and put it into a plastic bag that lined the small beige bin in the bathroom and then shoved it into his suitcase. He put the bottles back in the mini bar, checked out and hit the road again, this time with her next to him, securely held in place with the seatbelt. He was going to take her home.

'Would you like that? Would you like to go home? Perhaps you'll feel better there, with all your things around you.'

After picking up some fresh ice at a local supermarket he entered her address into his satnav.

'What would you like to listen to? I'm not sure what I've got in the CD player.'

He clicked it on and heard Britney Spears singing 'Oh baby, baby.'

'Damn, that's embarrassing. It not mine, it's... someone else's who uses the car every now

and then. I was going to play you a song that I
love, if you fancy it? It's a bit cheesy, a guilty
pleasure. It's from Breakfast in America by
Supertramp. I should say I don't normally listen to
that kind of stuff. Much more an Indie guy at heart,
Arctic Monkeys or the Little Comets, you know the
kind of thing, but I had this girlfriend when I was in
my late teens and she was really into Supertramp.
God, I used to hate it. I would always try to get her
to play the Smiths or the Cure, you know, always
doing her compilation tapes and stuff, but she'd
play them a couple of times and then it was back
to Supertramp. I used to hate their sickly sweet
sound, the lush harmonies, the orchestrated
backings, you know, it's got no edge or soul. But
when we split up, she sent me the album in the
post and there was a note with it saying, 'if you got
nothing else from this relationship, at least you got
this'. I didn't even play it for years, I think I just
threw it into a drawer and left it there. Then a
couple of years ago when we moved and I was
looking through a load of stuff in the attic, I found it
and put it on. It was amazing, I was right back
there with Amberley, I was eighteen again and
everything felt new and fresh and possible. I went
out and bought the CD and ever since then, I keep
it with me all the time. Does that make any sense?
I know it's a bit weird but there it is. Anyway let's
see if I can find it for you.'

He reached into the glove compartment
and as he began to scrabble around for it, he
remembered the last time he'd tried to find it just a
day earlier. It had been this search that had led to
him hitting her. He brought his hand back onto the

steering wheel and drove in silence for the rest of the journey.

Her home was a flat in a large village, pressing to become a town, about six miles from where he'd first come across her. He knew the place a little because at one time he'd taken karate classes in the village hall. Her address, 32b Exhibition Parade, rang a bell; not the number but the street. He knew he'd seen it before, so instead of stopping and asking for directions, he drove round until he came across it and the street sign brought the memory to the front of his mind. Opposite the quiet station, there was a turning that led down to a small parade of shops on the edge of an estate. He'd often gone there to buy a diet coke and chocolate after the sessions.

He parked his car in the row of spaces in front of the newsagents and sat there nervously for a couple of minutes. He left her in the car while he looked for her front door. He could see that there were two levels of flats above the shops with two rows of walkways in front of them but couldn't see any obvious way up to them. Number 32 itself was a launderette.

A snotty nosed child on a tricycle peddled furiously past him.

'Excuse me? Hello, do you know how to get up to those flats up there?'

The kid looked suspicious. 'Why? My mum says she's not in if anyone asks.' He blew a snot bubble from his nostril.

'No, a friend of mine lives around here. I'm not looking for your mum.'

'Who's your friend?' He said, not convinced by this stranger.

'A lady. Look do you know or shall I go and ask someone in the shops?'

The kid turned the trike round and took four or five pedals closer to him, examining his face in detail before answering.

'You have to go round the back and up the steps.'

'Thanks.' He began to walk off in the direction the child had pointed when the kid's voice called after him.

'She your girlfriend?'

'No… yes… kind of. It's kind of hard to explain.'

He found the wide concrete staircase to the right of the row of shops and climbed them noting the polite graffiti which informed him that 'Rachel was a slag.'

The first row of flats he found to be the 'a' flats, so he climbed again and found himself walking along the walkway outside the 'b' flats' doors. He looked down and saw his car and could just make her out through the tinted windscreen. The boy was nowhere in sight, obviously having other people to interrogate on another part of the estate.

The door of 32b was cobalt blue. He stopped outside it and looked at every scratch, every paint bubble on it. Its brass numbers were nicer than the white plastic ones on the front of all the others, as was the brass letterbox. She had made the most of her flat, just as he thought she would. He placed one hand on it, one open palm trying to get a sense of what was behind it. He could feel nothing, no vibrations. He wrapped on the door with his knuckle and then pressed her bell. He wondered if the little girl in the photo would answer the door, or if a husband might. Nothing. His heart was in his mouth. Perhaps they were all out; maybe the child was at school. He didn't believe there was a husband though; there were no pictures in the wallet of a man and no wedding ring to suggest any permanent relationship. Perhaps her daughter's father had been a one-night stand and was entirely unaware of her presence. She would be the kind of person who would do that, not to cause any bother or grief, but to bring up the daughter on her own, loving her enough for two.

He moved to the window and shaded his eyes with his hands to stop any reflection. He tried to peer through the closed curtains. He moved by tiny fractions trying to get a better angle. He could only see a sliver of a room. A light dusty grey elegant sofa stood against the far wall, above which he could see a painting – a full moon shone down upon a dark sea, it could have been naff but it had an unexpected depth and intensity. He wondered if she had painted it herself trying to come to terms with something. Art therapy?

'She's not in.'

The door to number 33b had opened and a diminutive white-haired lady in a vast grey cardigan was poking her head out. White hairs sprouted from her chin and although all the signs of advanced age were there, her voice and her eyes were bright and strong.

'She didn't come back last night.'

'Oh right.' He tried to look normal and a bit surprised as if he'd expected her to be in.

'What about her daughter?'

'What daughter, love? I didn't know she had a daughter, she's never mentioned it. Maybe she doesn't live with her or something. But to be honest what with her job and everything, she's not there that often anyway. She only moved in a few months ago and doesn't spend much more than a couple of nights a week here. Sometimes she's away for a couple of weeks at a time, so you might have a bit of a wait, I'm sorry to say.'

He wanted to ask her what her job was and anything else she could tell him about her, but he thought it was best to leave it there.

'Thanks. It was nothing that important anyway, just popping by on the off chance. Thanks for the information. I'll give her a ring next time, you know, so I don't miss her.'

He'd picked up a can of diet coke from the newsagents on the way back to the car and hissed it open.

'So, that's where you live.'

He took out her black pouch and opened it. He felt around for the keys he'd seen the day before. One looked like a car key, the other a front door key. When he found this one, he placed it on the dashboard and closed the bag back up.

'We'll take you home later. Maybe when it's dark?'

'Your auntie is a great healer, did you know that?'

The woman sitting next to him must have been somewhere in her seventies or eighties and was shrivelled like a white prune. She had a hearing aid in one ear which she was tapping as she spoke to him.

'I used to need this, but now I only wear it to make my daughter happy. I don't need it, not anymore. In fact I can hear better now than I could before. And she did that, your auntie. We're very lucky to have her here, very lucky indeed. Jesus be praised.'

She raised her palms skywards as she said this last phrase and rolled her eyes back. She began murmuring something under her breath, words that he found unintelligible in the whispered snatches he caught.

He was sitting in a small dark wood-panelled hall. There were fifty or sixty blue plastic seats facing towards a dais. Behind this was a simple wooden cross on the wall, lit from the vaulted ceiling by a pin spotlight. Apart from himself and the old lady, who'd introduced herself as Martha, there was no one currently in the Eltham Peace and Light Spiritualist Church.

As he sat there, he breathed in the smell of polish, flowers and old age. He looked at his watch; it was 10.25 in the morning.

'She'll be in any second and then we'll start. Small turn-out today.'

Steven looked round to see if there was anyone else in the room he'd missed. There wasn't. 'Small turn-out' was an understatement. Taking him out of the equation, the congregation amounted to precisely one person.

'Do you have any gifts? Have you inherited anything of your aunt's powers?'

Martha looked up at him from deep inside her herringbone pattern overcoat that dwarfed her.

'I'm not sure, really. I don't think so.'

'Sorry, what did you say, dear? I couldn't quite catch that.'

Steven spoke up a little. 'I just said, I don't think so, no.'

'Oh, that's a shame. I thought perhaps you'd come to us for a reason. Thought maybe you were the one your auntie had been speaking about all these years. It's just I'm sort of hoping he comes soon, because I'm not getting any younger. A lot of the others who used to come have passed over, and they never got to meet him. I'd like to meet him. You know, before I go. I just think that would be so lovely.'

The double doors behind him creaked opened and four more elderly people slowly made their way in like shuffling armadillos.

'Good turn-out today, Martha.' The blue-rinsed lady at the front called out looking at Steven. 'Who's the boy?'

'This is Steven. He's Doris' nephew.'

She pointed to each of them in turn with her crooked, withered forefinger and introduced them to him.

'That's Mabel.' The lady who had just spoken nodded to him and began the long process of removing her large red coat and her several scarves.

'That one there is Joan, she's Mabel's twin sister. Aren't you dear? Identical, look at them.'

Steven noticed that every detail of her was the same apart from the hair colour. Where her sister had opted for a daring silver blue rinse, her hair was pure white, reflecting any light that came anywhere near it.

'She doesn't really talk much. Do you, dear?' Joan shook her head and looked away from Steven as soon as he caught her eye.

'That lady there is, Rosa. She's a Mexican lady. Came here to help her cousin run a restaurant after her husband died. She's really a Catholic but she fell out with the priest and so comes here. We're a broad church and will accept everyone. But between you and I, I think we'll lose her if she can find another Catholic church on the number 41 bus route. She doesn't speak much English. Ola, Rosa.'

Rosa was the youngest of the bunch, probably no older than sixty-five and in her black shawl she looked exactly the way Steven thought a Mexican widow should look. Her hands were flicking through a rosary as she took her seat right at the back of the room.

'Ola, Martha. Ola.' She nodded to Steven and smiled.

'And that there's Bill. He lost his wife six months ago. He's a sweet man really but gets a little confused. You know, good days and bad.' She quickly looked him up and down.

'This is a good day; he's got his shoes on, not his house slippers. That's always a giveaway with him. Hello Bill, you well?'

The round red-faced man in the brown suit and flat cap waved a hand towards her and gave her a big smile.

'Not too bad, Marty. I think I saw her last night. I think she was in the kitchen. Didn't make me no tea though.' He chuckled to himself and also sat down on the back row, though a respectable ten seats away from Rosa.

They all sat there waiting. Joan and Mabel chatted quietly, Rosa said her rosary, Bill whistled to himself and counted the beams in the vaulted ceiling. Martha shut her eyes and looked as if she had gone to sleep. Steven heard a whisper just behind him, from one of the empty chairs.

'Here she comes.' It said and spoke no more.

The door to the right of the dais opened and Dodds appeared. She stepped on to the little stage, stood in front of them and bowed her head. Martha opened her eyes briefly and then closed them again this time with her hands held together in prayer. Steven took this as a sign that he should do the same, and as he shut his eyes, he felt himself bathed in bright blue light. He wanted it to soak it into his heart. He could hear his aunt leading the others in prayer. After the communal 'amen', he opened his eyes and for the first time he saw auric lights fizzing off his aunt. She had a bright purple cloud of shimmering electrical discharges glowing all around her. Her head was bathed in an intense mixture of light blue and purple. The colours were more intense around her head and hands and he was mesmerised by this new way of seeing. He looked to his right at Martha, and she was also bathed in light though hers was weaker and of orange and red hues. Each person in the room had their own aura like a fingerprint he could identify them by. He shut his eyes and shook his head, to see whether or not this was some momentary anomaly but to his great surprise with his eyes shut, he could still see them. The faces and bodies were removed as was the rest of the room but their auras remained. The anxiety was there again, as he felt himself falling out of control. His breathing became laboured. He started to sweat and wanted this to stop. If this was a gift, it was one he hadn't asked for but he didn't seem to be able to stop. It was in control of him not the other way round. He tried to focus on his aunt's face and ignore the light pulses shooting from her. She smiled at him.

'Everyone, I have a very special person with me today, I'm sure you'll all know who he is by now, but just in case, let me introduce to you, my lovely nephew, Steven.'

As he concentrated on her words, her aura slowly began to fade until after a few seconds it had entirely disappeared. He looked round at everyone else and they were also back to normal and smiling at him in welcome. Now that it had gone, he doubted whether or not it had ever been there and wondered what other games his addled brain might have for him before the day was out.

'Now all of you, come forward. No hiding at the back.' His aunt said in a playfully admonishing tone.

He was unaware of the procedure in this kind of church and wondered if they were to all go forward for some kind of Holy Communion, but it was something much more mundane.

'Come on, it's silly all of you being so far away when there are so few of us here. How many times must I tell you? Come on, all of you down to the front row. Don't be afraid, we're all friends here, we all know each other.'

All six of them dutifully shuffled with a distinct lack of enthusiasm to the front and sat with as many seats between them as they could get away with. Dodds giggled gently at them.

'Well, you're a fine brotherhood and no mistaking.'

The meeting was like no church service he had been to. It was part-clairvoyance, part-healing, part-counselling and part-gossip.

'Now, how are we all? Bill, how are you doing? You look very smart today, which is lovely.'

'I'm good, thank you, Doris. I was saying to the ladies I think she was in the kitchen last night, but she didn't cook me my tea or nothing.' He laughed again.

'Well, I think that's the last thing she'd be doing, don't you. I mean she did cook for you for how long? Fifty-six years? Goodness me, that's enough for anyone. Perhaps she was giving you a hint that you ought to spend more time in the kitchen cooking for yourself rather than relying on that Chinese chip shop down the road. With your dickey ticker, all that fat can't be good for you now can it.'

'Is that what she said to you, Doris?' Bill looked suddenly concerned and sad.

'No, Bill, that's what the woman in the chippy said. She said you've been in there every night this week and that you always have large cod and chips and a pickled egg. Just look after yourself a bit, eh Bill?'

After chatting to each one in turn like this, she sat herself in the chair in front of them, closed her eyes and began to move her head slowly from left to right. Watching her gentle rhythms, he was reminded of a cobra swaying from side to side following a fakir's flute, hypnotised by the music.

'Joan,' she said, her voice somewhat lower than it had been before.

'Joan, my love, I still miss you and think of you everyday. I am happy over here, but my happiness is only a reflection of the love we shared. And I know that when you are in spirit, as I am, we will be reunited.'

While she spoke, Martha explained. 'That's Jim she's channelling. Jim's Joan's husband. He died during a bombing raid during the war. He was a navigator in a Lancaster, terrible story. It had

The Blind Dog Gospels

made it nearly all the way back but the engines, which had been shot to pieces, finally gave out. The plane smashed into a hillside only three miles away from the airfield. Jim's twin brother John, was married to Mabel, and he died a week later, he was a fighter pilot and his plane got shot down somewhere over the Channel.'

'No he didn't.' Steven had a clear image of an old man walking down a lane. It was John and he knew it. It looked like a Cornish village to him but he couldn't be sure. He saw him posting a letter, and on the letter it said Mabel's name.

After giving each one a message from a loved one, Dodds had each one come up in turn and she laid her hands on any area they said they needed help with.

'Ooh, I love this part,' Martha said before climbing up to have Dodds hold her hands. 'My arthritis has been playing me up something chronic.'

Steven watched as, one by one, the lame and the sick five all went for their weekly dose of healing. All of them looked red and comforted after the laying on of hands. The final act of the service was the gift, and each one gave as much as they could to the little purple bag that Dodds passed around.

As they said their thank yous and started for the door, Steven caught up with Joan and Mabel.

'Mabel, could I have a word?'

She looked a little startled but nevertheless allowed him to sit her down at the back of the hall.

'It's all right, Joan. I'll only be a second.'

Joan took the hint and headed for the door.

'I'll wait for you down by the bus stop, Mabes.'

'It's about your husband.' He said holding her hand.

Instantly, she looked even more anxious.

'He didn't die in the war, did he? I got an image of a man in his elderly years writing to you. I have the feeling that he may have passed over now, however.'

She gently began to weep.

'No, no, it wasn't during the war, although, I didn't find out for many years after. His plane crashed in France and he fell in love with some French girl. He came back to live over here with her down in the West Country. She died twenty years or so ago, and like that out of the blue I got a letter from him, from the grave, explaining it all and asking for forgiveness. I couldn't tell anyone, it was mortifying. But you may be right, he may be dead. We wrote for a few years and the last letter I got from him said he was very unwell. I didn't hear anything after that. And that must have been six or seven years ago.' She was still crying. 'Nobody knows about this. And I don't want them to.' She added firmly.

'I won't say a thing.' He said honestly. 'I do have a message though, that I was given, and I think perhaps you could receive it.'

He leant forward and Dodds who had been watching all this from the podium while she counted her money, saw Mabel cry even louder and then begin to laugh. She cried and laughed as she pulled Steven close into an embrace and kept saying over and over again.

'Thank you.'

Over the next few months, Peter visited Lauren weekly and became one of her 'regulars'. She was chatty and he liked her company. He did occasionally go to other prostitutes but always felt a mixture of self-hatred and guilt as well as elation. With Lauren, it was different. She was intelligent, funny and a sensitive lover. She never gave him the feeling that he was just another punter. Her true GFE (girlfriend experience) service always made him feel that he was special. She was good at her job and because of this, he kept coming back.

On their third session, she kissed him. Her lips had never touched his before and he had understood that kissing was a thing that prostitutes rarely did. She had never even come close to kissing him before. She kissed him slowly and softly on the lips, her tongue flicked across his mouth. He lay there unsure how to respond, not knowing if this was an invitation to kiss her back or merely a gift to be accepted.

The next time they had sex, she kissed him again, and this time he returned the embrace. She kissed him with her tongue deep inside his mouth, exploring him with a tenderness he had never experienced with his wife. He just wanted to kiss her then and lay naked next to her. He didn't want the sex that he'd paid for; he wanted the intimacy that seemed extra. He fell in love with her for the time he was there. And when it was over, he saw from his watch that she had spent nearly two hours with him, far more time than he had actually paid for.

'That was beautiful, thank you.' He said as he put his clothes on.

'I'm glad you enjoyed it,' she replied as she disposed of the condom into a small white plastic bin by her bed.

'Was it nice for you?' He asked, unable to break an old habit he had had since he first began having sex. It was a nervous tick of insecurity.

'Of course. It was lovely. Same time next week?'

She was quite matter of fact but he didn't hear that, he only heard the words 'It was lovely.' He didn't see her check her watch eager for him to leave before her next client arrived. She needed time to shower and paint her smile back on. He drove home believing the experience had been as mutually profound as it had been for him. By the time he got into his house, another man was already inside her and she kissed him just as tenderly and just as deeply.

The house was in darkness as he pulled up. It would be another night on his own, another chance for the pizza delivery boy to get a tip. Recently she had not even bothered giving him an excuse. He suspected that she wasn't spending every night with Jim, because his wife would wonder where he was and because she was too selfish for that, it would cut down on her time to gossip with her coven. As he opened the front door into the cold dark hallway, he saw a bright green light shining out like a beacon under the hat stand. It was unmistakably the screen of Jill's phone which was normally welded to her hand. It was on silent mode and was gently vibrating, growling against the skirting board. Without putting the lights on, he reached down and picked it up. The caller recognition told him she had an answer phone message from Jane. He unlocked it and accessed her messages. An urgent voice babbled quickly.

'I'm so, so sorry, honey, I'm running really late. Fuck, I hope you get this before you leave. I think Peter has fucked something up and I've been trying to sort it out. Fuck knows where his head is at the moment. He's all over the place. He keeps missing appointments. You don't think he knows about us do you? Let's hope he is as dopey as you say. Anyway, I'm just leaving now, I'll be there in about half an hour. Love you.' Jim then blew a kiss before putting down the phone. A mechanical voice then announced.

'You have no more messages.'

He went into the kitchen and flicked through the phone to see if there was anything else of interest on it. He was shocked that she would have let it fall from her pocket or bag. It was normally the one thing she wouldn't leave home without. As he sipped away at his coffee he opened up her texts. There were six messages in her inbox from Jane all received within an hour that morning.

Message 6 'We'll talk tonite.'

Message 5 'Look the business wld be in danger, and I don't want to hurt Sandy and the boys. We had a deal.'

Message 4 'No u don't. and if he ever found out it cld ruin everything.'

Message 3 'We've talked about this b4.'

Message 2 'Well we'll hav fun tonite. 8?'

Message 1 'We still on for tonite?'

He then opened her outbox to see what she'd sent him.

Message 6 'Yes we will, and I want a decision.'

Message 5 'Fuck the deal! That was years ago. What about my boys?'

Message 4 'I don't care about money, I want out and I want you.'

Message 3 'I know but you don't hav to live with him. I want it out in the open.'

Massage 2. We hav to talk tho. I don't know how long I can keep doing this.'

Message 1 'Of course I am, you know I hate being in the house with him.'

He laughed out loud when he read the line 'I don't care about money.' He had never met anyone who cared more about it. None of this was particularly shocking to him, he had always known about the relationship although it was always through insinuation and suspicion. This was just the actual evidence.

The funny thing was he actually felt a little sorry for Jim. From what he could tell, she was also making his life a misery and was stirring things up that she didn't need to. He tried to put it all together and to give a timescale to it. He and Jim had started the business twelve years ago. They had been friends at college and after both going separate ways for a few years working for other companies, they had decided to start up on their own. He had suspected Jill and Jim had had a fling when the company was first set up and that it had been a fairly short-lived insignificant thing. She had a few years of fucking anything she could get away with, he knew of three people who had openly bragged about bedding her, so he presumed there must be at least another couple he didn't know about. Then by the sound of things she had got back with Jim, some time after he married Sandy. By the 'years ago' statement, he deduced the affair had been going on ever since. She sounded miserable in the texts but he suspected she wasn't; she was just being a petulant bitch who wasn't getting her own way all the time. If he knew her she would only be happy if he was there at her beck and call whenever she wanted him. He doubted very much that she actually wanted him full time. He wasn't sure she was capable of real love. Jim was in for a tough night.

Having ordered his food, he settled in front of the television to watch the football. As he sniffed back his amyl nitrate, he actually felt happy. He had someone he cared about that he was having sex with; his wife was probably in the middle of a row and, best of all, it wasn't with him and there was pizza on the way. He would feast, watch crap, take drugs and fall asleep. Life generally didn't get any better than that for him.

He woke up at the sound of the slamming door. He saw his wife storm past the living room door and head straight upstairs. In his half dozed state, he thought she looked as if she was crying.

'I don't feel well. I'm heading straight for bed.' She called down to him, with a definite catch in her throat.

He picked up the poppers bottle that had fallen from his hand on to the carpet when he had fallen asleep and tried to shake himself into some semblance of alertness. He still had her phone on the arm of the sofa. He walked out into the hall. Her handbag was on the side table. He picked it up and put the phone into it. It was so stuffed full of crap, she often found stuff in there that she was convinced hadn't been in there the night before, so there was every possibility that she might assume it had been with her all the time even if she'd looked for it. As he sat the bag up, he saw the cocaine.

It was an identical little sealable bag to the one the woman had at the party. He presumed she had made some arrangement to get some from her, as he couldn't think of any other way she would have found a dealer. He'd enjoyed the coke he'd tried with the girls in Brighton. He opened the bag and took it into the kitchen where he tipped about half of the powder on to a plate and chopped it into lines with a playing card he found lying on the Welsh dresser. He snorted it up with a rolled up twenty pound note and as it sparkled into him, he looked round the kitchen for something to cut the remaining powder with to make it look like none of it had gone. There was flour, icing sugar or scouring powder. He took two teaspoons of the scouring powder and put it in the bag before sealing it again and shaking it thoroughly to make sure it had all mixed together. He put it back into her handbag and went out for a walk; he wanted to wander in the moonlight and soak it up. He was wide, wide awake and felt wonderful.

Chapter 9

After my temporary blindness I redoubled my efforts to photograph everything and anything I came in contact with. I carried my cameras with me at all times and was always snapping away. It was a desperate attempt to hold onto images. I wanted to sear the things I saw not only onto the photos but also into my mind. I wanted to build up a collection of images that I could use as references when the lights were turned out. There was more to it as well. There was this terrible feeling of loneliness which had crept up on me over the last year. I had always been pretty independent and happy with my own company, but now, facing a dark world, I wanted to be able to reach out and capture other people. It was like my photos were attempts to catch people like a line and bait.

The pictures had become my own little universe quite apart from the real world. They were my imaginary friends. I would spend any spare moment I had flicking through them, making up stories about who the people in them were and what they had done just before and after they were taken.

It occurred to me how the phrase 'to die alone' was the worst phrase in the world. It was the reason I had married Baby so quickly. I needed to feel the love of someone before it all disappeared into darkness. I wanted to be able to see the person's face. I wanted to be able to kiss them and see the lips I was kissing. I wanted to suck her breasts and not just feel the nipple in my mouth but be able to see them, pink and delicious.

Rosa asked me over breakfast if I fancied coming with her to the Church. She told me that a man there could do wonderful things. He had a way of talking to people that helped them and she thought that I might appreciate seeing him. She wouldn't promise that he could help me, but she thought it might be nice anyway, just to be surrounded by the congregation. I had nothing else to do and I thought there might be some nice photo opportunities so I went.

Since the temporary blindness I felt a bit punchy and exhausted, so it was a groggy version of me that made its way down to the Church. I sat in the back row and Rosa sat next to me holding my hand. I was having some trouble staying awake. I put it down to the lack of sleep I had had the night before worrying about my episode. I was more worried about losing my vision than I was about death. My main fear was the helplessness of blindness. Whenever I imagined being blind, I was reminded of the blind puppies I looked after when I was a boy. Newly born and vulnerable, they snuffled and felt their way around without any clue of the world they had been born into. Their mother had been run over just three days after they were born and I was tasked with keeping the little things alive. I fed them hourly for weeks with a pipette full of enriched milk. I cleaned them, kept them warm and saw to their every need. They lay there blindly expecting to be fed and kept safe and the world provided for them. I, on the other hand, had no such expectations. There was no one to look after me. Depending on where and when my sight actually packed in, I could be totally lost. The only faces for comfort would be the ones I'd memorised from the photos, the army of stills that I had to animate in my subconscious.

The service was much like any other English spiritualist meeting I had been to, and I'd been to a few since I'd been diagnosed. There is a saying that states there are no atheists in the trenches. I was in the trenches as were most of the elderly people around me. We shared a common bond – the proximity of shuffling off this mortal coil. As I looked round, I realised I was more or less the youngest person there. There were some in that hall that I was pretty sure would be finding out the secrets to the afterlife before me, however little time I had left. The only person in the hall who was about my age, or perhaps a little older, was the quietly spoken man who sat at the front.

The older lady to whom I'd given a photo a few days before was sitting directly in front of him and every now and then she would turn round and look at me with the brightest smile, as if I had done something that she thought warranted such a grateful and wonderful beam.

At the end of the sermon when we were all shuffling our way out of the chapel, she pushed her way through the crowd to get to me.

'Thank you again for the picture. I know where the colours come from now. Funny, I think I always did but your picture helped me to see them more clearly. The colours come from him of course. How silly of me, of course they do. This place is full of them. No wonder you couldn't take a photo in there.'

She kissed me on the cheek. 'You should speak to him. Maybe show him one of your pictures. I think he'd like it, dear. I really do.'

'He is seeing him tomorrow.' Rosa stated plainly.

It was news to me.

'I never liked Hank.' He said.

He was chewing on the fried chicken she'd bought and rubbing his ankles with the grease where the cuffs had been. She had given him the key to take them off because of his help. She was eating dinner sitting in a chair on the other side of the bars. Between them, Hank lay fat and dead, sticky with his own blood. He was lying on his front so she could clearly see the three stab wounds she'd inflicted and, because of the way his head was resting on one side, she could also see the bloody socket where an eyeball had been.

'What you gonna do with him?' He asked.

She shrugged.

'Well you can't leave him here. Is his truck out front?'

She nodded.

'Then you gotta get rid of it and him.'

'What do you care?' She said wiping her mouth and reaching into the big paper bag hunting down any final fries.

'Like I said, there weren't no love lost between me and that piece of shit. Besides, I want you to rot for what you've done to me, not for what we did to this prick. You gotta do what I say.'

She snarled a little.

'I ain't gotta do shit that you say, or have you forgot, you're the one in the fucking cage.'

He let her calm down for a minute. He needed her to hear what he was saying and he needed her out of the house for a while.

'OK, but all I was going to say was, I know a place where you could get rid of him and his truck, that's all.'

She sucked slowly and noisily on her bucket of coke.

'Go on,' she nodded, 'go on, tell me what you're thinking.'

'There's a place out of town, down by the swamp where you can roll a truck in and no one ain't never gonna find it. Hell, you leave the window open and them gators'll come and eat Hank right outta there like eating stew outta can.'

He described the directions to her and even offered to draw her a map if she'd give him a piece of paper and a pencil. She had just seen what he could do to someone from within the cage without giving him a weapon like a pencil, so she let him dictate to her.

'You'll have to hitch back, unless you want to let me out and I'll drive behind you and then drive us both back once it's done. I'll come back in here after, honest.'

He laughed, a throaty hacking laugh, that reminded her he hadn't had a smoke since he'd been in there. She reached into her pocket and took out a cigarette, which she lit and tossed into the cage. It landed near his feet and he slowly bent down to pick it up. She could tell by the way he winced when he moved that he was still bruised and aching. He took a long toke and sucked the smoke deep down into his lungs as if unwilling to let it leave him in case this was the last one he ever got.

'You must be really fucking pissed with me to go through with all this.' As he spoke, the smoke slowly crept from his mouth making it look like he was on fire inside.

'You have no idea.' She offered.

'Oh, I think I have. It's not every day your wife decides to teach you a lesson like this. You gotta have really fucked her off. You wanna talk about it, darlin'.' He said in a mocking sarcastic way.

'I should just fucking shoot you now and be done with it.' There was an anger in her eyes that he was all too familiar with.

'Yeah and I should have shot you when you killed our child.' He looked away from her and waited for the impact of what he said to fully sink in.

'What did you say? What the fuck did you just say?'

'I think you heard me well enough.'

When they had first got together she had had an abortion. But he didn't know about that, he'd been away. She had taken off, paid for it herself and stayed with a friend for a couple of days until the worst of the bleeding had stopped. He didn't know anything about it. How could he? And why wouldn't he have mentioned this before in the heat of one of the thousands of other arguments they'd had over the years?

'You're fucking insane, that's what you are. A mean fucking bastard.'

'And you're a murderer, plain and simple. You had no right to have that abortion, you know that.'

This hit her in the chest like a punch.

'What? What are you saying, you fuck?'

'Did you honestly think that I wouldn't find out? Shit like that always comes out. And those people you think you tell as friends might quite happily tell other people who might quite happily tell me.'

He spat at her through the bars.

'I don't know what you're…' There was little conviction in her voice and she trailed off.

'You should have told me. What you did just ain't right.'

'How long have you known?' She asked.

Having not thought of this for years, it felt like a barely healed wound had been reopened with a swift stab of a jagged knife and that someone had thrown vinegar on it.

'I found out about three months after you had it.' He got out his cock and began to take a piss into the bucket.

'Why didn't you say anything?'

'What's to say? I married a woman who murdered my son or daughter. Kind of felt you had to be punished, but I weren't gonna go against God anymore by divorcing you. So I stuck it out. But I always knew you weren't human. No human being does something like that.'

'And no human does what you done to me. The beatings, the rape.'

'I ain't never raped you. You ain't never said no far as I can recall. Sure, you didn't look like you was enjoying it sometimes but after what you done, I didn't figure on how it was my job to make you happy.'

There was a pause as both of them thought about a secret which had fucked up both of their lives. She was the first to break the quiet, and there was renewed venom in her face and words.

'I did have an abortion, that's true. But firstly, it ain't murder, that weren't no murder, it was just a bunch of nothing when I had it flushed out. And you had no right to treat me the way you did. You never treated that fucking dog as badly as you treated me. And if you think some horseshit about my abortion gives you the right to have tortured me year on year, you're even more fucked up than I thought. And if you'd have asked earlier, maybe you'd found out why I did it in the first place and maybe now I should tell you. Seeing as how we're having a moment of truth-telling. I never murdered any child of yours, and you know why? 'Cos it weren't your kid. I made a mistake, I was told by Bobby that you'd fucked some girl on our weddin' night, so first chance I got I thought I'd get even. When you went on down to Tampa for the first time, I called up Jimmy and got him to fuck me all night. I didn't regret it, I figured that was it, we were even. I thought, hey, fair's fair, you got yours, so I got mine. Only thing was, I got mine in more ways than I'd wanted. I knew it wasn't yours; you'd only fucked me once in that first month and, as far as I could remember, you came in my ass. But I wanted to give us a chance, still loved you at that point, so I decided to get rid of it, didn't think it was right you bringing up someone else's kid. That's why I got scraped, you dumb fuck.'

He gave no expression of acknowledgement that he had even heard what she had said, and for a second she wondered whether or not she'd actually spoken them out loud at all, perhaps she had just wanted to tell him that for so long that she had imagined it. But then he spoke.

'Jimmy's kid, eh?'

She nodded.

'Still seems like murder to me, even if it was the child of some cocksucking motherfucker. I guess we just weren't right for each other, eh?'

He looked round at his iron barred cell, in the dark sweaty basement with Hank lying dead between them and the understatement of what he'd just said struck home and made him laugh. He gestured towards the bars and the bucket.

'No shit, we weren't made for each other, eh?'

'I guess that's one way of looking at it.' She began to laugh as well.

'So what happens now?' He asked, honestly not sure where this left them or, in particular, if it left him still stuck inside his hell hole.

'I guess I gotta find a way of dragging this sack o' shit outta here and down to the swamp. Perhaps if this fat fuck hadn't drunk so much and eaten so many glazed doughnuts, he wouldn't have been quite as much of a pain in the ass in death as he was in life, but there it is.'

'You could cut him up?' He suggested trying to be helpful. 'Reckon on how that might make it easier to carry him. If you hadn't killed the dog, he'd have done a god job chewing that cracker up for you.'

'I ain't gonna cut him up, I don't want anymore of his blood on me than I can help. It'll be all right once I get him in the truck.' And with that she grabbed Hank's feet and dragged him to the bottom of the stairs.

'I'd give you a hand but I'm kind of out of action at the moment. Sorry 'bout that.'

She tugged and scrambled him up the stairs, his dead weight always pulling against her. Gravity did its level best to defeat her, but eventually she got him up and sat on his fat bloated stomach to rest and sweat. Her weight made his thick blood pour out of the stab wounds in his back but she was too exhausted to worry about it. If she hadn't just murdered someone that needed disposing of and didn't have her husband locked in a cage downstairs, she'd have headed for bed and never have got up again, but facts were facts and if she didn't want to spend the rest of her life in the State Pen, she'd have to get her act together. It was time for Hank to become gator chow.

In the dim light of the car's internal light, he grabbed her front door key and, picking her up by her handles, he walked round the back of the flats and up to her door. He had the key ready, he didn't want to be caught fumbling and fiddling looking for it.

It slid into the groove with ease and he turned it first to the left then to the right and the door swung open. She was home. He closed the door quietly behind him with just the slightest of clicks. He stood there in the dark with his back pressed against the door letting his eyes acclimatise.

At first, the only things he could see were the small standby red dot of light on the television and the blue flashing numbers on the cooker in the kitchen telling him that it was 21:54, then 21:55, then 21:56. By 21:57, he could see all the furniture and the general layout of the room he was in. Now inside, he felt like a burglar.

He took three steps into the middle of the room and thought the first practical thing to do would be to get her into the freezer to stop any further deterioration. He bumped into the arm of the sofa on the way into the kitchen. Everything was small and compact, the whole place was neat, tidy and beautifully designed. He knew from looking at the cretins walking round the shops while he'd waited in the car all day chatting to her, that she wasn't like them. She wasn't one of the Neanderthals scraping their knuckles on the way to and from the betting shop, or one of the bag ladies that carried eight kids' washing down to the launderette, or the smoking disaffected generation who had heard of school but were blissfully unaware that they had to go every day. She was better than them, she was only here for convenience and perhaps through circumstances she couldn't help.

The kitchen units were, he imagined, a light maple although in the dark, the colour was somewhat muted. He opened the top half of the fridge freezer. It was the fridge. The light glared and stung his eyes. He shut it again and went back to close the kitchen door not sure if the light could be seen through the living room curtains. With the door shut, he opened the fridge again and looked at the food to see if he could glean anything more about Sandra from the contents.

There was very little to go on. A small carton of skimmed milk, three Yakult bacteria drink things, some salad bits, a salmon steak on a plate that had seen better days and some cottage cheese. It was either the food of someone on a serious diet or of someone who wasn't often at home. He closed it and opened the cabinet below it. The cold chill hit him in the face and sent a shiver down his back. The three drawers of the freezer were full. The top one contained microwave ready meals and the other two were packed with numerous tubs of Ben and Jerry's ice cream. He picked one up, and found it had already been opened; one spoonful of Phish Food had been gouged out.

He reached up from where he was sitting in the fridge light and opened a drawer to side of the fridge. It looked most likely to hold cutlery, his hand fished around being spiked by various knife ends and fork prongs before he found the teaspoons. He plunged into a carton of Chunky Monkey, its banana and walnut cold creaminess played on his tongue. It was heavenly and he could see her here just like him, crossed legged on the linoleum floor picking away sparingly, perhaps in her workout sweats after a spinning class.

He opened her bag and sat her in his lap. She was looking up at him or at least would have been if her eyes had been open and able to see. He took his left thumb and gently rolled back her right eyelid. The eye underneath was cloudy and opaque. He stared into it. Did she know he was there? He closed it again and moved his hand slowly across her cheek, over her nose and down onto her mouth. She had full fleshy lips and he let his fingers caress them for a while before sliding his finger between them and onto her teeth. The enamel was smooth and shiny. He held her lips apart so he could examine them. They were perfect, straight, whiter than white, no signs of coffee or red wine there at all.

He used both hands to prize her mouth open and looked in at the darkness that the light from the fridge couldn't reach into. Her tongue lay far back in her throat, a flaccid lump of flesh. He wondered if she wanted any ice cream and reached into the freezer for the plain vanilla. He took a mouthful himself and swilling it around his mouth, he waited until it was entirely melted and then lifted her up to his lips and kissed her. As they embraced, he slowly released the sweet cream into her waiting mouth. Somewhere deep inside himself, there was a dark shudder and he pulled away. The liquid was dripping out of her mouth and down the side of her face towards her ear. He carried her over to the sink and washed her again.

'Little Miss Messy.' He said playfully as he cleaned her up.

Leaving her to dry on the draining board, he emptied the freezer of all its shelves and contents. He shut the door for a second and was plunged back into darkness. Under its cover, he made his way back into the living room, found a cushion from the sofa and brought it back into the kitchen. He laid it on the freezer floor and brought her head over to it. She was still covered in drops of water and he wondered what this would look like when she froze again so he left them where they were and shut her in for the night.

He opened the drawers, fumbling around for a light and found a box of matches which he used to search around the kitchen until he found a small black metal torch on the window ledge. He used this to continue opening biscuit tins and coffee jars, packets of flour and a small sandalwood box, which contained joss sticks. That was the smell that pervaded everything, he had been immersed in it but not able to place the sweet patchouli smell that had soaked itself into the very fabric of the flat. As he flicked the torch around, he noticed the small discolouration made by the smoke from these incense sticks on the ceiling above the small marble pyramid with a single hole in the top which she obviously used to hold them after they were lit. It was the only imperfection in the whole flat as far as he could see.

When he had finished in the kitchen, he moved quietly back into the living room and looked through her books, her records and her DVDs. Next to the front door was a small table with a phone on a cradle, a Rolodex, and an answer phone. He noticed this but it took him twenty or so minutes to fully appreciate the significance of this particular discovery.

He flicked through her copy of Zen and the Art of Motorcycle Maintenance and wondered who Blake was who had wished her 'all the love in the world, my precious,' in nineteen ninety-five. He turned her stereo on and ejected the CD to see what the last music she'd been listening to was. It was the first Coldplay album. He had it at home. He sang to himself 'I wrote a song, I wrote a song for you, and it was called Yellow.'

Then it clicked and he walked over the answer phone. She was on here. He could hear her voice. He could see how much she sounded like the voice he had for her in his head. He weighed up whether or not it might make too much noise but decided to risk it. It took him a few fumbling button pushes to work it out but eventually there she was.

'Hello. I'm sorry but I can't make it to the phone at the moment. Either I'm out or I'm lying in the bath having a soak or I've fallen over in the kitchen and can't make it to the phone or I don't want to talk to you or I'm off doing an overnighter in some lovely city far away. If you're a burglar ignore the last bit. So anyway, you know what to do at the beeps.' It beeped.

She wasn't what he'd expected. He had imagined her voice to sound more Home Counties and slightly huskier but he loved the laugh in every word. She was a fun person, more alive and vivacious than he'd thought. He had her down as a thinker, a kind and calm person who exuded peace. But this person on the phone was very much more the 'life and soul of the party' type. It jarred a little, the shaking in his left arm began again and he massaged it as if it was a shiver that could be warmed and eradicated. He was living inside a snow globe and a crack had appeared in the glass dome above his head. He could feel the taste of her on his lips and it made him feel sick. He needed to lie down to stop the spinning.

He walked down the short corridor to the right of the room looking for a bed. The first door he opened went into the bathroom and so by purpose of elimination the door opposite had to be the bedroom door. It was. By the light of the torch, he saw her double bed and collapsed on it. He turned the torch off and lay there, just trying to breath. He was panting, unable to get a really good breath. There were pains all across his chest and he suspected he might in fact be having a heart attack. He wondered how the police would make sense of the scene if they found him dead on the bed and her in the freezer. He slowly calmed down and drifted into a fitful sleep.

His dreams felt more real than his current surreal waking existence as if his brain needed to retreat to a comforting conformity to calm him down and to bring him some peace. He was driving again and his wife was sitting next to him and she was smiling as wind blew her hair around. He looked at her for a second and when he looked back to the road, he saw a woman kneeling by a bike, he slammed on the brakes and dragged the car around her missing her by a hair's breadth and then flying on again, laughing the nervous laugh of someone who has just escaped death.

He put his hand on his wife's leg but the next time he looked across to see her, she was no longer his wife but Sandra. She was whole again and serene, there was music playing on the stereo and the car almost flew, it felt so free, as if on autopilot, driving through the most beautiful countryside on the most perfect day of the year. There was childlike giggling from the backseat but every time he looked in the mirror to catch a glimpse of the child, he would only see them for a second before they shot out of sight behind one or other of the seats. Suddenly his wife and child were in the road in front of him, and this time there was no time to stop. In the millisecond before he hit them, he caught in his peripheral vision a picture of Sandra's head back in the bowling ball bag staring up at him, her mouth opening and closing as if trying desperately to warn him. He hit them and felt the car bump and crunch over their bodies.

He woke with a jolt of horror, the morning light stinging his eyes.

The first thing he noticed in the room was a uniform hanging on a hanger from the wardrobe door. The scarf and winged badge told him immediately that Sandra had been an air stewardess. He pictured the head in the freezer on the uniform.

There was a knocking on the front door. A loud pounding rather than a knocking, which made him jump and he got off the bed and sat out of sight under the only window, just in case anyone tried to peek through the curtains. There was a voice as well, a shouting voice.

His ministry started without him really being aware of it.

Mabel brought three friends with her to the next meeting. They all sat politely listening to Doris as she led them through the service. She was particularly energised by the rise in attendance of fifty-percent. Her trance became deeper and more profound and she gave everyone messages from the Other Side.

Steven sat quietly on the end seat in the front row, observing. When it came time for the healing, they all lined up dutifully before Doris waiting for her to lay her hands on them. However, after Mabel had received her blessing from Dodds, she walked along the front row and, with some difficulty, knelt in front of Steven.

'Please, would you lay your hands on me?'

He could see that she was obviously in pain just being in that position and his knees ached in sympathy.

'But, I don't know...I have no... What do you want me to do?' He stumbled over his words.

He looked over at his aunt who was holding one of Mabel's friends by the hand, her eyes closed. When he looked back down to Mabel in front of him, he could see the lights around her again. His eyes scanned over the flashes coming from her. The colours were muted pastels and they moved in slow waves. Around her forehead, the rainbow of colours got darker and more intense, almost entirely black at the centre. The black unnerved him and the more he looked at it, the more sick he felt. He felt rising acid in his throat, and it made him choke, he coughed but couldn't clear it. He needed the black to go away. He raised his hands and plunged them into it. His hands were on fire, red radiant light burnt into the blackness, which he could feel on his hands like a sticky tar.

He gathered all the black up into a ball in his palms and then watched as it bubbled, melted, seared and shrank. When it was finally gone, he realised he had shut his eyes and was alone in the darkness with the colours. He opened his eyes and found Mabel no longer in front of him as she had been but now slumped on the floor weeping. This shocked him and it horrified him to see her like that. The rest of the congregation had all come to her assistance and his aunt had left her healing and come off the podium. She knelt down by

Mabel's side stroking her hair and whispering to her, trying to calm her down.

Bill grabbed Steven by the front of his jumper and lifted him to his feet, showing surprising strength for an old man. As he did this, Steven saw Bill as a young man, in a naval uniform holding someone else like this, his hair was short and immaculate and the short-sleeved shirt he wore allowed Steven to see the strong arms and the tattoo on his right forearm with a heart and a ribbon unfurling across it, on it were the words Tug and Kate. Then the image was gone and he was looking into Bill's older face again, red and angry.

'What have you done? What have you done to her?' He was shouting. 'Come on, tell me? What did you do to her?'

He pulled one arm back and Steven could see he had his fist clenched. He tried to move away from Bill but only succeeded in knocking over the chair behind him and nearly falling over.

'I… I don't know, honestly I don't.' He was desperate to know what had happened himself.

'Listen if you don't…' But before he could finish the sentence, Mabel screamed out.

'Bill, let go of him! Let go of him right this minute.'

Bill relaxed his grip on Steven a little but didn't entirely let go of him. Mabel pulled herself on to her knees and then with Rosa's help and her sister's she stood up. She wiped the tears away from her eyes and softly took hold of Bill's hand and removed it from Steven. She then cradled Bill's other hand still clenched until he loosened it and took her hand. She stared into Bill's eyes for a long time before reaching forward and kissing him on the cheek.

'It's all right Bill, it's all right.'

Bill eyes began to fill with tears and he sat down on the seat next to Steven's with his head in his hands. He began to cry. Every ounce of grief in his body came screaming out of him. He rocked back and forwards. Mabel took her sister's hand and looked round at everyone's stunned faces.

'It's all going to be all right. Steven has come to help us. I shouldn't have cried really but I found it overwhelming at first. It was silly of me, but I couldn't help it.'

Rosa had her arms around Bill trying to console him but was listening to every word Mabel was saying.

'And Bill will be all right too. He just needed some of the fire, the rapture, the love. I don't know what to call it. But I gave him a little bit of mine, just to show him, that it would all be all right. Now I think we should leave and give Bill some time alone with Steven. Come on girls.' There was an uncharacteristic confidence in her voice.

Mabel led Rosa, her sister and her friends out of the chapel and into the rain awaiting them outside.

'It's a baptism.' Mabel said happily as they stepped into the light shower.

'Are you all right, Steven?' Dodds had been looking at him throughout. She was unable to read his expression. She put her hand on his knee to reassure him.

'I think so. I'm not really sure. I feel strange but I think I'm fine. Let me have a couple of minutes with Bill and then perhaps we can talk.'

The only other person who hadn't left the chapel was Martha. She was beaming from head to toe, and looked as excited as a schoolgirl. She followed Doris out through the door by the stage that led into the little ante-room. Doris walked straight to the kettle and switched it on. Neither of them spoke until the instant coffee had been made, the biscuits were out on the table and they were sat down facing each other, a mirror of joy.

'Is he?' Martha asked.

'I think he is.' Doris whispered back. 'I think he might be.'

'What happens now?' Martha giggled as she dunked her digestive into her coffee; dripping little splashes of brown liquid on the table's white Formica top.

'I don't know.' Her smile slipped for a second as she got lost in some train of thought that she kept from Martha.

'It's been a long time, Dodds, a long wait. If I'm honest with you, I wasn't sure it would ever happen. Is that terrible of me? Does it mean my faith is weak? I'm sorry if I've doubted you, Dodds. It's just, well, you know, so many of them, of us, have passed over and missed this wondrous event. I was beginning to think that maybe I would miss it as well. I mean I'm not getting any younger and… I'm sorry.'

Doris reached out and touched her hand.

'Listen Marty, if I'm one hundred per cent honest with you, there have been times when I've doubted myself. And we still mustn't get too carried away but we need to hope that this is it, really it. 'Cos if it isn't, darling, then neither of us might be around to see Him when He does finally turn up.'

The door opened and Steven walked in, he nodded gently to both of them and started making himself a cup of tea.

'Are you okay, Steven?' Doris asked again.

'Yes, though I'm a little confused by everything that's going on. I'm not sure that I really feel myself, but I'm not sure who I do feel, if that makes any sense. I seem to know things and be able to see things that I couldn't before. Sounds crazy, doesn't it. I guess the scariest bit about it is the reactions and the need. I don't want to be what I think they want me to be. I don't want to answer their questions. I don't even know what I'm doing. I have no idea what happened with Mabel. I shut my eyes and then when I opened them she was on the

243

floor crying. What do you think is happening, Aunty Dodds?' He sat down with them and Martha passed him a biscuit.

'I'm not sure Steven.' She looked at Martha and Martha instantly got up and started making for the door.

'Well, I'll see you both next week, if not sooner. Thank you both again. God bless you both and may He send His angels to be with you.'

'Thank you, Marty. Have a good week.'

She waited before speaking again, sipping at her coffee, stirring it. They could hear Martha as she made her way across the echoey hall. Dodds gave it another few seconds while she collected her thoughts.

'When I lost Charlie, I found I had this gift. I could help people. Like I do here. But I was told that I was the one crying in the wilderness. I was the one who would recognise someone when they came and that this person would be very important.'

Steven got up and began pacing up and down again. He could feel everything slowing down. Time was stopping. Doris's mouth moved ever more slowly until it stopped altogether and he was staring at her inanimate face. Her hand was frozen in the middle of her stirring action. He walked over and looked at the minute wave circling around her coffee cup. They were still moving but so slowly it was almost imperceptible. He walked out into the hall leaving his aunt to her stillness.

He saw an image, a shadow shape of Bill sitting where Bill had been sitting. This spectral Bill looked up at him as he came in.

'I just wanted to thank you again, as I won't be seeing you again. But I wanted you to know you brought me a great deal of peace before my passing. I think I needed that.'

'It was a pleasure.' Steven said kindly.

Bill faded away into a ball of light that drifted upwards towards the roof and then through it and off to somewhere unknown.

Steven sat for minute in Bill's chair experiencing a vibration of him, then went back in to his aunt and stood where he had been when she'd started to slow down.

'This person would be very, very important. It may be that you are that person, Steven.'

He shrugged. 'I'm not sure that I am that important, Aunty Dodds.'

She continued stirring the coffee for a moment and then tapped the spoon against the side of the cup.

'How was Bill?'

'He was fine when he left. And I think he's fine now. But I don't think he'll be coming back again.'

'Why not, he comes every week, rain or shine.'

'I gave him the peace he needed to be able to rest. And now I think it's his time to sleep for a while.'

'We could all do with a rest.' Dodds said joking. 'I'm knackered myself. Come on, let's lock up and head home. What would you like for your dinner?'

'Anything, I'm not that fussed.'

Bill never did come back. They found him in his apartment four days later sitting in his favourite armchair with a lapful of fish and chips laid out on a sheet of white paper, a half eaten pickled egg in his right hand.

Peter's sons were twelve and fourteen and had been away at school for too much of their lives. Twice a term, he would travel down to see them at their expensive school on the coast to watch them play rugby and to take them out for the day afterwards. He would stay in a local hotel the night before because the matches always started at ungodly hours. This morning was no exception. It was foggy and the rugby pitch was lost in the morning's dim light. The main difficulty he had was watching both matches at the same time. He had a deal with the boys that they would draw lots for whose first half he watched and whose second half.

During half time, he would wander back to the club house for a cup of much needed hot tea before making his way to the other side of the playing fields to see his second match. The boys were both keen sportsmen and played every conceivable game possible. It was one of the few ways he communicated with them now. He could come and watch them play and then talk to them about their performance and through that their lives. He could take them off to a rugby match at Twickenham or a football match at White Hart Lane and do the same.

They were the only part of his life that was unsoiled, unsullied by the mess he had created for himself with their mother. If there was one thing he was grateful for, it was them, although he resented the lack of access he had to his own children because of their boarding. Nevertheless he did everything he could to be with them as often as possible and to ensure that when they did actually see each other, it was full of quality moments and laughter. In many ways, he only was the person he wanted to be when he was with them. He was funny and stupid and confident and content, there was no other realm of his life that he could say that about; at work he was uptight, in his marriage he was a failure and in his private moments he was a whoring drug abuser which wasn't exactly the way he wanted to been seen by the rest of the world.

On this freezing cold autumnal morning he stood on the sidelines waiting for the game to begin hugging himself for warmth. One of the other dads who he regularly saw at the matches came and stood by him. He always wore a huge sheepskin coat and smoked a pipe and looked as if the cold could never penetrate his rotund exterior. His son was the team captain of the under-fourteens. He never missed a match and Peter always felt slightly shamed by this.

'Morning, Peter.' He knew Peter's name, Peter on the other hand had no idea of his. So he just nodded back a hello.

'Your boy's playing well this season. Scored a wonderful try last week. He's really come on. Reads the game well as well. Jared says he's really pleased with him.' Jared was the sports master, who Peter merely knew as Mr Jenkins and the boys knew as JJ.

'Well, that's nice to know. How's your son doing?' Peter had little interest but it only seemed the polite response.

'He's doing well. I'm very pleased with him. Seems to have stopped clowning around and actually seems to be taking life a lot more seriously this year. He's upped his training regime and it's paying off. He's put on a lot of good bulk and he's got his second trial with the county side next week. He's a good lad.'

Small talk wasted lives. That's what Peter felt. He had heard a film director on the radio that morning say that after eighty years, the only purpose he could find in life was to avoid boredom. Boredom was a living death. Peter had been dead for most of his life in that case. Although he had been resurrected in the last few months when things had been anything but boring. Planning his wife's death and regular fucking certainly enlivened a person.

As the game kicked off, his mobile phone rang and he reached into his pocket and pressed the button to disconnect the call. He checked the screen to see who had phoned, it was Jill. It began to ring again as he looked at it. It was her again. He turned the phone off this time and watched the match. No doubt some disaster had happened, her credit card had gone over its limit or her car had run out of petrol.

'These black bastards have got hard heads.' His companion informed him, referring to the multi-racial nature of the opposition's team. 'I told my boy to go in hard, it's the only thing they understand. I remember playing some of the little fuckers when I was at school. Not built like us, they're as strong as gorillas, and fast to boot.'

His words proved prophetic. They were indeed strong and through the rising mist, both men could just about make out a tackle that ended a potentially glorious sporting career. As his companion's son got the ball and began to sprint down the flank, a black member of the opposing defence hit him head on, low and with force. His shoulder made excellent contact with a right shin and shattered it. The crack of the breaking bone could be heard all over the park as could the screams that followed it. Several games stopped briefly to ascertain the reason for this sudden outbreak of noise. Peter made his way on to the pitch with several other parents including the pipe smoker whose son had suffered the horrific injury. The normally straight leg now had a large dent in the middle at the front and several pieces of bones were poking through the skin down by the ankle underneath the long sock.

An ambulance was called for and it was decided that the game should be moved to another pitch while the boy's father waited for the medical assistance to arrive. As Mr Jenkins said,

'Let's not let this spoil a good game of rugby, eh lads? Let's play on for your captain.'

At half time there was much talk of the devastating blow this would be to the team over the remaining fixtures of the season. Peter was merely relieved it hadn't been either of his boys. Before heading off to watch the second half of the under twelves' game, he checked his phone again and saw Jill had left him a message.

'Peter, please phone me back, straight away. Something's happened, something terrible. Please come home as soon as you get this please.'

There was desperation in her voice that he had never heard before and she was crying. He watched his son score two tries and set up another one, took them out for afternoon tea and ignored the phone that kept ringing every ten minutes or so.

As he chatted away happily with the boys over muffins and crumpets with hot dripping butter and sweet strawberry jam, he wondered if she had snorted the coke. He pictured her nose bleeding, perhaps puking, high and paranoid, in agony. He would go back all in good time and make her confess to the doctor how she had got herself in such a state. He would act surprised at his wife's actions. She was a drug user, and an unfit mother, he would file for divorce and life might start again, perhaps he would take early retirement and persuade Lauren to come with him to some retreat in the South of France. The boys would stay at school but spend every holiday out there with them. They would never know what Lauren had been, or what he'd done. It would all be simple and beautiful.

After he'd said his goodbyes to his sons at the school gates, he reached into the car's glove compartment and took out a boiled sweet tin and opened it. It had a small collection of drugs he's bought from a girl who worked at a sex shop in London. He took half an E and put the stereo on and let Mozart's D minor Requiem glide him along the two-hour journey home. He cried and laughed and sped and flew.

He stopped for water at a service station and ate half a meal in the café while he watched ugly humanity sit and gorge themselves. The man in the next booth to him was lost in a world of his own. He was staring at a photo of what Peter assumed to be his wife and child. He look distressed and was talking under his breath. Peter had an overwhelming urge to hold him and tell him how much love there was in the world and that everything was going to be all right. He suspected that these entirely abnormal feelings of love and brotherhood were only present due to his own personal chemical enhancement so he left him sitting there and merely smiled at him as he left.

By the time he pulled up in his drive, the effects of the drug had more or less worn off and he was back to his numb depressed self.

Jill opened the door. She had none of the outward signs of injury he had half expected, half hoped for. There was no redness around her nose, no sign of bleeding. She looked pale and her eyes had obviously been crying for a long time. The cigarette in her hand was shaking. The effects had obviously been more minor than he'd hoped but they had undoubtedly shaken her up.

She led him through to the living room without speaking. Jim was lying dead on the carpet. There was dried blood all over his nose, chin and on the carpet where he'd fallen. Some ghastly liquid had obviously come from his mouth and left a yellow stain where he had projectile vomited it.

'Jim came over late last night to see you. And he just collapsed like this. And I didn't know what to do.'

She'd had the whole of the previous night and most of the day to come up with an excuse or an alibi and this was the best she could manage. She sat on the sofa, pulled hard on her cigarette and ran her hand through her dishevelled hair. She was wearing her jogging gear, there were patches of blood and vomit on it.

Looking more closely at the body, he could see drag marks in the blood, she had tried to pull the body a foot or so. He wondered whether or not she had considered disposing of the body somehow.

'Why didn't you phone for an ambulance?'

She began to sob and held her hands over her face.

Chapter 10

The following day I couldn't get out of bed. I couldn't move. My head felt as if it was going to explode. I lay there trying to hold the agony back, trying hard not to cry out, grinding my teeth. When Rosa came in and said she wanted to take me to her Church, I managed to hide the pain I was in but I told her I didn't feel well enough. She made me promise that if I rallied a bit I'd go down there with her. She left me lying in my darkened room, shutting the door gently behind her.

I lay there and, to take my mind off the pain, took pictures of anything I could see from where I was. I took some down the length of my body to my feet. I took close-up shots of the tassels on the lampshade by my bed.

I drifted in and out of consciousness all day and, at some point, I must have entered a deep sleep because when I woke up, it was the next morning, the clock next to me was telling me it was nine. I didn't remember the previous evening.

I climbed out of bed feeling better than I had the day before. I noticed, however, that my right leg was slightly stiffer and more difficult to move than normal, and I dragged it a little more heavily. Over breakfast I promised Rosa that I would leave her soon, I didn't want to be a burden to her. There was a measure of relief on her face, which she tried very hard to hide. But why should she have the responsibility of a stranger appearing out of nowhere to move into her house for their last days.

'Where will you go?' She asked.

'Oh, I have friends and some family up North, I might go back up there. Or I might get on a plane and head off somewhere, some new country. I like seeing new places.'

There was a look on her face that told me she obviously thought I was too ill to travel and that I was merely deluding myself. I was. I knew I was very ill and that any trip might be my last but I had an idea that it might be nice to die a long way away in a tropical climate in a hotel somewhere surrounded by my photos. But this was really reliant on me being able to see my way to the room I'd be dying in. If my sight failed before then I would just be a blind man wandering down strange alleys scared and absurd.

'Will you come and meet him?'

I knew immediately that she was talking about the preacher at her church.

'I can come, I feel well enough but I don't really believe. I would like to believe, I really would. It would be nice to feel that there's a reason behind everything and that there's something waiting for me afterwards, but I'm not sure that's true.'

'You come anyway.'

'If he lets me take his picture, I'll come along, how about that?'

She thought he would.

I packed up all my stuff and carried my bags with me as we walked down to the church. I don't know what I expected but it wasn't very much. Rosa pushed me through the door and pointed me towards the man sitting on his own looking up at the cross. I put my bags down in the entrance hall and walked in. He turned round and smiled. He looked at the Nikon in my hand.

'Nice camera.' He said.' Have you come to take a picture of me for your collection?'

'Maybe.' I said. 'If that's all right with you?'

'I don't see why not. Show me some of the other pictures you've taken.'

I felt around in my pocket and found a handful. I always kept some of my favourites on me, just in case I lost my suitcase that was by now packed-full of them. The ones I had on me were like a child's safety blanket. I loved them, as photos and as imaginary friends. I had a picture of Ma's friend in her orange jumpsuit. I had a picture of the man waiting in his car. I had a picture of the two women and the little boy at the airport and I had one of Baby silhouetted walking away. He looked at each one in turn.

'I like the photos. They have interesting stories. You can take mine. You have a rare gift.'

He asked me if I wanted him in any particular position and I told him I didn't. We talked and I shot off as many shots as I could. He talked about the music he liked and the films he'd seen that had moved him.

'It's A Wonderful Life. That's my favourite movie. I love it. Have you seen it?'

I had.

'I love the idea that whenever a bell rings an angel gets his wings. When I was a little boy my mother had a little handbell she would ring to call me down to dinner. Whenever I was left alone in the house, I would ring it convinced I was making new angels.'

He was transported by this memory to somewhere beautiful and I took a picture to capture it. The click of the lens brought him back from wherever he'd been.

'I think every time you take a picture it's a bit like the bell ringing. You're creating angels.'

'Rosa seemed to think you might be able to help me in some way?'

He was lost again somewhere in his last sentence as if he was weighing up the significance of what he had said. He flicked through the photos in his hands again and nodded.

'Did she?' He said after a time. 'I'm not sure what I can do for you.'

'Perhaps I could pay for a healing? I am not very well.'

'You can't buy healings.' He said softly and sadly.

I knew this speech too well so I jumped in before he had time to complete it.

'Of course, I mean I know that. But perhaps I could make an offering or a gift to the church.'

'No I don't think so.' He said weighing up the offer. 'No, I think you were brought here for me not the other way around. I can't do anything for you. Though all I can say is that your photos aren't what you think they are. You have more sight than most people do. And now you have me in your little camera as well.'

He walked me to the door and asked me to come back to that evening's service.

'Then I think you should head for wherever you want, but come tonight.'

It wasn't an easy drive down the winding creeper-covered tracks in the dark. She wasn't looking forward to the walk back to the freeway after, either. She would have to hope to pick up a late night ride or face a long walk home. As she weaved her way down to the water, she knew that she'd seen this horror movie and no good came from it. And then there it was, in the headlights – the gentle slope that led straight down into the green soup of the swamp.

She stopped, pulled up the handbrake and looked at Hank slumped in the passenger seat next to her. His head had lolled from side to side with each turn in the road like a small child asleep on the way home from too much excitement at the county fair.

'Well, Hank, I think this is it. Time for a bit of a moonlight dip.'

She unbuckled Hank's seatbelt and wound down the windows so the truck would fill up and sink quicker. She took out a hunting knife and stabbed Hank four times in the chest hoping to give the gators a better sniff of his blood. She wanted them to pick up their tasty drive-thru snack as quickly as they could. She wiped the blade clean on his trousers, grabbed the flashlight she'd remembered to bring with her, put the vehicle into neutral and climbed out of the cab.

Reaching in from the driver's doorway she took the handbrake off. As it began to inch forward she gave it one last push on its way. It picked up speed on the twenty yards leading down the mud track and then instantly slowed as it hit the water and the weeds with a loud smack and was then slowly consumed by the swamp, like a toy truck dropped into a tub of treacle. She'd left the lights on and they shone underwater as it ever so slowly went down and down. The headlights caught a thousand pairs of bullfrogs' eyes that twinkled in the dark like stars come to gaze into the water.

As she watched the roof of the truck go under and a final giant air bubble erupt from the cabin, the lights flickered and then shorted out. She thought she caught a glimpse of two or three huge monsters sliding and slipping their ways towards it in the flickering, dying illuminations.

The swamp was full of noise, croakings, splashings, crunching and crackings. She stood in the moonlight for a second waiting for some sign to tell her to leave but it never came so she picked her coat up and put it on, it was strangely chilly for that time of year. She turned the flashlight on and began the long walk back to the highway. She took out the hunting knife from its sheath on her belt and held it in the other hand, its blade reflecting the sharp artificial light. If anything or anyone jumped out on her, she'd slice it up before asking any questions.

As soon as he heard Hank's truck pulling away he started pulling and pushing away at the bars. He had no idea how long she would be away, but he calculated that, at the very least he had a good couple of hours. If she was unable to pick up a ride for a while on that road, which he knew would be quiet at this time, then he might have most of the night, but he knew he couldn't depend on that and having no clock down there, he had no real way of measuring the time. He knew as well that he had a lot of work still to do if he was going to actually get all the way out. He kicked and charged the bars, trying to get as much momentum as he could over the short space. It was shuddering and giving but he was weaker than he'd imagined. The blow to his head was aching and oozing puss and that combined with his lack of food or proper sleep meant he was exhausted after only a few minutes.

He was out of breath and sweating. He charged the cage one last time with his shoulder. He still had enough strength to break his own collarbone apparently because he distinctly heard it crack and felt a searing pain that made him hit the floor. He swore repeatedly and lashed out with his feet, but every kick only made the pain worse. It was only after several minutes that he saw what he'd done, three more bolts had come loose and were twisted and bent half way out of the wall, In fact, the whole cage was now slightly buckled and askew. He now had no choice. If she came home and saw the cage like this she'd know instantly that he had been trying to escape and she'd shoot him without so much as a blink.

He scrambled to his feet awkwardly unable to put any pressure on his right-hand side. He went to the back of the cage and started kicking out at the side that looked most likely to give. He was gritting his teeth as every shudder sent a sharp slicing pain into him – jagged bone cutting through muscle. Just as he felt he was getting nowhere and might pass out, two of the bolts flew out of the wall and fell to the floor. There were only a couple left now at the bottom of the cage holding it to the wall and with great difficulty he could just about get enough purchase to push it out nearly far enough for him to squirm through. Nearly, but not quite. It took him another whole hour to get free. His clothes were soaked with sweat and his mouth was foaming as he made one final excruciating attempt to squeeze himself out between the wall and the iron. It snapped back pinning him, crushing his chest and knocking all the wind out of him. He flapped around panicking before finding the adrenalin strength to push it off him and he fell to the floor and freedom.

He hobbled his way up the stairs and into the hallway. There was still no sign of her anywhere so he wandered through the house, picking up his rifle, which she left standing behind the kitchen door and three bullets he found lying on the kitchen table. In the living room he opened the fridge, pulled out a four-pack and settled down on the lazy boy in the dark to wait for her.

After walking for an hour she hit tarmac again and sheathed the knife. The flashlight arced left and right, there was no sign of anything – car, man or beast – in either direction. As she walked towards home in the dark, she had lots of time to think about the last few days and how fucked up it had all got. There was nothing in her childhood to suggest she was capable of the things that she'd done. Where had the girl in the pretty dresses always smiling in the pictures gone?

Her walking slowed down as she became weighed down by her life. All she wanted to do was to lie down by the side of the road and melt away. She wanted the moss and creepers to cradle her and absorb her. She didn't want to go back to the house. Now out here in the air, miles away, it seemed possible to just walk away as if she'd broken the length of chain that tied her to her old life. She had stopped and was looking up at the giant full moon above her when she heard the car behind her. She turned and could see the headlights through the trees winding down the road still some way off. The plan was to hitch a ride home, but then what? She didn't want to go on with this. She wanted him out of her life forever; in fact, she wanted him never to have been in it. She wanted never to have met him. She wanted to be eight again so that she could to start over.

She saw her shadow extend down the road as the lights got closer and without her even putting out a thumb, she could sense the car slowing down behind her. She looked down at her hand and caught a glint of her engagement ring. She took it off and simply dropped it to the ground and started walking again. The car now pulled up next to her. The big old Chevy's passenger window opened and she heard a voice from inside calling to her.

'Ma'am? I say, Ma'am? Are you okay? Do you need some help? Have you had car problems?'

His voice was soft, husky, full of concern and youth. She stopped and he stopped the car. She leaned into the window and saw him for the first time. He must have been no older than twenty, his cheeks were covered in a light stubble that suggested his rosy pink skin wasn't yet capable of growing a full beard even if he wanted to. There were silver rings on every finger that held the steering wheel and a red chequered shirt covered his white t-shirt. He was listening to Talking Heads on the stereo.

'You okay? Need a lift to town? It's mighty late to be wandering around the roads.'

She opened the door and sat down on the springy leather armchair of a passenger seat.

'Where are you going?' She asked.

'Well, you know, ma'am, I'm not really sure.'

His eyes quickly darted on to the back seat and she followed the glance. It was a mess of clothing, boots, skateboards, CDs, pictures, books, beers and a guitar – all the detritus of a person on the move.

'Kind of had a change of circumstance. Life doesn't seem to be working out the way I thought it would down here. So I thought what the Hell, there's a big old country out there and if I can't find happiness in one part of it, maybe I should try somewhere else. So, at the moment, the plan is I'm just gonna drive and see where I end up. Always fancied Vegas.' He had a laugh in his voice, which was infectious.

'So where can I take you? What you doing out here so late, anyhow?'

'I had some car trouble, crock-o'-shit thing packed up a little way back.'

'Oh really, I didn't see a car. Where was it? Do you want us to drive back and see if I can do something about it? I'm not much of a mechanic but I know my way round a little.'

'It's a bit late for that, it's at the bottom of the swamp. It's a long story. But if you could just drop me off at the next town, it's about twenty minutes along here, that would be great.'

He turned up the music as he pulled away.

'He's right, you know. It's a fucking wild life. Time to get me a piece of it.'

She wound down the window as they drove and let the cold night air chill her cheeks and whip her hair around her face.

'Time to get me a piece of it too.' She repeated.

'Miss Sandra Simpson? Are you in there? Sandra Simpson?'

He could hear the letterbox being opened and the voice suddenly became louder.

'Sandra Simpson? I'm the bailiff, here on behalf of Jamieson Debt Collection Agency. Are you in there?'

He tried not to breathe, though his heart alone seemed to be making enough noise to wake the dead. The dead currently waiting to be discovered in the freezer. Would they break down the door and come straight in? Might they take the freezer as an asset? He could hear the man outside walking up and down in front of the flat, looking through the windows. The letterbox opened again.

'Listen if you're in there, there's no point in hiding. We'll be back tomorrow and this time either you have the money you owe or we'll enter by force if need be and take your property up to the value that we require. I hope you understand me, Miss Simpson. In the meantime, I'll leave my card, if you want to pay before then, just phone my mobile and we can make arrangements for that to happen.'

Waiting in the darkened room for the man to finally walk away, he wondered what debts she could have run up and whether or not he could pay them off for her. He heard the door of a car slam shut down in the car park outside and after another thirty seconds or so heard it pull away. He waited for another couple of minutes and then emerged from the bedroom. A small slit of light bisected the living room, it was the gap he'd looked through in the curtains only the day before. He had to get out of there and quickly. Suddenly he could see all the madness of the last two days, what the fuck had he been thinking. He put it all down to shock, maybe some kind of post-traumatic stress disorder.

He picked up his keys from where he'd left them on one of the kitchen units and turned to leave. The freezer sat there waiting for him to open it. She was waiting for him to say goodbye. He knew that he should just leave but he could hear her, a muffled voice calling from inside the freezer.

'Come, kiss me. Say goodbye.'

'This is crazy, you're not talking. This is all in my head. This is all just shit. This is my head just fucking me over.'

But the voice he could hear in his head was getting louder in its pleading.

'Please, my love, just kiss me once before we're parted. Please.'

It was her voice all right, it was the voice he'd heard on the answer phone but there was no laugh in it now, only desperation and tears. He opened the door and there she was. Her skin was blue and thinly frosted making her look like an actress made up to play the Ice Queen. The water droplets on her face from the night before her frozen into ice tears falling from her eyes. She was more beautiful now than he had ever seen her and yet at the same time more tragic. He found himself mesmerised by her, unable to take his eyes away for the longest time. It was only the sound of another knock at the door that made him start and break his hypnotic state.

'Are you in there, dear? I thought I heard someone moving around in there. Are you all right, love? I couldn't help overhear what those men were saying, nasty rotten bleeders.'

It was the lady from next door and he could see from the shadow on the curtains that she was trying to peer through for signs of life. He slowly eased the kitchen door shut, hoping the movement wouldn't catch her eye. Like the other intruder, she stayed outside for a long time. He couldn't be caught there.

As soon as he heard her front door close behind her, he left the kitchen and peaked through the curtains. He checked both ways along the walkway to make sure that the coast was clear and then left pulling the door shut behind him almost silently. He hurried along the concrete pathway, down the concrete steps and finally into his car and was away. It was still early, so he did what he normally did, he went to work, hoping that familiar surroundings would bring him back to his senses.

He sat through meeting after meeting, dishevelled and distracted. Several people commented on the cuts and bruises he had from the bomb blast and asked if he was 'really okay to be at work'. He told them he was but his ears were still ringing from the explosion. For some reason he hadn't noticed this whilst he'd been alone with her. It was as if she had taken all his pain away and the longer he was away from her, the more the pain came back.

All he could think about was the flat and the head. Why had he left it there? But what else was he meant to do with it? Make it disappear like the rest of her. But, where? Even if she was found, there was nothing to link him with the crime, was there? It wasn't even really a crime was it? It was simply an accident, wasn't it? But he had left his fingerprints all over the place and probably DNA from his hair or skin or something. Then of course there was the other major give-away to link him to the death, the bowling bag. He'd left it there. When his mother had given it to him she made him write clearly in indelible ink his name, address and telephone number on the inside of the bag so that, 'Somebody could return it if you leave it somewhere. I mean you're always leaving stuff places'.

He had to go back, not just to clear up any evidence of him having been there but because he couldn't stand the idea of her being there all alone. As soon it was dark, he made his excuses and left. On the way he planned his movements in advance; he would open the door, walk straight into the kitchen, grab the bag, check the flat over for any other evidence of his intrusion and leave. But as he drove, he revised his plan. If he left her there as she was, there would be a full investigation when she was eventually found, without any doubt. They would check the flat meticulously for any signs of foreign bodies. It occurred to him now just how stupid he'd been. He could easily have taken the head somewhere and buried it and no one would have been any the wiser. There was no other option. She had to come with him again.

He turned the key, stepped quietly across the dark room. He found the bag where he'd left it. He picked it up, opened the freezer door and took her out. Her hair was crunchy with ice. She was frozen solid. He tried not to look at her too closely, afraid he would get lost again in his fantasies. He zipped her in and replaced the trays of the now melted Ben and Jerry's back into place. He washed the spoon he'd used and put it back in the drawer.

In the bedroom he straightened out the bedclothes and checked the pillow under torchlight for any stray hairs that might incriminate him. That done, he checked the balcony again, through the curtains, and stepped out closing the door behind him as quietly as possible again. He took two steps away from it and then had a moment of hesitation; something was nagging him. Had he left something behind, had he in his rush left anything that might connect him to the place. His indecision led him back to the door and he stood outside it, mentally replaying all the things he'd done. No, he was fine, everything was as it should be, and everything was as it had been when he'd found it. He turned to leave again when a voice called to him.

'Excuse me?'

He turned round. It was coming from the far end of the walkway in the shadows, just by the top of the stairs. Someone was walking towards him. She flicked in and out of the lights from the windows of the other flats as she came closer. He caught glimpses of her. Her head turned at each doorway obviously looking at the numbers, checking them for something.

'I'm really sorry, but you don't happen to know where number 32b is by any chance.'

The clipped tones of her accent matched the clipped clicking of her heels as she approached. She reached him, and even in the dark, he could tell who it was.

Sandra stood there in front of him, whole once more, complete and alive. He took a step back from her, almost tripping over his own feet in his surprise. What new tricks was his mind playing on him now? He only needed to reach out a hand and he could touch her, he could even smell her perfume. He had gone deathly white and thought for a second he might sink to his knees but instead he leaned against the wall to steady himself. She stared at him, concern in her eyes. Her lips moved on their own with no help from him, cold dead lips he'd kissed were now red, full and vibrant.

'Are you okay? I'm sorry I didn't mean to startle you? I was just looking for number 32b. It's so dark up here, I was having trouble finding it.'

Her eyes checked the number on the door he was standing by and a look of surprise came over her face.

'Oh, I'm sorry, are you here to see Sandra as well? Is she in?'

He couldn't speak, his throat was closing, and his tongue seemed to have swollen.

'It all looks pretty dark in there, doesn't it? I was worried about that. Have you knocked?'

His brain was swimming trying to make sense of everything. How could she be here? Why was she talking about herself in the third person?

'Are you okay? You look like a startled rabbit? Is there a bell? Perhaps we could try that.'

She looked around at the side of the door and pressed the buzzer. Both of them heard it ring inside.

'Doesn't look like we're in luck, does it?'

'No'. He managed to get out.

'Typical. I had a horrible feeling she might've gone already. Sorry, I haven't introduced myself. I'm Sukie.'

She held out a hand. He looked at it in bewilderment. Hadn't he buried that hand? He took it just to feel if it was really there. It was; it was solid, tangible, warm even. He looked into her eyes but in the darkness outside the flat, it was difficult to tell if those were the eyes he'd stared into.

'I'm a friend of Sandra's from way back. How do you know her?'

Then it all made sense. The woman in the photograph wasn't Sandra Simpson at all. It was just a picture she kept in her wallet of her friend. The woman that he'd been haunted by, that he created a whole life for, that he'd fallen in love with, was not the head that he carried with him, but this woman standing in front of him.

'Well I…I had… I'm her…'

'Don't tell me she arranged a date with you, didn't she? Looks like she's stood both of us up, doesn't it? To be honest, I don't think she's coming back anytime soon.'

His eyes strayed unintentionally down to the bowling bag.

'Why do you say that?'

'Oh, it's a long story, and it's too cold to go through it all here. Listen, do you fancy a drink? There's a pub just down the road that's actually quite nice. We could go there for a quickie and a chat? What do you say? You look frozen, you're white as a ghost. Have you been waiting ages for her?'

'A little while, yes.'

'Well, what do you say?'

He was still reeling. 'If you think it's okay?'

She laughed at him kindly. 'Well you hardly look like a murderer, do you, so I guess we'll be all right. You got a car?'

He nodded.

'Good, then you can follow me.'

Word spread quickly through South London's spiritualist community about Steven. Each week more people would turn up hoping for healing or words from him. Although he was reluctant to take on the heavy mantle they were thrusting upon him, he seemed to have little option.

He was moved onto the stage with Doris, although he never felt comfortable with them staring at him. He never addressed the group as a whole and most weeks Doris got on with her normal service and he would sit there with his head bowed. He very rarely laid his hands on anyone and it was even more infrequent that he would actually give the message. But when he did, it had a profound effect on the person and on the congregation and the following weeks the numbers would have swelled again.

He watched as the rows began to fill; the first three rows, then the next four, then the next and the next. Within two months, the hall was full and Doris wanted to offer more services. Steven wasn't keen on this. After every session, whether he had done anything or not, he felt physically drained for hours. It was as if they were sucking his life energy from him.

He was, however, getting better at controlling his visions. Occasionally, someone came into the hall whose aura shone out like a beacon of pain and it was these people he felt compelled to offer something to.

Most evenings he would talk to Doris about her beliefs and philosophy, and he would try to fit what he was experiencing into this tight framework, her singular worldview. More often than not, he found himself at odds with her morally and religiously, though he never told her. She was so convinced he had been sent to the church for a reason and that he had a mission to fulfil. He, on the other hand, was by no means as certain.

After one service, Rosa approached him and asked if she could speak to him. He was pleased she had come forward because, of all the people in the room, she was one of the few that never stole from him. She would take nothing unless it was offered, while others seemed to be able to leach a part of him just by their deep desire to be close to him.

'Shall we go somewhere away from here? Would you like a coffee perhaps?'

She seemed somewhat taken aback by this offer, and he realised he was seen as 'different' again, he was still an outsider. They had a place for him and a need for him, they didn't want him to be like them or one of them, they wanted him to be something else, someone who didn't ask them if they fancied going for a chat over a coffee. Rosa accepted despite the fact that it made her feel awkward.

'I think there's a café down at the end of the street, isn't there?'

'I…think so, yes.' She said with her strong Mexican accent.

They put on their coats and walked along the road. She kept three or four steps behind him and every time he looked back, she looked away, averting her eyes from any meaningful contact.

The café was loud and bright; it was full of cabbies, labourers and old ladies. The giant Thai man behind the counter in his sweaty grease-stained apron greeted them happily.

'All right mate, what you want?'

'A coffee for me please and Rosa, what would you like?'

She shyly asked for a glass of milk.

'No problem, take a seat. I'll bring it over in a minute.'

Steven handed him some change and as he came into contact with the other man's hand, he felt a jolt in his chest. His heart pulsed and squirmed, it was struggling to perform. It knocked the breath out of him for a second and he coughed to try and clear his throat. He looked into the man's face.

'I would take your wife's advice and go and see the doctor.' He said.

'What has she been saying now, eh? She always worried. What she say, eh? She tell anyone and everyone that comes in here everything?'

Steven held the man's left wrist and both he and the man felt a sharp pain shoot down it followed by strong pins and needles. The man pulled his hand away quickly and started massaging his arm.

'Like I said, I think you should see someone? That can't be nice.' He left the man looking worried but nodding in agreement.

Rosa waited for her milk to arrive and took a large sip of it as if it was the hard liquor she needed to get her courage up.

'I am sorry to take up your time. But I have worries.'

'About what?'

'About you.'

'Oh,' Steven said quite surprised, 'why?'

'I don't know who you are. I mean, I don't know what you are. I am worried that you are not good.'

'In what way, Rosa?' He could see in her eyes that she was highly agitated about this.

'I have been coming to see your Aunt for some few months and she is good, I think. It is not a service like in my church, and I would like that more. But your Aunt is a good woman and she knows to pray and to help. And I don't think she does any harm. She has no power, I believe. Which is good, I think. She helps people by being there and giving them hope, I think.'

She stopped speaking and he could tell she felt she had been disloyal to Doris in some way.

'I mean, I like that she has no power, she touches people or gives them messages but I don't think that she heals people. She tells them what they need to hear. But she isn't lying, I think.

Because she does help people and I think she believes it but…'

She took another big gulp of milk and then wiped her mouth with her fingertips before continuing.

'You do things and you know things. How?'

'I honestly don't know.' She was asking the questions that he had been asking himself.

'And what do you do? When you wave your hands around them. When you whisper to them?'

Steven thought carefully before answering. 'I'm not sure I can really describe it. I don't know what it is I do. It's like I can see when people are ill.'

'How?' Rosa jumped in.

'I can see colours around them and if there's a black spot that I can see, it makes me feel ill and I think that means they're ill in some way. So I reach in and sort of burn it out of them.'

Rosa was fascinated by the description but concerned as well. It brought up more questions than it answered.

'What is the black thing? How do you burn it? Where does the power come from?'

'I can only tell you what I feel, because I don't know anything for sure.'

He closed his eyes and slipped inside of himself to find the answers.

'I think the black stuff is fear. I think that's all it is. I don't think I do anything except maybe take people's fear away.'

'But you make people better, you give them healing, no?' Rosa interrupted.

'No, I don't think I do, I don't think I make anything better physically, I don't think I cure any real ailments. It's just that everyone is so frightened of the possibility of dying, and that can form itself into these clouds, these darknesses which make living hard. I think all I do is help people to let that go and so start living instead of worrying all the time about dying. I don't heal anyone because that would be pointless. We're all going to die at some point, when and how are irrelevant. It's finding a peace in your head while you're alive that I think is important. I don't know how I get rid of it. I feel my hands get very hot and I can touch this bit of the person which is around them reaching deep into them. As for where the power comes from, I don't know.'

'What if it comes from El Senor?'

'El Senor?'

'El Diablo! The Devil' She said, crossing herself to ward off the Evil One, as if just mentioning his name might bring her into jeopardy.

'You don't know where it comes from, why do you think it is good?'

'I don't. I don't think it's good or bad. I think it's just a thing that happens. But it doesn't feel bad to me, does it to you?'

'I don't know. These things are beyond me to understand but they make me scared, I think.'

He could tell that she wanted to believe that there was nothing bad in him but needed reassurance.

'He is a trickster you see, he can be beautiful and charming and yet it's still Him underneath. He's there to steal your soul. What do you tell people when you whisper in their ears?'

'I tell them something I was told.'

'What?'

'It's a thing that I was told to tell certain people. People who needed to hear it, people who would know what it means.'

'But what is it?' She was insistent.

'You don't need to be told it. I don't know how I know, I just do. And I don't really think you want to hear it, do you?' He paused to let her answer.

She shook her head.

'No, I don't, you're right. But who are you then?'

'I don't know what you mean by that. Who do people say I am?'

'They say that you are the One. Some say you are the Rapture, that you will usher in the end of days. Others, that you are just a great healer sent to help us prepare for the One.'

Sitting in this greasy smoke-filled café in South London, she was aware of how ridiculous the words sounded.

He looked stunned.

'Rosa, I am none of these things. This isn't what... I'm not anything like that. I'm just here at the moment. I'm not here for any big reason. I'm not here to start anything.'

He was gabbling faster and faster, stuttering over his words. Doris had hinted at things but he hadn't thought she meant anything like this. He now realised as he replayed all her cryptic conversations that this was what she had been hinting at all along.

'I have to go, Rosa.' He stood up and his chair scraped and screeched its way along the floor. 'Do forgive me.'

He was out of the door and running down the street. He wanted to escape but couldn't think of anywhere to go. He felt trapped, he wanted to be back in the bath or in his squat or anywhere away from this oppressive sense of responsibility.

As he ran, he felt the burning in his chest that reminded him of how unfit he was. He couldn't remember the last time he had actually run anywhere and as he had no idea where he was running to, he slowed down to a fast walk. Without consciously thinking about it, he had retraced his steps back to the church and as soon as he realised he was outside it he turned to walk away, not wanting to be near it. A woman's voice called after him.

'Excuse me? Are you the man who works here? The man who does things?'

He looked back to find a woman sat on the stone steps leading up to the front doors. She was huddled in a large brown coat and he could tell from her face that somewhere underneath her mass of brown hair she had been crying.

'I don't know what I'm doing here. I saw you walk out a little while ago and I wanted to say something then but you looked busy. I can come back another time if you want. If you are the person I want that is.'

Before he could answer her, a rush of purple and blue light flew from his chest and surrounded her. As it did so, she passed out and slid unconscious to the floor.

There was something about looking down at Jim's dead body that made Peter want to laugh and cry at the same time. This man, who had mocked and humiliated him for so long, had died and was lying in his own filth on their living room carpet. He hadn't planned this at all; if anyone should have been lying there, it was Jill. He had fantasised about killing her a million times whilst slicing up the roast beef on a Sunday afternoon or mowing his immaculate lawn.

He asked her what Jim had done before he collapsed.

'Nothing, he just collapsed.' Was her answer.

'Then I don't understand why you didn't just phone someone, an ambulance or the police even.'

'I've told you, I just panicked that's all. I didn't know what to do for the best'

'That doesn't sound particularly likely. I think anyone would have phoned for an ambulance unless they had a reason why they didn't want one to come straight away. Was there some reason why you didn't want them here?' His voice was steady with only the slightest hint of malice.

'What is this? The fucking Spanish Inquisition? I don't know why I didn't phone and besides he was dead so quickly anyway, there didn't seem like a lot of a point. Can't you just sort it all out? Can't you say you were in the house when he collapsed?'

'No, I can't.' He replied coldly.

He called the ambulance. They came, took the body and called in the police.

As it turned out, she had flushed the rest of the bag of coke down the toilet. This made the investigation that followed difficult. She got stronger over the weeks that followed, stronger, more cunning and harder. She refined her story to clear herself from any blame. She was shocked that he had cocaine in his blood stream and had no idea how it had got there, and badly cut cocaine at that.

Peter waited for it turn into a murder investigation and for the truth about their affair to come out in the open, but Jill weaved a magic web of lies which entirely exonerated her from any blame.

In the end, this was the story that she told and that was accepted by everyone, everyone except Peter of course.

Jim had been under a lot of stress at work because Peter had become erratic. To relieve the stress, he had obviously got hold of some cocaine from someone unknown to all involved who had told him it would make him feel great for while. He had come over that night, late at night, to have a showdown with Peter about work. In order to pluck up the courage, he had snorted the coke just before coming in. Jill had let him in and he had collapsed there on the carpet in the living room. She had repeatedly tried to get hold of Peter, who was away with the children, for advice but he didn't answer his phone and she had watched Jim die. She tried to help him but he had died so quickly that she thought there was no point in calling the ambulance. She knew she should have called them or the police but had gone into a state of shock.

There were holes and inconsistencies everywhere but Peter was in awe of her ability to spin lies upon lies. Over the two weeks after Jim's death, she was at her most creative. In fact, of all the people that came out worse in the story, it was him. The police questioned Peter about why he had been missing so much from work and why his actions had caused this normally model citizen to turn to drugs. He put it down to stress and a mid-life crisis. They even asked him if he had supplied Jim with the cocaine. He denied this and as this seemed like an unlikely line of enquiry, they left it and him alone.

At Jim's funeral, Peter was overwhelmed by Jill's amazing hypocrisy. She spent the whole event glued to his widow's side, holding her arm, whispering comforting words when she broke down and even weeping with her as the coffin was lowered into the ground. It was only Peter who saw the picture for what it was – it was two widows mourning together.

Peter couldn't face the wake and so he slunk off, leaving Jill and his sons there and headed to see Lauren. He wanted to fuck himself out of the increasing depression that had been growing over him since Jim had died. In reality, he wanted to be held and kissed. The fucking side of his relationship with Lauren was a very minor part of it. Although most visits would end with him reaching some kind of climax, he was more into the slow intimacy of her touch or the way they talked.

He phoned on the way to her flat but only got an answer phone message saying that the number was not available. He presumed she was busy with another client so drove on regardless. He parked across the road from her flat and waited listening to music in the car pressing the redial button on his phone every fifteen minutes or so. Every time he got the same message. He looked up regularly to see if he could work out what was happening in the flat. The curtains were closed like always. At first, he assumed a client had paid for a long session. He felt a stab of jealousy as he thought about this, picturing the images of what she might be doing to him, but as one hour turned into two, he came to the conclusion that she must, in fact, not be working today. He knew that she was like everyone else and took days off and even went on holiday but she hadn't told him that she would be away. Perhaps she was on her period, he knew she took a few days off every month for that, or perhaps she had caught a cold or a virus of some kind.

As he sat there with only time for company, he wondered whether or not she had caught some venereal disease which had caused her to stop working for a while, waiting for the antibiotics to clear it up. It was the one subject he had never brought up with her, and one of his main concerns about visiting Lauren. How often had she caught things? How careful was she? What were the chances of him catching something from her?

When he had been to see other prostitutes, he had always washed his cock and then dipped it in salt water afterwards hoping this would ward off any possible infection. He would check it for spots and signs of redness for days and would consider every time he peed if there were any sensations of pain or stinging. There never had been but he was worried about it nonetheless.

He got out of the car, walked across the street and rang the bell to her flat. He waited, conscious of the possibility of being seen by anyone passing that might know him. He kept his face facing the door, his mouth near the intercom ready to speak.

'I was just passing and thought...' He practised to himself. And just thought what? It was irrelevant anyway as no answer came. He buzzed four times and stood there for a good five minutes. He tried her phone another few times on the way home but got the same lack of response. He had a sick feeling in his stomach as he realised that he had no other way of contacting her. Her records at work all related to the flat and if she wasn't there and she didn't answer her phone, then he was totally cut off from her. He felt like a heroine addict whose dealer had just been put inside. He was shaking, she had become the way he dealt with his anxiety. He considered going to another hooker but this only made him feel more anxious. He now felt that that was cheating on Lauren, he wanted to be true to her. She was the only one he had sex with or made love to in a long time and he didn't want to spoil it.

The house was deserted when he got home. He found a note from his wife saying she had taken the boys back to school and wouldn't be back until late. He didn't like being in the house on his own since Jim's death. The living room had that distinctive new carpet smell. It had been impossible to get the stain of his death out of the carpet so they had it taken up and thrown it away and replaced with another identical one. His blood had gone right through the fabric and had soaked into the floorboards beneath. His wife had the cleaner scrub at the stain for hours with bleach and wire wool but to little avail. Like the spot of blood on Lady Macbeth's hand, it was still there underneath his feet, a small mark but a reminder of his ocean of guilt.

He had become obsessed by the death and whenever he closed his eyes, he would see Jim writhing on the floor, blood pouring from his nose, trying desperately to breath as his lungs bubbled and dissolved. What he wanted to do most in the entire world was to confess. To tell the world what he had done and what had driven him to do it. He wanted a way to scrub himself clean of the punishing weight of his actions and his distracted mind. He wanted to take something to make him feel at peace, but all the drugs he had tried never made him feel like that. He went back to an old friend, alcohol. He poured himself a huge tumbler full of scotch and went out on the patio to look over the garden. He sat wrapped in a large coat being warmed by every sip.

The garden was in the last throws of Autumn, decaying and turning to mulch. Where there had been flowers and colour now stood empty beds and spiky sticks that only a few months before had been abundant with roses of all hues. The horse chestnut had dropped its leaves neatly to the floor around its base, as if a carpet of gold had been laid for the arrival of some visiting dignitary. The lawn needed cutting, not a lot, it was still short enough for most but he would like to get one more cut before putting it to bed for the winter. He looked up into the sky. It was overcast and the light was rapidly failing but he wasn't sure it would rain. If it held off all night and the dew wasn't too heavy, he would get the mower out before lunch and perhaps drift off in the smell of cut grass and poppers or take an E.

Tomorrow he would give the lawn its final cut.

Chapter 11

He whispered something into my ear. I couldn't quite make out what he was saying. He was so close his breath was on my ear. Although I couldn't hear the words clearly, I felt them. They slipped their way into me and flooded through my body. He kissed my cheek, started speaking again and this time I heard him.

'Thank you. For giving me a gift, I will give you one. If you want it.'

I said I did and he touched me on the shoulder. I didn't feel anything at the time, but later I replayed the moment over and over again and at times I imagined I did – that I saw lights, that his voice seemed to change, that I felt a charge hit my body, but none of that happened. In fact, I didn't discover what he had given me until a few hours later.

'Write me a gospel.'

As I left the Church everything it seemed was slightly brighter. I could hear more clearly and my limp was less pronounced.

I said goodbye to Rosa who was radiant and speechless about the night. She promised me she would send the pictures I had taken of her to Ma and my love with them. We kissed and hugged each other on the steps amid the mass of hugging and kissing and crying that was going on.

I hailed a taxi and told him to take me to an airport, I didn't care which. He drove me to

Gatwick which was nearest and I booked the first flight I could get. There were seats on a KLM flight to Bangkok. My final farewell to England was in a departure lounge full of sleepy travellers and duty free shops.

It was only when I checked in that I realised I was one bag light. I had my clothes, I had my cameras but I had no photos. I had left them in the boot of the taxi or maybe even back at the Church, either way, they weren't with me. I would have to take new ones.

During the flight I reached into my pocket to find a pen and found the four pictures I always carried with me. They weren't who I thought they were though. There was the lady in the orange jumpsuit. There was the man waiting in his car. There was the picture of the two women and the girl, although only the airhostess who had first asked me to take the picture could be seen clearly, the mother and daughter had faded and blurred. But, like a magician revealing his final trick, I found no picture of Baby. On the fourth photo was the silhouette of someone walking away from the café in Las Vegas but it wasn't her. It was unmistakably the silhouette of the man in the Church, his outline surrounded by the sparkling lights of my visual anomalies. This in itself wasn't the gift, it was just a neat trick, the real gift was something far more powerful.

If I shut my eyes as I held each picture, I could step into them. I was able to experience their entire lives from start to finish. I could feel everything they felt, taste whatever they tasted. I would only have to hold a picture to know the person. From that day onwards I was never alone.

'Sure is a beautiful night.'

His slow calm way of speaking soothed her. She wanted him to talk to her all the way to Las Vegas. He was enthusiastic about everything, music he'd listened to, films he'd seen, places he'd been and even books he'd read. In half an hour of driving, she knew more about this boy than she had managed to discover about her husband in ten years. He was excited about life and this made him stand out. She didn't know anyone like him. He saw possibilities where none existed. Her town was a dead pool, the folks in it, bloated fish floating on the top of the scum, but he was alive.

'I'm sorry, I've been talking all the way. I haven't let you get a word in. I guess I'm just pumped about starting over. Feels like everything has been wiped clean. As long as my car keeps going and I've got enough cash for gas, then I'm just gonna see where this old road takes me.'

They were parked up at the end of her street. She didn't want to get out of the car. She didn't want to walk back into all the mess inside the house.

'Drive, just drive me away from here', she wanted to say.

He looked in her eyes.

'Well, I guess this is you then. It's been nice sharing a little bit of the journey with you. I hope the next car you buy doesn't have as much of a passion for swimming as your last one.' There was that lovely smile again.

She ached for him. He was all the pure things, all the hope that she had lost or had beaten out of her. He smelt of some scent, some delicate perfume he'd put on hours before but which was now mixed with his sweat. She was overpowered by it. She leant forward and kissed his cheek before climbing out of the car. She shut the door and started to walk away without saying goodbye or thank you.

'Hey.' He called after her. She turned and leant back into the car through the window.

'Is there a diner round here? Somewhere I can get a coffee and a burger at this time of night?'

She pointed down the road.

'Take a left on Mulberry, you'll see Jake's place. He's always open and always there. Some folks reckon he ain't slept a wink since he got back from Vietnam in '75. The coffee ain't nothing special but try the pancakes.'

Before she could turn to leave again, he reached across and touched her hand.

'You want a coffee?'

His touch was gentle, not possessive, not aggressive. She didn't know what to do with this kind of attention.

'I have some stuff to do.'

'And I guess you ought to hit the hay as well.'

'I'm not tired. But I have to clean up the house a bit. You go on. If I can get out, I will. We'll see.'

'I'm Josh, by the way, pleased to meet you, ma'am. Is it all right if I tell you what a fine looking woman you are? I don't mean to be rude or nothin', just thought you might like to know, that's all.'

'Thanks, Josh. Maybe catch you later. If not, you have a good trip, you hear.'

She watched him all the way down the road until he took the left on Mulberry, then walked across the road and up the path through her yard to the front porch. This would be the last time she would enter the house. She knew what she was going to do. She would pack her things, put them all in the truck and at the last moment throw him the keys and be gone. She would try and find the boy and follow him wherever he led her. If she couldn't find him, she'd just keep driving herself until the gas ran out, then she'd hitch her way as far away from there as possible. Wherever she got to, it wouldn't matter. It wouldn't be there and it wouldn't be with him.

She heard the merest click of the gun before the crack and the flash from the darkness. She tilted her head instinctively, years of slaps and cuffs had given her a sixth sense for blows. This nervous tick saved her life. Her head went down and to the right. The bullet passed exactly where her forehead had been. She felt like she'd been smacked round the side of the face.

In that split second she saw him sitting in the chair illuminated dimly by the cigarette in his mouth. From the movement of his hands, she knew he was re-loading for another shot. Without thinking she pulled his hunting knife from her belt and ran towards him, as she knocked the gun out of his hands with a swipe of her left arm, it went off again deafeningly close to her ear. She plunged the knife into his chest but to her amazement it stopped only an inch or so in, caught up on two of his ribs. Looking straight into his eyes she instantly changed her grip and used her right hand as a hammer, slamming it against the handle with every piece of force her ten years of abuse could muster. It sank deep into his chest, right up to the hilt and beyond, until her hand was actually inside him feeling the final pulses of his black heart. His eyes closed and she moved closer to catch his last breath on her face. She breathed it in, took it inside.

'You stole my life, you rotten son of a bitch. Let's call it evens.'

In the bathroom upstairs the cold water she splashed over herself stung her ear and caused the blood to run freely down into the basin.

She turned her head and examined it in the mirror, she wanted to see the damage. At first she began to panic that it was as bad as it looked. The whole left side of her head was a mess. All she could do was to slowly lift the hair away from the wound to examine it in more detail. She felt sick. She didn't want to find that half her head had been blown away.

Her hands were shaking and her legs buckled slightly under her. Her fingers slid through the blood. She had been luckier than she could have hoped, the bullet had merely taken the top of her ear off. More accurately it had torn it in two, both sides flapping apart, glistening in the flickering light thrown by the swinging bulb above her. It was pouring blood, and she looked in the cabinet to find something to quench the flow. She found a sanitary towel and some gauze bandage and made a crude patch after cleaning it up as well as she could. It was throbbing and painful but she knew she'd live.

She put one of her husband's cowboy hats on to cover the bandage. She knew she'd have to get to a hospital soon but she wanted to be out of Florida before then. She threw a few t-shirts and pairs of jeans into a big carpetbag her mother had left her. She took one final look at his corpse as she headed out of the back door.

In the backyard she found a can of gasoline and splashed it all over the house's foundations. She lit herself a cigarette and then was about to drop the Zippo she'd stolen from Hank's pocket when she remembered there was one thing she wanted to keep. She walked back in and went straight downstairs to the cellar. She could see how he'd escaped now, the twisted metal a testament to his determination. She opened the top of the CD player and removed the Supertramp album. She wiped it on her shirt to clean it and slid it into her top pocket.

Standing by the spot the dog had been spiked out in the yard, she looked at the lighter. It was a good lighter and better than any she'd ever had before. It had an American eagle taking flight embossed on it, which seemed somehow apt for her, so she changed her mind and threw her cigarette on the gas instead. She was surprised by the speed it caught. Tinder-dry, the whole house exploded into flame burning her face.

She walked away silhouetted by the glow and headed down to the diner.

She wanted three things: a hamburger to go, Josh and a new life.

———————————————————

The pub, called the 'The Diamond', was down a small country lane a good five miles away from Sandra's flat. As he parked up next to Sukie's car, he was unsure whether or not he should bring Sandra in with him. He turned on the internal light and saw there was a dark puddle on the carpet down in the footwell where she was sitting. He left her behind.

Inside, the pub was small and cosy. Sukie found them a table at the back out of the way, while he went and got the drinks.

'Cheers.'

'Cheers.' He repeated and clinked her glass.

She sank half of the large glass of white wine in one gulp.

'Fuck, I needed that! I've been nervous about seeing Sandy all day. All that fucking stress and she's buggered off already.'

She was happy to talk and he was happy to listen. It gave him time to think.

'If I'm honest with you, I haven't seen Sandy properly for a year or so. I bumped into her the other day at the airport quite by accident and that's how we got back in touch. This was the first time I'd even been to her new place. I mean, I don't know how well you know her...'

'Hardly at all, really.' He said honestly.

'Well she can be a bit of a liability. Don't get me wrong, I love her to bits and she's one of the loveliest people you could ever wish to meet on loads of levels but she's got these weaknesses. Just stupid things really and I shouldn't have let them get to me but I did and we had this falling out and I haven't seen a lot her since.'

'What did you fall out over?'

She fished around in her handbag looking for something. She pulled out an identical picture to the one he had in his top pocket.

'That's me obviously, and that's Poppy, my little girl. It's a long story but she doesn't live with me anymore, she lives with her father down in New York. Anyway, before we split up and when we'd first had Poppy, I asked Sandy if she'd be her godmother. She was over the moon about it and I was really glad I'd asked her. But then on the day of the Christening, she turned up three quarters of an hour late, drunk, with some stoned poet in tow. That was ages ago and we got over that but she just couldn't grow up.

Last year we met up for a meal in town, the night was going really well, we'd had a nice meal and then she decides we need to go dancing. I mean I like a boogie as much as the next person but I was tired and not really up for it, but she insisted. Anyway to cut a long story short, we got into this club, with this awful pounding dance music, and within ten minutes she leaves me for this guy that hits on her. She comes back ten minutes later with two pills in her hands and she says "Sukes come on have an 'E', it'll be fun". Honestly. Do I look like the kind of woman who'd take an E? I said she was being silly and that I wanted to head home, but she just popped one of the pills in her mouth and said "you can't leave me now, Sukes. You've got to stay, come on don't let me take this on my own, you've got to take the other one". I hate that side of her, so I just left her there. We hadn't really spoken since. I missed her loads, but I'm really trying to sort my life out and she's like a fucking hurricane, blowing everything to pieces in her path.' She downed the rest of her glass of wine.

'That's not fair of me, she's one of the kindest, most loyal friends I've got. But I just couldn't take all the other shit that comes with her.'

They sat in silence. She stroked the picture of her daughter that laid on the table in front of them. He felt a terrible guilt that he had looked at that private picture, stolen that intimate moment between mother and daughter and distorted it in his mind over the last forty-eight hours.

'Why were you coming over to see her tonight then? What made you change your mind?'

'After I bumped into her, when I was putting Poppy on the plane to see her dad, she sent me a letter. It was a kind of apology I suppose, although without including the word sorry. But it was also a goodbye. She's always been crap with money and she's always bought things when she shouldn't have, and if there wasn't a man there to buy her the champagne or the coke she wanted, she'd buy it herself even though the airline paid her peanuts. I thought, when I opened it, that she was asking for a loan again, but she wasn't, not this time. She just said she'd really fucked up this time and that her debts were way, way out of control. But basically her plans were to leave them all behind and disappear. She had met some guy on a flight, some Texan, I think. Anyway, he had a load of money and had flown over to see her a couple of times and he'd proposed. She said she was going to leave the country, and leave all the debt and that whole life behind her. She thought the bailiffs would be calling any day and so she planned to just hitch a ride with cabin crew on the next flight to the States and never come back. Well, not until she had enough money to not worry about any of the debts.

I guess I just wanted to say goodbye. Or maybe I wanted to make sure she really knew what she was doing. She doesn't have any family to speak of, and I was just worried about her.'

'So where do you think she is?' He asked.

'Probably in the States by now, I guess. She did a runner once before, left everything behind and headed off to Australia for three years, working in bars. Then one day like a bad penny, she was there on my doorstep again. She's very beautiful and men just seem to fall all over her. She can always find a bed for the night and someone to bail her out. I guess she'll come back when she's drained this guy dry. Or maybe this'll be the one for her and she'll settle down. Who knows? Do you want another drink?'

He watched her as she made her way to the bar. Her small skirt was tight and squeezed her arse as it wiggled. He was trying to work out in his head what all this meant. He had created a person, and this person's name was Sandra Simpson. But Sandra Simpson was now only a name and a head. She was nothing like the visual image he had of her, nothing like the person he thought she was. She didn't speak like he'd imagined, she didn't act in the way he thought she would. In fact, Sandra Simpson, who had seemed so real to him only three hours before was now little more than a shadow being eradicated by a rising sun. Sukie on the other hand was real, did speak like he'd imagined, had the child he thought she had, and in fact in every way except for her name was the living embodiment of his Sandra Simpson. And she was alive which was a decided bonus.

'So tell me about you? How did you meet Sandy again? What did you think you were letting yourself in for?'

'I met her out cycling. My car had had an accident and she…'

'And she hit on you as she cycled past! She is shameless.' Sukie laughed. 'Mind you, you've got to admire her, she never lets an opportunity pass. She must have been all sweaty though, didn't that put you off?'

'She was in a bit of a state. But I was in a state of shock, I think. The accident had shaken me up and I wasn't thinking straight.'

'And she gave you her number and the rest is history, I suppose.'

'Something like that.'

That was how the story would go for years to come when they told anyone how they'd met. Sandy had done a runner but had forgotten to tell the lovely man she tried to pick up just after he'd been involved in an accident. He would say in her defence that he was the one doing most of the picking up. But that was the last they saw of her. They'd heard all her stuff had been repossessed and sold off. She hadn't even given her notice in to her work, she'd just upped stumps and left.

Sukie wanted to know about his life, and he told her about his wife and his boy and that they were separated. He just needed more from life and his wife wanted them to settle down and be a normal suburban couple.

'I feel guilty, but I knew it was a mistake right from the start. I should have had the guts to get out then but it took something like the last couple of days to really wake me up.'

'Why? What's happened these last couple of days to change you so much?'

'A bomb hit my life, metaphorically and as it turned out literally. It just took something like that to make me reassess everything. I've been too safe, and if I'm not careful, I'll go through my whole life being afraid of change. Then one day a bomb goes off and you realise you could have been dead in an instant.'

They chatted away until closing time. She took the piss out of him whenever he got up himself too much and touched his hand when he opened himself up. He told her everything, everything except about Sandra. She told him about her film-making ex-husband who had their daughter six months of the year over in New York and how she was trying to be okay with that. They left the pub after they took the final hint from the landlord when he began to turn the lights out. She turned to him outside and said.

'Would you like to fuck me?'

'What?'

'Would you like to fuck me? I'm sorry, I'm not really good at this. But I could really do with having someone inside me tonight. And I really like you. I know it's a crap thing to say but I'm glad Sandy wasn't there tonight.'

He looked down at her and couldn't find the words he wanted to say.

'I...I...'

'Oh, shit.' She took his lack of response as a rejection.

'I should have just shut up, shouldn't I? Fuck, I'm embarrassed now. Will you forgive me? I don't know what came over me. Let's put it down to the wine. I'll go. It's been really nice meeting you.'

She turned to leave but his hand reached out without any thought at all and grabbed hers pulling her round and back towards him.

'I didn't say no. I was just thrown for a second. This has been a very weird week for me.'

They climbed into the passenger seat of his car and fucked. She frenziedly hitched her skirt up and undid his belt. She found his hard dick and used one hand to pull her panties aside, the other to guide him into her. There was none of the tenderness he'd experienced with Sandra over the last few days. This was a raw living thing. She was biting him and licking him. Her hot tongue was in his mouth, his cock sliding into her.

'Shit, wait we gotta stop!' He was on the verge of cumming.

'Why? Don't you dare stop!'

'No I've got to, sorry, or I'm gonna cum right away.'

'So? Cum! I want to feel you cum inside me.'

'But I haven't got any condoms and I...'

'I'm on the pill, now fuck me and cum.'

Pretty much on the word pill he felt his balls tighten just before he climaxed. His body bucked and bucked with every shudder of his orgasm. In all, the whole act can have taken no longer than five minutes. But it was intense and somehow just what both of them needed. She sat astride him for another ten minutes as they kissed. They both agreed it was probably best if he came back to her place for the night, as he didn't have anywhere else to stay.

She straightened herself out outside the car while he sat inside with the window open.

'So you'll follow me. It's only down the road really, shouldn't take more than twenty minutes.'

She leaned in and gave him a kiss.

'Oh and I wasn't going to tell you, but… well I think I might have put a hole through your bag. Sorry, it's just, I kicked out during… well you know…and my heel went through it. I had to yank it out. It got quite stuck. I hope I haven't broken anything.'

'I heard about you from my grandfather. He sent me a letter. Said you'd helped him loads and that if I ever felt lost, then maybe you could help me.'

The colour had come back into her cheeks now and the redness around her eyes was fading nicely back to a quiet pink.

Steven had carried her into the hall and had laid her down on the dais. Dodds had splashed some cold water in her face to bring her round. She was sitting up now looking at the two of them looking at her.

'Who was your grandfather, darling?' Dodds was patting her knee for comfort.

'William Caster.'

'I don't think I know him…'

'Bill, he was known by everyone as Bill. In his letter he said he started coming here after mum died.'

The penny dropped.

'Bill! You're Bill's granddaughter! Oh my goodness. It's Charlotte, isn't it?'

'I'm sorry about your loss. I didn't really know him very well. But he seemed like a very lovely man.' Steven said and helped her over to a chair.

There was something about the way her hand felt on his that shook him slightly. Its soft warmth reminded him of how his mother would take his hand on cold dark nights and lead him through the nightmares that tortured his childhood. She would sit on his bed and hold him as he feverishly tried to escape from the fear that gripped him, this act could chase away the demons haunting him. It was the feeling of unconditional love.

'I think he must have written it to me on the day he died. After I got the letter, I tried to phone a few times but got no answer, eventually I called the neighbour to see if he was all right, and that's when they found him.'

She looked like she might weep again but she held it back.

'I'm sorry. I don't even know what I'm doing here. I feel stupid for being like this. This really isn't me at all. I think it's just the fact that I hadn't seen him for a few years and the last time I did we had a discussion which got very angry and we hadn't spoken at all since then. I didn't even know he knew my address. But the letter was so beautiful, so full of love. He was the only family I had.'

Now she did begin to weep again. Dodds went off to make her a cup of tea and left Steven alone with her. If it had been anyone else, he would have put his arm round them to console them, but he felt differently about her and he thought that if he did hold her, it would be as much for him as it would be for her. There was no voice either in his head telling him what to say or do, it was as if everything had left him the moment he'd seen her. He wanted to be able to say something to reassure her but anything that he would say at this point would only be from himself and that he felt wasn't sufficient, so he just sat there patiently until Doris returned with a sweet tea.

'I need to know that he really forgives me, I suppose. I know in his letter he said he did, but he said perhaps you,' here she looked straight at Steven, 'might be able to contact him or give me something that would make me understand. He said you spoke to him and gave him something, some kind of gift and he said that perhaps you could give it to me. I don't know if I even believe in any of this, but this has hit me much harder than I thought it would. Maybe because now they're all gone, I suddenly feel very alone.'

'What do you want forgiveness for?' Steven asked flatly and bluntly.

'I... I've just done things that I know he didn't like me doing. I don't feel bad about doing them. But I know it caused him pain and I'm sorry for that, he never really understood.'

'I have no message for you.'

Steven left her and his aunt and walked out of the chapel.

He found himself in a large park at the top of Shooter's Hill. He sat on a bench and watched the sun go down on London. The purples and pinks made the city look like a painting. He stayed there well into the night and when it had got very cold and his limbs ached, he stood up and walked and walked again. He had nowhere to go but back to Dodds.

She was already asleep by the time he got there and when he climbed into his bed, he found she had warmed it with an electric blanket.

He couldn't stop his mind racing. Every time he shut his eyes a thousand images and thoughts infested his brain. Faces and places and seasons flicked through him and her face was always there, slipped subliminally in, all over his imagination. At some point he fell asleep and at some point he woke up.

He made his mind up to leave the Church. He didn't want to hold people's lives and expectations in his hands any longer. What he wanted was to be normal. It was as if a veil had been lifted. He would like to start a new life and he wanted to start it with someone he hardly knew.

Dodds was flying around all morning, cleaning and writing letters and there seemed no good time to break the news to her. So he left it. He went to the service with her that evening. By now, there were three services a week all oversubscribed, two mornings and one evening. He sat there quietly on the stage in front of the audience and as he looked out on them, he could only just about make out the auras that he had been able to see so clearly only a day before. It was as if he was tuning them out, as if he had finally got some control over when and what he wanted to see. A mist of colours of all hues drifted above them dimly, but at the back of the hall there was one bright aura. He recognised it before he had even seen her face. She had come again.

He stood up to see her and as he did all eyes were drawn from Doris to him. A murmur of expectation ran around the room. He had never stood up before and now it looked like he was going to address them all, another thing he'd never done. Most of them had never even heard his voice. As their hopes rose, he found himself blinded by the jump in the colour and intensity of the energy all around them. The whole hall right up to the ceiling was filled with hope; it was becoming a collective curtain of electricity, like the aurora borealis contained in a small box. Doris stopped speaking and turned to look at him.

'Steven, did you want to speak?'

He then began what would later come to be known as The Transformation. He looked at his hands but found he couldn't actually see the fingers or palms; all he could see was a brilliant ball of white light which surrounded them. He turned them up to the heavens and light shot out from him, across the room. As it hit each of them, it raised them to their feet. Like a Mexican wave they began standing. He stepped down into them and laid his hands on them one by one letting each sit down as he released them. There were four people in the hall that he whispered to. They were the last ones to hear 'the message' from his actual lips.

As with many events of this nature, in years to come many of the people in the room at that time would come to claim he spoke to them, and in fact many people would claim they were in the room who had never even heard of Steven at that time. The last person he reached was Charlotte. He looked deep into her eyes and they fell into each other. For a brief moment nothing else existed except the two of them. He gave everything he had to her.

'All this I did for you and I give it all away to be with you.'

She looked frightened but nodded and that was all it took to make a contract that would last for as long as he lived. A small smile came over his face and he took her hand and kissed it. He walked back to the podium and stood in front of them all. He opened his arms again and clapped his hands together suddenly with a loud clack. With that it was over, with that he stepped away from whatever 'it' was, for the last time.

He spoke to them quietly, barely above a whisper, but everyone heard him clearly.

'I release you. This is my final gift. I have given you all I have. Now you must release me. You will not see me again.'

With that he walked down the aisle and taking Charlotte's hand he entered the world again, a normal person. He had been on a journey for over twenty years and now he arrived at the end of it and it was a journey to normalcy, from the sacred to the wonderful beauty of the profane. His head had sorted itself out.

They kissed on the steps outside and there were no fireworks, no auras, no energy exchanges, it was just a kiss. The most perfect kiss he could ever have imagined.

'I don't love you and haven't done for a long time. I'm not sure if I ever really loved you, if I'm honest with you. I think it's best if we call it a day.'

Peter had woken up in the middle of the night, found himself still on the patio lying on a lounger, a smashed glass and bottle at his feet and had made it as far as the living room before crashing for the rest of the night on the couch. Jill had woken him at nine by opening the curtains. She was already showered, dressed and looked immaculate. She had asked if they could have a chat. She looked serious and business-like.

'You go and shower and get yourself shaved. I'll make you a coffee.'

He knew from this that something fairly monumental was coming as she never offered to make him anything without wanting something in return.

Twenty minutes later he was sitting at the kitchen table, a coffee steaming away in front of him, and she was openly proclaiming her lack of love for him. She was speaking to him in the same unemotional way that she had always spoken to him. Even when telling him that their marriage was over, she showed no sign of remorse, guilt or even sympathy.

'I would like a divorce, I guess, is what I'm saying. I want to sell this place and move on with my life. I can't stay here, not after… well, you know, after what happened. '

She was wiping the surfaces of the kitchen as she spoke. As if attempting to clean up the mess her life had got itself in to. To her it was just as simple as that. She was just wiping him away.

'I've had someone draw up a settlement that I think is more than reasonable. I'll keep all the profits from the house sale. I'll keep my car and all the belongings in the house and we'll divide all the current savings we have in half. You'll continue to pay for the children's education and give me a monthly income but it's well within what you earn.'

This amounted to a lot of money and as he sipped his coffee and nodded agreement, he tried to work out roughly how much it was and then tried to average that out by the amount of times they'd had sex over their marriage. He was pretty sure that in purely monetary terms it would have been far cheaper for him to have just spent the last two decades hiring a hooker full time.

He couldn't work out how he felt. He had wanted to be out of this marriage for so long that he couldn't remember a time when he had wanted to actually be in it. But now, faced with the reality of it, he once again felt disempowered. She was doing it *to* him, again. She was controlling his life just as she had done all the way down the line. He should have been the one to do this. He should have been the one to make the break. At least she could have the decency to show some kind of sense of regret. He could feel an anger building up him that he was afraid of. It was bubbling away.

'I see, and why do you think I'll give you all that?' He was quiet as he said this, it was almost a whisper.

'What?' She looked somewhat shocked that he had even spoken back to her.

'What if I find those terms unreasonable? What if I don't even want to give you a divorce?'

'Look, Peter, let's not even do this, okay? Let's just make this as amicable as possible, shall we? And anyway, you can't be happy?'

He wasn't happy that was true enough but this wasn't making him any happier.

'What grounds for the divorce were you thinking of citing?'

'I was just going to put it down to irreconcilable differences and leave it at that. Look, these things are quite straightforward nowadays, there's no need to make a big deal out of it.'

'Or perhaps we could divorce on the grounds of you fucking my business partner for over a decade and in that time also fucking anything else with two legs that happened to cross your path, how about that? Although I'm not sure how that would go down with the ladies at the bridge club or the golf club. Especially as you fucked half their husbands.' His voice had risen just a little and he bit out every word, spitting them from him like acid he hoped would burn her face.

'Are you out of your fucking mind? How dare you…' She shouted slamming her hand down on the draining board.'

'How dare I? How dare I?' He repeated, shouting back at her. 'How dare you! You fucking cunt. I came home and saw you fucking him in our own bed. Years ago now, and I've caught you out so many times, it's beyond a fucking joke. Do you know what they call you down at the squash club when they think I can't hear them? You're the "bike". You're the one anyone can fuck. And I've taken this for years. I've had every shred of dignity taken from me by you. I've sucked up your shit all this time. Don't ask me why, because I honestly have no idea. And then you stand there having the audacity to say you're divorcing me. You killed your lover in our own house, you drained me dry of everything I am, and now you want to take the house and my money as well? And you expect me to just roll over like I always have done?'

By now he was shouting right into her face, his spit flying from him all over her. She tried to push past him to leave. There was fear in her eyes. He hadn't seen this before in his whole life with her and he liked it.

'Where do you think you're going?' He grabbed her and squeezed her arms hard. She screamed.

'Let me go.'

He dragged her over to the table and forced her to sit down.

'You're not going anywhere until we've got this finished. You're going to apologise to me for everything you've done to me, for stealing my fucking life and throwing it away. And then *I'm* going to tell *you* what's going to happen, I'll tell you what the settlement will be.'

She was shaking and there were tears in her eyes and she was wildly looking around the room for a way out.

'I don't know what you're talking about. I have nothing to say or apologise for. I've been everything you needed; I've been your trophy wife, haven't I? I've been to your stupid work dinners; I've made this house for you. I've made you what you are. You couldn't even dress yourself properly without me.'

There was still fire in her and two minutes of shouting at her wasn't going to shift a power balance that had existed for years. The more she spoke, the more she grew in confidence and strength again.

'I should have married a real man when I had the chance. You're a weak spineless mouse. So what if I slept with some other men? What, did you really expect me to do? Stay faithful to you? Christ, consign myself to a life without orgasms, I don't think so, and besides I presumed you were doing the same thing. I thought it was an accepted arrangement.'

He was shaken again by her words. She knew how to manipulate him even now when he had finally found the strength to stand up to her. He knew he could never beat her in an argument, he just didn't have the stomach for it and however much he wanted to lash out at her physically right at that precise moment, he couldn't do it. He had missed his chance to kill her when Jim had snorted the coke instead of her. That was the only kind of murder he would have been capable of, something at a distance.

'You can have the house. You can have all the shit in it that you've bought over the years, you can have all of that. But there's only one thing I won't let you have. I won't let you have the boys. I won't let you fuck them up in the same way you've done to me. You can have everything you want but the boys stay with me.' He calmed down when he said this.

His prior sudden outburst had exhausted him and he was on the point of crying when he started talking about the boys. They were the only things he truly cared about in the world. He could lose everything else; in fact he would be relieved to start again free of all the clutter he hated, but he wanted to start again with them. He would take them out of boarding school and be there for them every day.

'I don't think that's appropriate. I'm sorry.' She was in control again and the fear in her eyes had gone as she watched him slump down in the chair opposite her.

'I want them, Jill. I'll give you all the money you want, for fuck sake, have all the savings, all the money, I know that's all you care about. Take it all but leave me the boys.'

'I can't.' She wanted that to be the end of the conversation but Peter wouldn't leave it alone.

'It's all I'm asking for. You don't even really love them. The boys are…'

'Jim's.'

He knew just by looking at her face that she wasn't lying. It would have been quite within her to make something like this up, some final coup de grace to win an argument or to crush him, but she wasn't saying this with any of her usual triumphalism. She was just stating a fact. If there was any part of him that had not been broken, it was shattered now. He suddenly felt as if he was falling. The world was spinning and he had to hold onto the table to keep himself upright. He was aware of her standing near the door and he knew that she was looking at him but he couldn't move. He was having difficulty breathing and he wanted to slip to the floor and curl up in a ball.

'I'm going out for a bit to my sister's. I'll be back later just to pick up some things. I'll give you some time to think about everything. If you're not around when I come back, I'll understand. I think it's probably best if I stay at Lisa's for a few days until you find yourself somewhere to live and then I'll move back in to arrange the sale and make all the moving arrangements. I'm using John as my solicitor, I'm sure we can talk through him if you need to know anything.'

With that she left.

He heard her walk down the corridor, open the door and drive away. He heard everything but saw nothing. His eyes weren't working properly everything had gone very dark. He slowly passed out.

Chapter 12

'And if that don't work, we'll try again and again 'til it does – besides all this practice sure is fun.'

He was still inside her and she looked up at his beautiful red face as a bead of sex sweat dripped from his nose on to her top lip, she flicked out her tongue and licked the salt tear. He slowly took himself out of her. She grabbed his tight arse and slammed him back. She held him there kissing his neck.

'I love you!' She whispered with every kiss.

He started to laugh as it tickled and eventually he had to take her hands off him and pin her down to actually escape her clutch.

'I love you too, you crazy bitch. Now come on, let me go, will you. I gotta be at work by ten and it's already fifteen after nine. If you're a good girl, we can try again and again tonight when I get back after my second shift.'

She watched as his sculpted young body walked out of the bedroom. She heard the shower turn on. Remaining on the bed, she lifted her legs over her head and supported this gymnastic move with her hands underneath her lower back. She shut her eyes and visualised the sperm inside swimming through the dark of her vagina in a desperate race to be the first to find the magic prize egg. In her head, they all wore Fifties-style swimming hats and bathing costumes and when they got close enough to see the huge egg, it wasn't in fact an egg at all but a giant birthday cake covered in cream and bright candles which acted like landing lights, guiding them in to a successful completion of this marathon mission.

'What are you doing?' He was laughing again.

He was always laughing. She loved it, she even laughed herself now, a noise that her body had had to re-learn. He was dressed in his tuxedo and looked like James Bond.

'Just helping them, I figure on how they might be quicker if they was swimming downhill.'

'My boys don't need any help. Believe me, they come from good stock, everyone in my family has always been a great strong swimmer. Now shouldn't you be getting off your beautiful arse and getting to work as well?'

She dropped her legs back down and rolled over, burying her head in the pillow.

'Don't want to,' She said barely audibly through her self-imposed muffler.

The sudden stinging of a smack hit her arse and she flipped over angry with that black look in her eyes. But there was Josh smiling again, and she knew it was only a playful thing. She smiled back. It was a reminder that she hadn't totally left everything behind, even after she had stabbed him through the heart, he was still capable of reaching out from the dead to slap her again.

'All right I'll get out of bed in a minute. I don't have to be at the store until eleven. Damn, I hate that shit hole.'

He knelt down by the side of the bed and took her hand and kissed it.

'I know you do, honey, but it'll only be for a little while. If I finish off all these croupier qualifications, I'll be earning enough to keep us and the kids, when they come along. Until then, if we want to keep this place, or get out of here to a nicer place in a better part of the town, we need your income as well.'

He had real love in his eyes, and everything he said to her was thought out and reasoned. She was unused to this, and she sometimes had to stop herself from kicking against it. She was so conditioned to arguing and fighting against everything that dumbfuck had said, it was hard to listen when someone was talking to you, not at you, and even harder to accept that they truly had your best interest at heart.

She leant over and kissed his soft lips and then off he went downtown.

She got up slowly and walked around the blind-shaded apartment tidying up the remains from last night's 'pizza and beer' DVD watching session. In the shower she washed and hated the fact that some of his cum dripped from her. Was there enough left inside her to do the job? She would try and try again until she got pregnant.

She watched television while she dried her hair, smoked a cigarette and drank a coffee almost simultaneously. By the time she put the nasty nylon brown uniform on, she only had twenty minutes to get the fourteen blocks to the store.

Checking herself in the mirror before she left, she looked at the name stitched onto the uniform, Eve. She liked that name, it was the name she wished she'd been called. Josh only knew her as Eve, as did everyone else here.

She was slowly pulling a life for Eve together, she faked and lied her way into getting a new bank account, new ID, new all sorts of things. Vegas she had found was an ideal city to reinvent yourself in if you could hook up with the right people. For the first few months she'd work in a strip joint behind the bar, dancing occasionally if she needed extra cash to pay for her new self to be created. Everyone that came into the seedy bar she considered a possible contact, someone who might be able to help her smoke screen existence. It was easier than she had imagined and she had only blown a couple of guys for help, but this she saw as a necessary evil to be with Josh. He would never need to know, and he would certainly never understand but what she did to keep them together was small potatoes, nothing worth even feeling guilty about. After all, this time it was all done out of love not hate, and that made all the difference.

She only worked there until she'd got everything she needed to move on and then she quit to work at a local Seven Eleven. This was only meant to be a temporary thing until she could find a proper job. Eve fancied being a realtor but that might take a little while. For now she was happy just being what she was and happy to have wages that were her own but that helped keep them together.

As she stepped out of the apartment, the desert heat hit her. It was dry and baking, unlike the clammy sweltering humidity of Florida. In this heat, the sweat dried on you quick as it seeped out. The sky above her was a brilliant blue even through her pink heart-shaped shades.

There wasn't a bruise on her body. Her legs, so long kept in the dark of sweat pants to avoid the stares of people who might want explanations as to what the large welts were, were now no longer pallid white, but a rich brown and she liked watching them as she walked, especially in her red 'fuck me' heels. Everything about her was reborn. She actually felt younger than her thirty years. The scars of her previous existence were fading slowly, now only thin white line reminders of the red gashes.

She clocked in, took the trainers out of her bag, put her shades away and started work, glad to be out of the heat and into the chilled air-conditioned shop. Maria was on the next checkout. She loved Maria and Maria loved Eve. She had adopted her as her surrogate daughter. Her own daughter had come with her from Mexico but had soon fallen in with a bad crowd and had left her alone here in Vegas, this city without a heart. Or if it did have a heart, it wasn't a real one. It was a mechanic ticking slot machine of a heart.

No one belonged here, but everyone was accepted in this manmade Sodom in the sand. Eve loved it.

Maria hadn't heard from Juana, her real daughter, for two years, the last contact she'd heard was that she was in Texas but that was a while ago and now she didn't know if she was alive or dead.

'How are you, my darlin'?' She would always ask as Eve sat down behind the till.

'Good, mama, how are you?'

'Still no word, but I went to the chapel twice yesterday, and lit candles for her. Perhaps her name will protect her, it means 'gracious is God', did you know that?'

She had told her that everyday they had worked together.

'No, I didn't know that. It's a beautiful name. I'm sure, she'll be fine. I'm sure, there's nothing to worry about. People sometimes just need some time to find out who they really are. She'll walk through that door someday and it will all be better.'

She knew that this was unlikely but then when she looked at her own life, perhaps anything was possible. Perhaps Juana was sleeping like she had been and would wake up like she had, crack open the chrysalis and fly home to her mother.

'Tell me, have you done the test?'

Eve loved listening to Maria's thick accent and the way she spoke so quickly, like everything she said was important and had an urgency to it. Floridians spoke slowly and lazily as if weighed down by boredom and a sense that life was pointless and that there was really little point in talking, after all, what difference would it make.

'I done the test.'

She served another customer as she chatted away. They always spoke like this, just chatting away and swiping items as they were put in front of them, just taking time to look up enough to say the amount needed and a cursory

'Thank you, have a nice day.'

'And… well… what'd it say?'

'Not this time, Mama. But we had fun this morning trying again.'

Maria giggled at the innuendo.

'He's a good man that Josh. I see the way he looks at you when he comes to pick you up. He's hungry for you. Hungry in love is a good way to be. It means there's passion. He wants to eat you all up. You are a lucky girl. If I could find me a man like that I would spend all day in bed trying again as well. You are lucky I'm not twenty years younger. I would have given you a run for your money. I was beautiful once. Hey, don't laugh, it's true.'

Eve could see how beautiful she must have been. Although her hips and arse had spread from years of sitting on chairs, shift after shift, she still had a fine and exquisite face. As a younger lady, she must have been stunning. She could see her dancing into the night with that little giggle exactly the same, drawing men in like bees to a honey pot, and like many good Catholic girls, she would have teased and pleased many of them and then be cleansed by confession.

'What do you mean, Mama, you were beautiful once? You are now. That's why I won't leave you alone with him. You keep your hands off, you hear!'

They both laughed.

She picked up the gum scanned it and noticed the thin black belt with its silver buckle, simple plain and perfect holding up the black suit trousers. She looked up the white shirt and dark blue tie into the man's black shades.

'That'll be...'

She stopped as he reached into his jacket pocket for something that she already knew was not small change. He flipped open the leather wallet that he'd produced and showed her his ID. He began to speak but she couldn't hear the words, everything went into slow motion. She stood, walked around to him, turned her back and offered him her wrists, which he dutifully cuffed. Maria she knew was screaming and crying but there was nothing she could say or do to comfort her. She sounded a long way off anyhow, like she was calling to her from the end of a long tunnel, and besides she wasn't crying out for her she was crying out for Eve and as quickly as she had made up Eve that night outside the diner in Florida, this man had made her disappear when called her by her given name.

As the two agents led her out of the store to the car on the pavement, she knew that this had been a dream, all of this, and now it was time to really wake up.

'That's life, that's what all the people say...' He sang along with Frank Sinatra blasting out of the French windows.

The barbecue sizzled as he squashed a burger onto the grill, squeezing out the excess fat onto the hot coals. Dan passed him a chilled bottle of beer from the cool box next to his lounger and squinted up into the sun as he reached up.

'I still don't understand how you pulled all this off.'

'All what off?'

Before Dan could answer, Sukie's head poked out of the bedroom window.

'Oi, shitface?'

'Yes, my love', he said turning round to look at her, Juliet on her balcony.

'Where's the ladder?'

'What ladder?'

'The stepladder, dimbo. I need to find some of Poppy's stuff before she gets here next week. I think I put it in those high cupboards above her bed.'

'It's er... is it in the utility room downstairs? I think that's where I saw it. The removal men had it when they were putting the stuff in the library.'

Her head disappeared inside.

He popped the cap off the beer by knocking it down on the side of the barbecue. It fizzed and frothed. He slurped it back, then wiped his lips with the back of the hand.

'All this. The new house, the beautiful wife, your own company. How did you get from being that fuck-up at the bowling alley to this?' Dan continued.

'Yeah that was the low point, I think. I was having a really bad couple of days, and I think I needed to go through all of that to stop treading water and start actually living. That's what the company's all about, I guess. Helping people to deal with change on a corporate level. It was Sukie's idea and who'd have guessed we'd work so well together.' He chinked his beer bottle with Dan's.

'Cheers.'

She climbed up the ladder and pulled down all the boxes one by one. They were full of old letters and chequebooks and receipts. This stuff should have gone into the office and not into the bedrooms. There was none of Poppy's stuff in any of them. She wanted to decorate her room before she got there to make sure she didn't feel too weird about being in a new house. With the baby on the way, she wanted her to know that this was still very much her home as well. Most of the rooms had been cleared of the mountains of boxes and crap and had started to take shape. She hoped Poppy loved it here as much as she did.

She looked out of the window down at him hooking a burger into a bun and passing it over to Dan. She liked Dan. He reminded her a lot of the relationship she had with Sandra. He was their fucked-up single mate who turned up to drink too much and talk about all the fun he was having while at the same time feeling desperately sad at how his life was turning out. At least Sandy didn't do that anymore, in fact her life seemed to have calmed down remarkably. Dan took a big bite of his burger and then hopped around wafting a hand across his open mouth. She opened the window again.

'That'll teach you, you greedy sod. Patience is a virtue.'

'Fuck, that's hot!' He managed to garble out through the ball of hot meat he was juggling in his mouth.

She laughed but then all of a sudden was taken over by a wave of pain like a knife slicing across her abdomen. She let out a loud exhalation of air and a low growl. Both he and Dan turned round to look at her. Her face was a tight grimace of agony. However, almost as suddenly as it had come, it went and she was left feeling shaken up and pale but fine again.

'You okay?' he called up.

'Yeah. Sorry to scare you. Just got a nasty twinge. Really weird.'

'Do you want me to call the doctor?'

'No silly, I'm fine, it's just one of those pregnancy things. Who knows what's going on? But maybe you ought to get on with painting the nursery and not leave it until next weekend after all.'

The muscles in her stomach although not actually still in pain, had the memory of pain in them like a dull ache and she tried to stretch them out, however, with the bump this big it was difficult to do any meaningful callisthenics. She was determined to continue her hunt for Poppy's stuff so she wandered around the upstairs looking in cupboards and under beds but to no avail. On the landing it occurred to her that maybe they had gone up into the loft. She looked up at the trap door in the ceiling and noticed a padlock across it that she hadn't noticed before. She got the ladder and climbed up, slowly and carefully. A small lock had been fixed to the right-hand side just by the brass ring used to pull the door downwards. She put her finger in the ring and pulled to see how strong the lock was, she pulled again harder hoping to pull it off.

'What are you doing up there?' He shouted as he ran up the stairs towards her.

She was so surprised by this sudden outburst that for a second she lost her balance and wobbled on the steps. He was there at the bottom of them in a flash, steadying them and her. He looked angrily at her as she climbed down.

'What were you doing up there?'

'I was just looking for Poppy's stuff. I thought it might be up there.'

'Well it's not!'

'How do you know?'

'Because I know what's in the attic, and Poppy stuff isn't up there.' He softened his face and brought her into him for a cuddle. 'You've got to be careful. You can't go climbing up ladders in your condition. I'd hate anything to happen to you or the baby. Sorry if I snapped, I just got scared seeing you up there, that's all.'

'Why's there a lock on the door? Was that there when we moved in?'

'No. I put it on for safety. It's to stop the thing from coming down on its own. It was a bit loose and I had horrible visions of the internal ladder coming down some time and knocking someone's head off. Just thought it was safer to keep it in place with that lock until I've got the time to get up there and properly fix it.'

He shepherded her downstairs and sat her down on the patio. They ate, drank and laughed with Dan until the heat of the summer's day began to cool and the sun dipped behind the house. Dan made his excuses and headed out to meet another date from the internet dating site he'd joined.

They settled down in front of the television and cuddled. They played 'Who Wants To Be A Millionaire' against each other and the stupid contestants on the telly and then when that ended, flicked up the menu showing them what other delights might be on later. Sukie noticed something on Sky Movies.

'Look at that, Sandy would kick herself, she's missing "It's A Wonderful Life" it's on in half an hour. She loves that movie. Shall we watch it? I haven't seen it for ages. Then I might email her and tell her we were thinking about her. Haven't heard from her for a couple of weeks.'

'Perhaps she's busy, you know what she's like. Well, if we're going to snuggle down, do you fancy some ice cream? I've got some Ben and Jerry's in the fridge.'

'That would be perfect.'

He kissed her forehead and headed for the kitchen. In the corridor, he called back.

'Do you fancy a coffee?'

'Yes, please.'

He could hear her purring like a cat with joy.

First he went into the downstairs bathroom and took something from the cabinet. In the kitchen he took out a pot of Chunky Monkey from the freezer and put three small tablets that looked like sweeteners into Sukie's cup and stirred it well as he poured the coffee from their filter machine. As he pulled the spoon out, he was about to lick it clean before throwing in the sink but had second thoughts.

He watched her drink her coffee, then watched as her head began to nod downwards and then snap up again as she tried to shake the effects off. It was a losing battle and within ten minutes she was out cold. He lifted her up and carried her to bed. Although she was only slender, with the extra weight of the baby and the awkwardness of her new shape, it was quite a struggle. He sat with her for ten minutes stroking her head and looking at how beautiful she was. He kissed her tummy and held his hands on it, hoping for a kick from his new son or daughter.

'I love you', he whispered to it.

He unlocked the padlock, took the pole with its brass hook out of his wardrobe and pulled down the hatch. The ladder came down towards him as the door swung open. He caught it and pulled it down the last few feet before climbing up and into the loft space. He moved some boxes around until he found two marked with a big red marker pen reading 'Poppy's Stuff'. He carefully took them both downstairs and mingled them in with the boxes in the utility room.

Back in the loft, he rearranged more of the boxes until he could gain clear access to the humming small box freezer hidden under the eaves. He opened the door and sat in front of her again.

'Hello lovely, how've you been? Sorry it's been a while but things have been kind of manic.'

She stared back at him with only one eye. She now wore a patch over the other eye to cover the damage done by Sukie's heel, which had pierced right through her left eye and into her brain. He had plaited her hair and she was wearing the diamond necklace that he had bought her for their anniversary two years earlier. There were some signs of deterioration on her flesh, which was now a translucent light blue. He had designed a metal plate and collar for her, which was screwed into her frozen neck. This made her look much neater her thought. He lifted her out and kissed her softly.

'We must write Sukie an email later, she's been missing you, but before that I've got a real treat for you. What would you say to an old movie and some Ben and Jerry's?'

He brushed the light dusting of frost from her cheeks.

'Yes, I think it is, James Stewart, you're right.' And with that he closed the freezer door and headed downstairs.

Steven woke up and watched the way the light seeping through the curtains played over her body. She was lying on her side half under the duvet. If he let his eyes drift out of focus her contours looked like a beautiful series of rolling hills, gently undulating in silky smooth perfection.

He hadn't had sex with a woman in years, and he had never experienced anything like the night before. She had run him a bath when they got back to her flat, bathed him with oils and massaged his head. She'd shaved him and then dried him in large hot towels straight from the radiators.

She laid him down on her bed and kissed him softly over every part of his body. When she reached his lips she lay naked on top of him down the full length of his body. Her tongue entered his mouth as she slowly pushed down to take him inside her. They lay like that for what seemed like hours, her lightly moving up and down the shaft of his cock. He had never experienced this kind of intimacy, there was something happening, a type of joining of two people or two souls that he had never known was possible. Without making any sound she wept on to his chest but wouldn't let him try to talk or ask any questions. They continued in silence, he kissed her face and let the tears roll onto his lips, his tongue tasting the salt, he wanted to take these inside him to absorb her sadness. He knew though that these were tears for a life now finished and the tears of rebirth. Behind them, she was smiling and he knew that she felt the same wholeness being with him that he felt being with her. Perhaps this was what he knew was different about it, it was a two-way experience, not only did he give her all his heart and love, she did the same and he was able to accept it without any filter of scepticism or past experience. This was a pure act of love for both of them.

He was pleased to be able to watch her while she slept so soundly and deeply. He had a great desire to touch her, to just place his hand on her hip to make sure she was really there and that this was reality and not just another dream or hallucination. All he wanted from now on was solid, grounded, real things. He wanted to able to trust his five senses again.

She sighed deeply and opened one eye scrunching up her face.

'Morning.'

'Morning.' He said back, wondering what would happen next. He was worried it would be awkward but she snuggled into him and kissed his neck. He held her in his arms and it was all right, there was no break in the continuity of affection.

'I need to brush my teeth.' She laughed. 'I've got terrible morning dragon breath. What do you fancy for breakfast? I fancy something scrummy, something like smoked salmon and scrambled eggs. Something deliciously decadent.'

When she finished saying this, a look of concern came over her face, perhaps he might prefer a more ascetic start to the day and would be offended by her suggestion, but she needn't have worried.

'God, that sounds lovely. Can I help you with it?'

'Of course, if you'd like. Do you want to use the bathroom after me? I thought I might jump in the shower. You could hop in as well.' She kissed him again and nuzzled into to his chest.

'I haven't got anything with me.'

'That's okay, you can borrow anything of mine. I think I've even got a spare toothbrush somewhere if you want.'

'No. I meant I haven't got anything. I've pissed my life away. I've fucked up everything I've ever touched. And now I have nothing, apart from a few clothes back at my aunt's. I just thought I ought to tell you. I didn't want to start anything under false pretences. Pretty much what you see now is what you get. I did have a house and some money, but I signed it over to the Church.'

He felt this was a bit like a confessional or a statement to AA. Now he waited to find out whether or not he was at the start of his rehabilitation or whether or not this was just a pleasant interlude before it began.

'So?' Was all she said.

She kissed him again and climbed out of the bed. He watched her perfect body stretch. She peeked out at the day and gave a disappointed moan at the grey day that met her.

'So, I can't give you things. I don't even know what I can do now to actually earn money or even who I am really.' He apologised.

'I've made loads of money over the last few years. I've got a couple of flats that I rent out. I don't need anything financially if that's what you're worried about. As for you not knowing who you are, you can join the club. But I think if you're up for it, I'd like to have a go at this. I'd like to try to make this work, and see where life takes us. How does that sound?'

They made love in the shower until their legs were both shaking like jelly and they were in serious need of some nourishment. They ate together and stared a lot. They each took it in turn to tell the story of their lives and Steven left nothing out. He told her about his drugs. He told her about his ex-wife and the child he had but didn't know. He told her about the two years in the bath and every two minutes or so he told her loved her to reassure her and himself that it would all be okay. She told him about her childhood, about her father's death, about her degree and about her life as a prostitute. He had always sort of known this about her even without knowing and it made no difference to him whatsoever, but for her it was the major confession of her life. She was so worried that he would leave when he heard it that she cried when all he did was give her a kiss and ask if she wanted more tea.

They went back to bed and made love again and slept well into the afternoon.

'I should really go back to my aunt's and talk to her about everything. I guess I'll pick up the few bits and pieces I have and find somewhere else to stay tonight. But can I see you again, very soon?'

'You'll see me tonight. Bring your stuff here. I want you to.'

Walking up the path to his aunt's house, he could see her through the front windows ironing in the living room while she watched some chat show on the telly.

He let himself in. She was overjoyed to see him.

'Steven, where've you been? I was worried about you. Last night was amazing. I don't know where to begin, after you left, the whole room… everyone… it was like a fire spreading through the…'

'Can we have a tea and a chat, Dodds?'

'Of course we can.' She picked up the remote control that was lying next to the iron on the ironing board and switched off the TV. She put the ironing away and headed for the kitchen to put the kettle on. He followed her and got the mugs down from the cupboard.

'Dodds, I won't be coming back to the Church again. You know that, don't you? And I'll be moving out of here today. I know it's sudden but I think I need to do it.'

'What do you mean? Don't be a silly boy.' Although she had a joking tone in her voice, he could tell that underneath she was shaking.

'I can't thank you enough, really I can't but I just need...'

'You just need a nice cup of tea and a sit down. Last night was probably exhausting for you, that's all. But there's work to be done now, so much work, this is just the start.'

With the tea made, they went back into the living room.

'No, Dodds. Whatever happened last night was the end for me. I don't even know what that was. It may have all been in my head anyway or something. I just don't know. But all I do know is that it's over. I have a chance to start over. I think I'm going to try and give it a go with Charlotte.'

He could tell that Dodds was trying desperately to not let go of the anger and panic that was rising up inside her. He could hear it in her voice when she spoke.

'You can't stop it. It's not your choice. Can't you see what this is? This is just the Temptation. And she's the whore of Babylon.' She was unable to keep from spitting out the last words. He had never seen anything like this from his aunt. He was shocked and a little frightened of her. He stood up and made for the door.

'I think it's best if I just get my stuff and perhaps we'll talk about this another time.'

In his room it only took him a minute or so to pull his stuff together into a small backpack.

She was waiting at the bottom of the stairs looking sad and sorry.

'Please don't go like this. What I said was stupid. It was a silly thing. I was just thinking of myself, I got scared. Please stay for another tea. Just stay for another five minutes and then go with my blessing and without any bad feelings.'

He sat back down where he had been two minutes earlier and she put the telly on for him as she went off into the kitchen to make a fresh pot. The guy on the screen was showing the way a brand new cleaning product could remove any stain however old or stubborn. He asked Dodds if she needed any help but she said she was fine. She came back in with a tray of tea and biscuits.

'Here we go. Doesn't that look nice? I remember you as a boy, you used to love these.'

He noticed that there were jammy dodgers on the plate, and she was right, he had loved those as a small boy. He smiled at her and took one with his tea.

She chatted away about the television, about the Church and what she might do with it now, about how much he had meant to everyone down there and that no one would ever forget him. He dipped his biscuit in the tea and when it was cool enough, he picked it up and drank it down quickly. Still a bit uncomfortable after her outburst and feeling that the pleasantries had now been completed, he thought he should be making a move. As the last of the tea slipped down his throat, he noticed a bitter aftertaste in his mouth. He knew just by looking at his aunt that she had done something. She was watching him for some reaction.

Within seconds he could feel the effects of the poison. His throat began to swell and close and his stomach felt like it was on fire. The spasms sent him to the floor retching, but nothing came out. There was yellow foam of saliva and bile dripping from his mouth. He was having great difficulty getting any air inside him. His aunt came and knelt by him and began stroking his back. He tried to flap her away but all strength had gone and he lost his balance, his face hit the carpet. His vision was blurring and he knew it was only a matter of seconds before he lost consciousness. He could hear Dodds talking in soft tones to him while she kept stroking him, like a parent strokes their child while they vomit. Her voice though sounded miles away and as if he was underwater.

'There, there. There's a good boy. This is for you, Steven. This is just for you. You have to realise who you are. You can't see it, you see. She's blinded you. She's led you away from the path. You will see though. You will rise again, you see, my love. Then you'll see. When you rise again, then you can complete what you are here to do. And people will see, everyone will see. I've waited for you for so long. I hate doing this, but this body of yours is only a vessel, all the pain will pass, and you'll come back to me. Do you understand?'

All he knew was that he was dying. He could no longer breathe at all and his body shuddered in a fit, shaking violently on the carpet. His arms flailed around grasping for help that would never come. Everything went black and he lay still.

It was a grey miserable afternoon day. Peter got into the car and drove over to Lauren's flat. He didn't ring ahead. He got out of the car and rang the buzzer straight away. After a minute's pause he heard her voice a little out of breath on the other end of the intercom.

'Hello, can I help you?'

'It's Peter. Can I come up?'

'Oh, Peter. No, not really. I'm not working today. In fact, I'm not sure that I'll be working again. I'm sorry about that.'

'I really need to talk. Can I come up?' There was a desperation in his voice that Lauren found hard to turn away.

'Of course, but just briefly, okay?'

'All right.'

He made his way up the tight staircase and found the door open when he got to the landing. He looked in and saw a number of cardboard boxes full of stuff from the kitchen and another two boxes filled with things from the bedroom. Lauren came out of the bedroom carrying a chair with another box on its seat. She was dressed in jeans and a purple jumper. She looked like everyone else. She smiled when she saw him. A smile so genuine and happy that he wanted to break down there and then.

'Hello, Peter. I'm glad I got to see you before… well, before I disappeared, I guess. Come through to the front room. Sorry it's a bit of a mess. But I've got to get everything out this afternoon. I'd offer you a tea but I've packed all the mugs and the kettle.'

'Where are you going?' He said without moving.

'You okay, you look upset?'

'Where are you going?' He repeated. 'Were you just going to go and not tell me?'

'I was hoping to see you before I went, like I said.'

'Where are you going though?'

She could see the strange lost look behind his eyes.

'I'm stopping doing this, Peter.' She tried to break the news as gently as she could.

Of all her clients, she knew that Peter would take it hardest, he used her more like a therapist than a prostitute. She was also aware that over the months he had become fond of her.

'That's good, I think.' He was stuck in the doorway and didn't want to come in. 'We could still…' He looked in through the bedroom door to the bed. She followed his eyes.

'No, Peter.' She was firm but kind. She wanted him to really understand what she meant. 'I'm not going to be doing this anymore. I'm stopping altogether.'

'I know. I came over here because I wanted to say that I'm free. I've left my wife and I'm free for the first time in years. And I was going to say that if you wanted to we could… well I was hoping we could maybe…'

'Peter, I'm flattered, really I am. But there's nothing between us. I have met someone. That's why I'm stopping now. I have met someone who's changed my whole life. I just want to be with him now.'

'But, you can't…I thought we… I thought it was different…' He was stammering and falling again.

'Peter, you're just confused at the moment. You don't really feel anything for me. Not really. It's just a fantasy that you've let yourself believe. You don't really know me, not really.'

'That's not true. I do know you. I know you have feelings for me as well. I just know it.'

'Peter, what's my name?'

'What? What do you mean?' He was even more confused now.

'What's my name?'

'Lauren.'

'Lauren what?' She said plainly.

He didn't know, or at least couldn't remember. When she had worked for him, he knew it but put simply like that, he had no recollection.

'I don't…'

'And what's my middle name. And where do I actually live? And how old am I? What's my star sign? What's my favourite colour, flower, music?'

'I…I…I don't.'

'You don't know any of those things and that's as it should be. That's not what I was there for. I was there for you and in return you paid me money. It was a monetary transaction, nothing more.'

'No.'

It had never simply been business for him. There were other hookers for that kind of thing. Those questions she'd asked were nothing more than tiny details all of which could be answered in a matter or seconds. He couldn't have misread things so profoundly, he just couldn't have.

'My name isn't Lauren, it's Charlotte. Or at least that's the name I was born with. Lauren is actually my middle name and only punters call me it. I'm sorry you thought there was more to it but that's all there is to say. I have to finish packing. Goodbye, Peter.'

He staggered his way down the stairs.

He was numb.

He was numb as he drove home.

He was numb as he mowed the lawn.

He was numb when he entered the shed.

He wanted each letter he wrote to say something profound but it's difficult summing up forty-five years of failure succinctly and in such a way as to add meaning to everybody else's life. The first letter he wrote was to his eldest son, or rather Jim's eldest son.

Dear Jake,

I am doing this for too many reasons to explain here in this short letter. There are a few things I want to tell you though. Firstly, I have always loved you and my actions have nothing whatsoever to do with either you or your brother. You two have been the single greatest joy of my life. I leave you because I can no longer see a way forward. I'm sure there is one out there somewhere, but at

this moment I am too tired and beaten to find it. This will give me peace, a thing I have lacked for most of my life. If I have always appeared to be one thing whilst inside I have been another, then perhaps that is a lesson for you to learn from. Don't let yourself ever be led or forced down any routes you don't want. You are your own man. Don't let your mother or wife or brother or friends ever decide the direction your life goes. Be certain in every action or decision you take that they are your own. Lead a good life however you see fit, have the courage to follow your heart and never suppress who you are, you are a wonderful, bright and funny young man. You have many great gifts. Use them. I pray you find contentment. Goodbye, my son.

To Jim's youngest son, he composed a new letter. He didn't want to repeat himself because he wanted the boys to know how special both of them were to him individually.

Hello kiddo.

I'm sorry that you should ever have to read a letter like this in your life and I'm sure that you must find this upsetting. For causing you any pain, I am forever sorry. You and your brother have been the most wonderful thing in my whole life, and if I have any regrets, it is that I won't be there to watch you both grow up into fine men. You are so funny and creative, please never lose that. Don't let this one event change you in any way. You have the world ahead of you and if you meet it the way I know you can with enthusiasm and fearlessness, you will be happy and successful. But let the success you get be your own. Don't measure it in monetary terms or by possessions but by how happy you are or how fulfilled you feel. If I had taken this advice many years ago, I would not be leaving you now. I am going to be happier believe it or not.

Although I might not have always have shown it, I have been sad for a long time and I really can't keep going on pretending. So for me, it is time to put an end to all the darkness that I have held inside me. I go in the knowledge that in both of you I have a wonderful, strong and beautiful memorial. Strike out to find your happiness and never let the world consume you the way it has me. You have the power to change things whenever you want. I love you.

       He folded both of these letters perfectly and placed them in their envelopes, licking them and sealing them, writing their names on the front in as steady a hand as he could manage.

The next letter he wrote was to all his employees.

Dear Derek,

I would like this to be read to all employees. I have for a long time been unhappy and with Jim's passing I no longer wanted to continue at the company we had started up together. The other senior partners will no doubt continue to run the business, so all your jobs should be safe. I know I hardly knew any of you but I wish you all well. Well, that's not entirely true there are a lot of you that I don't really give a shit for. Many of you won't shed a single tear for me and those that do will be faking them so save yourself the effort.

We make most of our money from the misery of others and it is this misery that has consumed me and brought me to this. I hate more than I love and wish more people harm than wellbeing. I know this is no way for anyone to live his life, so I am going out with a bang rather than a whimper. Those of you who are young enough to change your lives, do it and do it now. Travel the world, have sex with as many beautiful people as you can and tell the boss to go fuck himself. Well, that's about it. Please take my name off the company logo. Goodbye.

The last letter and the briefest he saved for his wife.

Dear Cunt,

You are a spiteful, hateful little woman and if you have any ounce of love in your heart, I pray you give it to the boys who are far better human beings than you ever deserve to have in your life. Be kind to them. You have destroyed every part of me over many years and my crime was to let you. Small victory though it is, I will now have the last say. You are ageing and you already look like mutton dressed as lamb, perhaps ageing and watching everything you built yourself on sagging and putrefying will bring some humility to you but I doubt it. I wish you nothing but a joyless life and a painful death but as we all know life rarely turns out the way we want it. Cheerio, chin chin and all that.

He put these final letters in their envelopes a little less carefully and then placed some clear plastic sheeting over all of them on the workbench so they wouldn't get splashed with blood.

With the barrel of the gun in his mouth and the hammers cocked, he could feel the shaking of his hands making the black metal chink against his teeth as he bit down gently on them. His thumb was on the two triggers. His last thoughts were would he be able to pull both triggers at the same time and would he hear anything of the noise that was about to happen. As he looked down the barrel, he caught the briefest glimpse out of his peripheral vision of his wife's car pulling into the drive. He waited until her door opened. Even if he didn't hear anything, it would be nice to know that she had and that perhaps that sound might echo through her for the rest of her life. He heard the click of the hammers as they fell and nothing more.

I have a room in a hotel in Bangkok. There are photos covering every inch of the walls. There are faces of all colours, ages and sex, and each one of them can tell me a story.

The four I keep by my bed are the four that came with me, and the four stories I have written as dark gospels

I know that the Church is still thriving and that the Word has spread far and wide. The internet is full of sites dedicated to him and his amazing works. Go check them out for yourself.

Ma's friend was executed. At least that's what I heard from Rosa when we last Skyped, though Ma won't talk about it in her emails.

I don't know anything more about the guy with the head. Love comes in all shapes and sizes though I guess.

As for myself? I have a girl that I am seeing here, or at least nearly seeing. She's a housemaid in the hotel and I've left her everything. I knew she was the one for me because when I took a picture of her, all I saw in it was pure grace and love and for me that's a nice and rare thing. Like Steven said, I seem to be a magnet for some things.

I took a picture of myself to see what the future holds for me but nothing came out. Like all awfully big adventures, there are still unknowns and surprises ahead.

I'm not sure these were the Gospels he wanted but these are all I have to give. I am more or less bedridden now and it has taken all my energy to finish what I have.

I sleep more and more and my eyes are failing but I am held often by my love and when I can't take it anymore, I have enough morphine to help me drift off gently, there are worst fates.